Shielded Mates Volume 2

A Guardians of Chaos Duet

C.D. Gorri

Shielded Mates Volume 2
A Guardians of Chaos Duet

Featuring:
Stallion Shield
Panther Shield

Guardians of Chaos Books 3 & 4
by C.D. Gorri
Edited by BookNookNuts
Copyright 2021, 2022 C.D. Gorri, NJ

To the loyal readers of LLS,
You are the best! <3
Xoxo,
C.D.

STOP! Before you go, sign up for my newsletter and get the latest on
my releases, giveaways, freebies and more:
https://www.cdgorri.com/newsletter

Stallion Shield

Guardians of Chaos 3

BLURB

He knows she's his mate, but this stubborn kitchen Witch isn't making things easy.

Furio Lo Duca is a Stallion Shifter with serious problem. Set in his ways, the Guardian has a reputation for being tough as nails, but a certain kitchen Witch sees straight through to the heart of things. Will he continue to fight his destiny? With Loyalists threatening to disrupt the balance of magic, the Guardians must pull together. They need to be at their strongest.

Can this Jersey boy claim the sassy, smart-mouthed Jessenia, taking his rightful place among his team, or will self-doubt destroy all he's worked for?

Guardians of Chaos Pledge

I am the watcher in the storm.
I am the sword who strikes true.
I am the iron shield.
I protect against those who seek to control the wild nature
of magic.
I am the guardian of chaos.
To thrive, we must be free.
From chaos comes creation.

PROLOGUE

Chop, chop. Scrape, scrape. Place in bowl. And repeat.

Jessenia smiled for her followers as she demonstrated the proper way to choose, clean, and prep fresh herbs for her latest delectable recipe. It was difficult to concentrate when she had so many things crowding in on her already full mind, but she muddled through. Cooking was her jam and vlogging both her successes and failures was how she paid the bills.

Putting together dishes based on her experiences with cuisine from across multiple cultures, and new cooking fads had always brought her a sense of peace and purpose. Jessenia supposed it was a good thing she was trained to be a kitchen Witch.

Her powers really seemed to shine when she was

brewing potions and healing salves. And she was getting better at both every day since she'd started living at the Keep and taking lessons from Holley.

Of course, thinking about Holley made her think of Furio, and that led to even more complicated emotions. It was an eye-opening experience for the young American kitchen Witch. Holley was able to bring her knowledge of the past and both her European and Native American cultures to the present. Jessenia was grateful for any knowledge she imparted to her. Heck, she was happy just to be allowed in the door.

"Whoops," she stopped and plucked a stem from the sprig of thyme she'd been stripping out of her pile of herbs, "You want to make sure you don't rush this step. There's nothing worse than biting into a hard, wiry stem from a thyme plant." She smiled, already feeling her cheeks heat up with embarrassment.

But that was nothing new. She'd polled her audience early on in her vlogging endeavors, and it seemed they loved she could admit her mistakes to them. To err was a very human trait, she supposed, and was glad her followers knew she understood that.

Perfection was not her goal. In fact, Jessenia often emphasized the opposite on her show. She wanted folks to know that cooking was messy, but awesome fun. Recipes should be fluid and based on what was accessible to the chef in their own home arena.

"Remember, any fresh herbs will work for this souffle," she spoke with a smile on her lips, listing various combinations that went well together as she worked.

Where the careful cleaning and preparation of the herbs for this dish might have seemed like a boring waste of time back when she'd been a young Witch, Jessenia had come a long way since then.

She used to follow her poor Nana Carol around like a little lost kitten back in the day. Tugging on the older woman's apron strings while she snacked on whatever yummy goodness her grandmother had been preparing, bombarding her with mountains of questions at the same time.

Gosh, she had been so annoying back then. She shook her head at the memories with a momentary self-indulgence. And yet, her Nana had always had infinite patience with her. The older Witch had taught her so much before she'd passed far too soon in Jessenia's opinion.

Memories of her childhood warmed her almost as much as the superb quadruple ovens in the Keep's superb, restaurant quality kitchen. All of the appliances were in exquisite condition, and better yet, they were on some kind of magical warranty. In other words, they were entirely self-cleaning.

Sigh. That alone was worth moving in for, but really, it had seemed natural in the heat of the moment. With Fergie gone, the apartment they had shared was just too costly. Besides, she was there all the time.

She worried her lower lip as she added the herbs and shredded cheese to the egg mixture, showing the audience as she went. Yes, she loved it there, and yet Jessenia had been doubting her decision to live inside the Keep just recently. Pushing the thought aside, Jessenia tried to focus on the task at hand.

"There, now we fold this in with our other ingredients. Doesn't that smell great?" she smiled and breathed in the herb scented air.

Tilting the stainless-steel mixing bowl, she whisked the contents to a froth. Technique was something a chef developed, and she had hers down. But the people watching her were not trained in culinary arts, they were regular people, and it was her job to make recipes like this accessible and less frightening.

"Okay, this is the big payoff for all that hard work peeling the leaves off the thyme, and quadruple rinsing the sand off the basil and parsley. You see, this requires patience, but in just a few minutes the results will prove worth it," she winked at the camera and continued to whip the mixture for her *light-as-air* ricotta and herb souffle.

Her weekly vlog was important to her. It not only provided her with enough money to maintain her old truck and chip in for food and things in the Keep, but it was her way of connecting with people.

"Okay, just pour it into your ramekins like this. Now, who is ready for the results? Check this out."

Setting aside the mixture, she opened the oven. Jessenia always had a finished product waiting to show her followers since cooking in real-time took actual time that neither she nor her viewers had. The fragrant souffle filled the kitchen with a delightful aroma, and she pulled it out carefully with her oven mitts on, lifting it to show her online audience.

A flurry of hearts and thumbs up emojis flooded her screen, and gratification filled her. Jessenia's vlog currently had over one-hundred-thousand followers, and her sponsors were thrilled with her steady progress.

Still small time, for sure, but she was happy. And that counted for a lot these days, given the fact her emotions were in constant upheaval. How could they not be when she was being driven crazy by an arrogant, cocky male who thought he was above all reproach?

Furio Do Luca was the bane of her existence. He'd

not only made life difficult for her mentor and newest best friend, Holley, but he spent most of his time either staring at her like she was some damn science experiment or ignoring her.

The jerk. Still, he was pretty darn cute, and he had the nicest ass she had ever seen. Perfectly muscled and rounded, her hands itched to give it a slap every time he walked by.

What? She had eyes, and they worked. The man was hot. Even if he was an arrogant jerk face, it didn't lesson her attraction to him. Jessenia was still allowed to look and appreciate. So, what if she wasn't exactly talking to him at the moment? It did not detract from his good looks.

A shame. Yeah, right. Sniff. Whatever.

She could judge herself to death later. Right then, she had to concentrate on her audience. Making good, home cooked food less scary for folks was kinda her thing.

So? Jessenia loved food and wanted to share that love with the world. Growing up with working parents, she absolutely hated the way they'd grabbed fast food almost every night instead of cooking for her and themselves. Like a real family did at least once in a while.

Her grandmother was the total opposite, and she'd

loved the older woman to pieces. She'd passed on her love of food to her granddaughter, which only grew once she'd inherited her powers, and embraced her kitchen Witch heritage.

Whoever said chicken soup was a cure all had no idea. It totally was. The ritual of cleaning, preparing, chopping, and adding ingredients was highly ritualized. Good cooks knew this. That was why they had their favorites.

Favorite knives, cutting boards, pots, pans, utensils. All of it was based in Witchcraft, though normals denied its existence. It was part of who she was, and she wanted to bring that sort of holistic approach to tackling kitchen tasks to her followers as well.

Just imagine being able to ease the mind and body through comfort food readily prepared at home. Jessenia understood the convenience of eating take out. Heck, it wasn't like she never grabbed a hot dog or burger on the run. She just wanted people to know cooking wasn't half as scary as it seemed. Anyone could do it.

"And there you have it!" She smiled and presented the perfectly golden souffle, "Remember folks, magic can happen in any kitchen. Even yours."

The back door to the kitchen slammed open, and she suddenly stopped filming. With a click of a button, she switched on the usual credits and the jingle she'd prepared for the end of the show.

Nerves fluttered around her stomach. How irritating! She ignored those pesky butterflies and began to clear away her mess as the group of Guardians, whose kitchen and home she'd recently invaded, ambled in from their recent scouting mission.

"Something smells good," a familiar voice called out.

Eeek! It was *him*. The only man in the entire manse who could set her heart to pounding like she'd just run a hundred yard dash.

Furio. The youngest Shifter in the bunch, he was still decades older than her. Not that he looked it. The man shared his body and soul with his equine half, a Draft Horse, she'd learned in passing.

He was absolutely gorgeous with his long, dark hair, emerald eyes, and olive toned skin. His Italian heritage evident in his Roman nose, and tendency to use traditionally recognized Italian American colloquialisms in his speech.

He entered the room, and she stopped like a deer in headlights. His lips curled, and she recalled the movement meant something different to Horse Shifters than a mere smile. He was tasting the air, testing the atmosphere.

Shit. She only hoped her body didn't betray her feelings. Turning quickly to see to the oven, she worked hard to ignore his presence. Some secrets had to be kept for a reason, she reminded herself. Hardening her resolve, she stopped her heart's foolery before it could run away with her.

He is not for you. She told herself and went back to getting lunch on the table.

ONE

"Hey Jessenia, you cookin' in here?" Storm called and pulled himself up short before he could bump straight into Furio's back.

He'd recognized the Wolf's voice and knew he was simply being friendly. Shifters were always hungry, but Furio still did not like the idea of his buddy being so casual with Jessenia.

The female in question turned and grinned. Not at him. No, never at him. The warm, wide smile was for Storm. That just made him want to punch the fucker in the gut. She'd probably be pissed if he did that.

With a heavy sigh, he refrained and stalked past her to the dining room. It was getting to the point where he could hardly walk into the room without getting all growly and pissed. But that was what happened when you denied yourself, he supposed. Having Jessenia so close but being unable to claim her was wreaking havoc with his emotions.

Unable? The fuck you say, his Stallion snorted. The beast was more than able. And he assured his human half of that little fact.

Shut the fuck up. He gritted his teeth and talked down his baser side. Not that he didn't want her or could not claim her. Actually, it was pretty fucking complicated. After the morning they'd just had, he didn't want to think about it.

"Lunch is ready," her voice broke the blissful silence that had settled on his mind, and he winced.

Not because he did not like her voice. On the contrary. He liked it far too much. Spent many a restless night imaging her using it to call his name.

Mincha! That's all he needed. A fucking hard on at the table. He growled again, but an elbow hit his arm and he met Storm's confused stare.

"Dude?"

"What?"

"Nothin'," the man shrugged, "This looks great, Jess," he said warmly.

Furio allowed himself to look across the table, and his chest squeezed. The mostly vegetarian meal she'd prepared, with the help of the Keep, comprised almost all his favorite things. He didn't know if she did that on purpose or not, but it touched him either way.

She knew the home where they all lived was magical. Knew the kitchen would present him with a vegetarian option had she made meat for the rest of the group, but it was almost as if she wanted to cook for him. No one had ever done that before, and it touched him deeply.

Tell her, the Stallion pushed. Furio ignored the pesky Horse and grabbed a fork. Next, he reached for one of the steaming ramekins, which cooled by the time his fingers grabbed it.

The *manetuwak*, or the spirits of the Keep, as Holley called them, liked to take care of the inhabitants of the residence. She was their resident Witch/Shaman and mated to their Alpha, a Diamond Dragon named Kingston.

She was also the reason everyone was walking on eggshells around him. Totally his fault. He knew that. His Stallion was pissed as hell at him because of the bad way he'd handled his Alpha mating the Witch.

Now that Jessenia was currently studying under Holley, she probably hated him too. He didn't blame her at all, but it was one more reason he could never tell her the truth about what she meant to him.

Pain lanced his heart, and the delicious meal turned to dust in his mouth. Still, he kept eating, acting nonchalant. He'd even joked with the others, though he could tell they were more reticent with him than normal. It had been that way for months now.

"This is so good," Fergie said to Jessenia, and everyone echoed the sentiment.

Everyone but him. He could hardly look at her, much less tell her that her food was amazing. He felt Storm frowning at him, but he kept his head down and went through the motions of eating. Same as he had for months now.

Hell, it was all he could do. Work, eat, sleep, and repeat. Like he was stuck in his version of *Groundhog's Day* hell. Unable to confess to the woman he loved what she meant to him. Unworthy of her in every way.

Fucking hell, he stood up and brought his dish to the sink. He needed to go work out or something. Anything to get away from the sweet heavenly scent of her. A Guardian should always be in top form, he figured, and headed for the training room.

Thoughts plagued him of the night when all his hopes for the future had gone sour. He'd been looking for Jessenia and had finally tracked her down in the old library.

No one else was around, and his sweet, curvy

piccolina was curled up on the chaise reading one ancient book or other. Furio was not a big reader. Hell, he hardly passed school, but it wasn't because he was stupid. Hardly.

Kingston would never allow any ward of his to be anything other than educated. Furio simply preferred action to more intellectual pursuits. He liked running, playing guitar, and sparring. He also liked fucking. What could he say? Ever since he was a teenager, he knew it was something he was exceptionally good at it.

But ever since he'd seen the little kitchen Witch something had gone wrong inside of him. Furio was not interested in sex with anyone else. Hell, his Stallion went nuts if he even thought about it.

No two ways about it, she was different. Special even. And he wanted her.

"Whatcha doin' there by yourself?"

He stalked over to her and gave her a slow grin that had melted the panties off many a female in his day.

Jessenia had barely glanced his way. Lifting her big, brown eyes a fraction, she'd returned them to the page she'd been studying just as quickly.

"Reading," she replied.

"I know something else we could do that's more fun," he tried again.

"Are you serious? Do you really think that line is going to work with me?"

"Hey, I know you're just as curious as I am."

"How would you know that? You've never even tried to talk to me."

"Talkin' is only one way to communicate," he said, "I know others."

"I bet you do, Mr. Italian Stallion, but you don't know me," she said, "and you have no idea what I want or need."

"Piccolina, I know I got what you need right here," he growled.

Chest heaving, he crossed the room, more than able to meet her challenge. Placing his hands on either side of her head, he mashed his mouth to hers. Stealing a kiss that rocked his entire fucking world for the first time. Like ever.

"No," she pulled back, "We can't do this. I can't do this. Not after the way you treated Holley."

"What does she have to do with us?" he asked, utterly confused.

He knew the little kitchen Witch wanted him. Hell, he wanted her too. And he thought he'd proved himself by being part of the effort to retrieve Holley from Offner's clutches.

"She is my friend, Furio, and you made her feel

unwelcomed here," Jessenia shook her head sadly, "I just, I can't do this," she pushed past him, rushing out of the library leaving her book on the chaise.

Furio had fucked up. Apparently, he'd been wrong in thinking that his mate wanted him back with just as much heat and surety as he'd wanted her.

Thank fuck, he'd kept that little tidbit of information to himself. Rejection was a familiar if unwanted emotion in his lifetime.

Fuck if he'd give anyone another opportunity to do so formally. No, he would keep the fact she was his mate to himself.

It was safer that way.

Two

L unch had started off so promising. And yet, as Jessenia watched Furio stalk away, the mood had turned decidedly sour in her opinion.

The Guardians of Chaos did not exactly advertise. They were an organization made up of groups of elite supernaturals. She only knew about it for two reasons. One, she was a Witch. Two, her BFF was mated to a Guardian.

Fergie had been kidnapped by the Loyalist's a few months ago and Jessenia met up with the group to get her back. She would do anything for her bestie. That much hasn't changed, though a lot of other things had.

"So, what's cookin'?"

Speak of the devil. She turned to see Fergie

wagging her eyebrows at her. Jessenia had to squint at the redhead's newest fashion ensemble. Her bestie was a fan of red despite her orangey locks. She wore a clinging red wrap around dress and, of course, a pair of spiky silver heels. Her choice in footwear made Jessenia cringe when she thought about taking a step in those things.

Hell to the no. More of a combat boot in the winter, flip flops in the summer kinda gal, Jessenia shook her head and pointed at the table. Her best friend's obsession with high end footwear was unhealthy, in her not-so-humble opinion. Detrimental was another word that came to mind.

The last time she wore heels she was at her senior prom, and she'd kept them on all of two minutes before slipping on a pair of ankle socks and rocking out to *Nirvana* with Sergio, her best guy friend *evah*. The Jersey Bull was one hell of a dancer. Like someone took genes from Fred Astaire, the Jacksons, and John Travolta and made one badass Shifter cocktail.

Hmm. What was with her and hoof-footed Shifters with Italian heritages, anyway? Not that she ever had the hots for Sergio, but Furio, well that was another story.

Jessenia wanted the Stallion with every fiber of her being. Once upon a time, she'd thought he'd returned that interest, but after she'd turned him down after one passionate kiss, he hadn't tried again.

Maybe she should've went for it when he'd given her the chance. But Jessenia didn't do casual sex. It wasn't how she was built. If the stories Fergie's mate had imparted about the Stallion were true, then she'd gotten away easy.

The man was a heartbreaker. Collecting notches on his bedpost was a way of life, and she could never be just that. Not even for him.

"Smells wonderful, Jessenia," Kingston nodded his customary polite greeting, jarring her from her unpleasant reverie.

The Alpha of the Group and a Dragon Shifter, Kingston was enormous. The tallest, widest, and perhaps scariest fucker there. At least, Jessenia thought he was. Which was saying something, considering they had a Vampire in residence.

Then again, she kind of liked the mysterious Vamp. Hell, she liked all of them. Byram was nothing if not courteous to her in an old world sort of way she found charming. Egros, a male Witch whose specialty was portals, was a bit more standoffish, but she was used to that kind of thing from other Witches.

Many supernaturals paid little mind to her or her kind. They thought a mere kitchen Witch beneath them. That was cool with her. She just ignored them right back.

"I'll fetch Holley, and we will join you in a moment," Kingston announced, clearly communicating with his mate via their special telepathic link that only bonded mates could afford.

The interaction was so amazing to watch, though it made her feel slightly voyeuristic. Jessenia smiled sadly. Would she ever have that? Would her mate search for her with eyes blazing?

She could only hope and dream, she supposed. As it was, Holley beat him to the punch. The tiny Witch came hunting for her mate in the dining room before he had time to stand. Three months swollen with their young, Holley was either in a tizzy of energy or asleep.

She'd taken to napping most mornings as her pregnancy kept her up during the night. Or Kingston did. Either way, she was not resting now.

"Hello," she said, smiling around the words.

"Mate," he seemed to breathe the word as she nuzzled his lips with hers.

It was their customary greeting, and Jessenia stopped and averted her gaze. She realized she was staring, and that wasn't exactly cool. Crap. She really needed a life of her own.

But the truth was, Holley's pregnancy was another

reason Jessenia was in residence. Everyone worried about the Alpha's tiny mate wearing herself out, so Jessenia stayed to help with things. Like the preparations for the herb garden.

Cooking and taking care of the Keep was her pleasure. She wanted to learn from Holley, and if that meant lightening the expectant mother's load, then she was only too happy to help.

"So, you make any meat for us carnivores?" Fergie growled a bit, eyes flashing as they romanced over the many veggies and sides she'd prepared.

Jessenia rolled her eyes. She'd never get used to Fergie's new Wolfish side, she supposed.

"Of course," she said, and nodded to the tray that seemed to be one of the Keep's favorite.

Sitting beside a smaller tray full of individual ricotta-herb souffles that were each identical to the one she'd prepared for her vlog, *courtesy of the Keep*, was a huge rack of lamb beautifully cooked with rosemary and garlic. Fergie sighed and began to load her plate while Jessenia opted for a souffle.

"Thanks," she murmured when Storm handed her a bowl of fresh spring greens she'd made into a salad.

She set the bowl down and sighed. She'd made it for *him*. Of course, Furio had eaten and gone before she had a chance to even catch her breath, much less offer him any.

The dang Stallion was driving her bonkers. Usually, she could tell the second he'd left a room, but he'd snuck in and out in record speed this time.

"Good?" she asked and waited a beat for Fergie to sample the salad before she went back to her meat.

"Yeah, but Jess, you know I'm carnivorously inclined these days," she said and nodded towards the corridor where Furio had disappeared, "So. I was wondering if anything has happened on that front yet? Ow!"

Jessenia grunted when Fergie's elbow connected with her side, causing her to drop her fork. Thank goodness the rest of the Guardians were engaged in their own conversations and no one was paying them any mind.

"Ow," Jessenia grunted, "How many times do I have to tell you, you are stronger now?"

"Sorry! My bad," Fergie snorted, and opened a covered platter that suddenly appeared on the table in front of her.

Jessenia frowned. Beef enchiladas in red sauce? Sometimes, the Keep was just plain nosy, she thought. At least the darn magical manse could stick with the menu. *Ugh.*

"Mexican? Yes!"

"Are you seriously going to eat that after that lamb you just put away?"

"What? I'm a growing she-Wolf, right babe" the insufferable redhead winked at her mate, whose growled answer was incomprehensible to the kitchen Witch.

Thank God, she shook her head and sighed again. Those two were a little too much with their PDAs. Fergie barked a reply, *like really barked*, then tossed her head back and shouted to the *manetuwak*.

"Thanks, Keep!"

"I still can't believe you identified the Keep as a magical entity before everyone else here," Jessenia shook her head and grabbed the glass bottle of home-made salad dressing she'd made.

It was a simple vinaigrette with some mustard seed and honey, but the fresh herbs made all the difference. She was leaning more towards vegetarian just lately and knowing the reason made her chomp the lettuce a little more roughly than she normally would have.

Oh well, she sighed. It wasn't like the greens had feelings. Not like she did anyway.

"Same," Fergie was already munching her second enchilada happily and agreeing with Jessenia's heartfelt sentiment.

She loved her friend, but the woman was hardly what she would've called empathetic only a few months prior. But that quality only grew as she got to know her mate and her Wolfish side better. It was wondrous and new, and Jessenia was happy for her. Really.

Okay, maybe she was a tad envious, but that would never get in the way of their friendship. They'd been through too much for that. Lunch at the Keep, like most mealtimes, was busy and noisy one minute, then over the next.

Jessenia mused at how quickly the food went, as did the people. Before finding their fated mates, the Guardians ate most meals on the run, though some were prepared magically by the Keep. Yes, the castle did a good job. The food was wholesome, but this was different. This was family.

"I am going to take my mate to bed. She needs her rest. Thank you again for lunch, Jessenia," Kingston said before standing and picking his mate off the floor princess style.

"What is that?" Storm looked at Furio's half-eaten ramekin skeptically.

"A souffle," she said.

"Is it vegetarian?"

"Yes. No meat. Eggs, cheese, and herbs."

"Sounds like Furio's favorites, I wonder why he left it," he said, then grunted when Fergie's elbow connected with his ribs.

"Shh," her bestie growled.

Jessenia grinned, mildly amused at the byplay. Yes, he'd tried it. And yes, he left it half-way through. Maybe he just did not care for her cooking. She shrugged and ate her own food. The Stallion was so not her business.

"No, I meant, uh, it smells incredible," Storm turned a deep shade of red and smiled at his mate carefully.

"Thanks," she murmured, looking look at her own plate and not the two of them.

Would they ever stop tripping over the elephant, or in this case *horse*, in the room? Probably not.

"Look, Jess, I know he's rough, but give him time," Storm said, his hand clasping Fergie's.

Jessenia did not know what to think. Did everyone know she pined for the man? Shit. Even Fergie looked ready to beg on his behalf.

"Guys, there is absolutely nothing going on between me and Furio. I don't have to give him a chance to do anything."

"But I thought—"

"Well, you thought wrong. Excuse me," she blurted, then stood up and cleared her place.

Dammit. She needed to work on hiding how she felt. Especially in a room full of supernaturals. Things had been strained ever since he'd objected, and loudly, to Holley's presence. It wasn't that he disliked the Witch. It was more that he felt disloyal to the memory of Kingston's fallen mate.

Jessenia was there the day the Alpha had told his sorry tale. Neela was not a mate in the traditional sense. Kingston had explained the circumstances of their mating in painful detail, and Jessenia's heart ached for them both. But Holley was the Dragon's fated mate, his *conpar*, and she completed him in a way the she-Dragon never could.

Jessenia hardly recognized Furio when he'd lashed out. It was like a bus-sized bug had crawled up his ass and died wherever Holley was concerned. Oh sure, he'd come around. Eventually. He'd even defended her from the Gila Shifters working with that crazy ass Warlock. The Stallion obviously had hang-ups. Besides, he'd made it abundantly clear that she meant nothing to him.

Jessenia would just have to get over her annoying little attraction to the man. That wasn't going to be hard. Right? She only liked him a little. Very little.

Yeah. Right. Okay, fine, so she wanted to jump him, but she refrained. Playing it close to the chest, as it were.

Not that it matters, she reminded her inner Witch. He hardly even talked to her.

Whatever small amount of lust she'd thought was there in the beginning, was gone now. Maybe she had been mistaken. Jessenia would do better to keep her head down and learn what she could about her powers and casting as a whole. Then, when she had enough money saved, she could leave the Keep.

Her heart hurt at the thought, but she didn't belong there. She was not a Guardian, and she obviously was not mated to one.

No, she did not belong there.

THREE

"*Cump*, I fucked this all up," Furio snorted. He shook his head from side to side, causing his thick hair to tumble from its confines. He tried to catch his breath, but aside from the physical strain of the work they were doing, he was all torn up inside.

The end of February meant the heart of winter in the Garden State, but that wasn't going to stop either Shifter from getting the job done. Kingston had started the project, but Furio jumped on board from the get-go. It was the least he could do to make amends.

The greenhouse was a surprise for the Alpha's mate, and coincidentally for Jessenia. The cold could suck his dick, for all he cared. He was a motherfucking

Stallion baby. Cold meant shit to him. He would always do what was required of him, regardless of any weather.

Besides, this was something close to his heart. He had been watching for months, storing away tiny fragments of information about the curvy little kitchen Witch as he noticed them. Jessenia was a marvelous chef. She was always running to the market for fresh herbs and things like that.

All for the wonderful concoctions she constantly whipped together for the Guardians. He hated that she had to work so hard to get them, and her disappointment when they were out of something was his own.

Fucking hell. He sounded like a goddamn pussy. His Stallion stomped at the description, and he closed his eyes to rein in the animal. Nah, the beast was right. If it meant something to her, it meant something to him. Even though she'd rebuffed him after the first *and only* time he'd kissed her, Furio was still hooked.

She was his mate. That was how these things worked, he figured. It didn't matter how she acted towards him. Not that she behaved badly, she just wasn't into him. Shit, that sucked to admit, but there it was.

Even though now and then he swore he'd caught a whiff of her arousal, he could bever be sure, fleeting as the scent was. Anyway, back to the reason he was outside in the freezing cold. His fated mate was a chef and a Witch. She would damn well have fresh herbs at her disposal year-round if he had anything to say about it.

"What are you talking about? You fucked what up? The frame looks straight," the Dragon grunted, and lifted a huge pane of glass to fit into the slot.

"Yeah, the frame is fine," he growled, and held it while the Dragon slid that last piece into the metal frame.

Furio had only just finished securing the hunk of metal to the frozen ground with four feet of rebar and a big fucking sledgehammer. Good thing they had plenty of Shifter strength between the two of them to complete the project.

Sure, they'd already prepped the outdoor kitchen garden for planting in the spring, but that would not be useable for another few months at least. Holley and Jessenia had already used up every free inch of space to sit their potted herbs and plants on in the kitchen, dining, and living rooms. It was getting to the point where they had to stand to eat.

Kingston had finally realized there was no stopping his mate when it came to growing things, so he planned this greenhouse as a Valentine's Day surprise.

Unfortunately, rounding up the remaining Loyalists in the area was proving more difficult than they'd imagined, and they were already late with the little project.

"So, what are you talking about then? The gutters?" Kingston asked and wiped his brow.

"I don't mean the greenhouse."

"Ah, you are speaking of our resident kitchen Witch then," the Dragon smirked, and Furio's Stallion whinnied.

The fucker always knew what was going on within the Keep and among his Guardians. Furio supposed it came with his job. He could not have had a more patient and knowledgeable Alpha if he'd gone and searched for one.

And yet, Kingston was so much more than that to him. The Diamond Dragon deserved his respect and unwavering loyalty.

"Yeah," he said honestly, "She still isn't talking to me. Well, not really. Every time I walk into a room, she runs the other way."

"I've noticed things seem tense," Kingston grunted as he tried to delicately drive in the screws holding the last pane in place.

"It all started when I was being an ass to you and Holley," he fessed up, shrugging, and trying like hell to not completely wuss out.

"I see," Kingston returned carefully.

"I can't even tell you how much I regret that, bro."

"I understand, Furio," his Alpha turned to him, "You loved Neela. We all did, in our own ways. I get that you thought I was being disloyal."

"It wasn't my place, *cump*," he clenched his jaw, "I am so sorry about that. Seriously, Holley is wonderful, and she deserved better from me. Neela was a great friend, and no, she didn't deserve to die. Not the way she did," he shook his head emphatically, "But that wasn't your fault. I knew that then, and I know it now. She was great, but she wasn't your fated mate."

"Furio, you don't have to say this," he placed a hand on the other man's shoulder, and the Stallion trembled under the weight of his good Alpha's stare.

"I just, I wanted you to know, I can tell the difference now, between one who is a mate and one who is not. I am so sorry for giving you shit, bro," he closed his eyes, feeling a lighter now that he'd said it all.

"It's all good," Kingston said, "I know you were going through something. Maybe the circumstances with your own parents too, yeah?"

"Yeah," he sniffed, turning his head.

Kingston knew the whole sad fucking story of his past, and Furio didn't want to rehash it. Not here. Not now. Especially not when he could hear footsteps in the snow, and he knew exactly who they belonged to.

Neigh. Stomp. Fuck yeah.

Shit. His Stallion whinnied and stomped inside his mind's eye. The huge Draft Horse had a thick-muscled white body, with a dark ebony mane and tale. Unique among Shifter species, he was the only one left of his kind that he knew of.

Truth was, he did not know what to expect from his Horse. A prey animal, it was odd for a warrior like him to not be a large predator, but instinct wise, he was on the money when it came to fighting. In battle, there was no more reliable a fighter than Furio. He was proud of his rep in that respect.

Of course, he was not so proud of his behavior the last few months. But he would work on regaining some of what he'd lost. Even if it killed him.

His human hair was much the same as his animal side. Long, dark, thick tresses that he kept back from his face with a vegan leather thong. He kept a close-cropped beard year-round, nothing more than scruff really, and he preferred flannel and denim to suits or leather.

Unlike many of the supernaturals in his group of Guardians, Furio was a vegetarian. And like his Italian heritage suggested, he preferred pasta to steak any day of the week. Of course, greens were his chocolate.

It was another reason he'd volunteered to help build the greenhouse. Also, there was the tiny fact he was a trained carpenter. After his parents had died, but before he'd become a Guardian, Furio had spent weekends doing carpentry work.

Papa was a Shifter like him, but his Mama was a *normal*. A wonderful chef and brilliant mother. Damn, he missed them like hell. Could still hear their screams sounding off inside his head when the car his father had been driving had spun out of control.

They'd been on their way home from the shore after a weekend getaway, and the weather had turned bad suddenly. The freak storm was unnatural, a manifestation of Dark Witches, he'd later found out.

Furio had been twelve at the time. Neither of his parents survived the accident. Just him. Afterwards, he went where most destitute male Shifters in the Garden State ended up, St. Christopher's Orphanage.

Not something that was widely advertised, the orphanage used to be run by the Hounds of God. An old Werewolf organization who used to answer to the Catholic Church. As far as he knew, the Wardens of Terra had taken over after the Hounds were disbanded, but the place was still up and running.

And his old principal, Sister Margaret, still worked on keeping little shits like himself in line. Furio sent the older nun and Doe Shifter, a fruit basket and hefty donation every Christmas like clockwork. It was the least he could do, considering she'd saved his life.

"You know, they would be proud of you, Fur," Kingston said, squeezing his shoulder, but the Horse merely grunted.

By the time he'd turned seventeen, Furio was into anything that could help him forget about his past. He'd tried drinking, drugs, wild parties, and even a misdemeanor or two. It wasn't until another boy he was hanging around with almost died after an allergic reaction to some pills they'd scored, that he'd wised up.

He'd gone to Sister Margaret's office, red-eyed from crying, and she had called a number. Twenty minutes later, a silver car pulled up, and out stepped the most ferocious looking fucker he'd ever seen.

Kingston Baldric. The badass Diamond Dragon was there to whip Furio into shape. And did he? Fuck yeah.

"My name is Kingston," he'd said, *"You about ready to stop fucking around, and be part of something valuable?"*

"Whatcha talkin' 'bout?" an incredibly young and stupid Furio had returned.

"I am talking about bad guys. Real ones. Like the ones who conjured the storm that killed your parents."

"You know who killed Papa and Mama?"

"I know the group claiming responsibility for that thunderstorm. What I want to know, is do you have what it takes to best them?"

"Fuck yeah, cump," he'd growled.

"We'll see, cump," the Dragon spat back.

Sister Margaret had hugged him goodbye, and he still hadn't realized then how much she had helped him. Wouldn't know what she did for him until years later.

Kingston had driven him home to the Keep. He'd been patient with the streetwise kid and helped turn him into a man. Hell, they all had. Each of the Guardians had taught him something. Shit, they taught him *everything* he knew.

He'd met Byram, Egros, Elena and Storm. And of course, Neela too. The she-Dragon was the most beautiful woman he'd ever seen, and she'd smiled at him. She made the Keep feel like a home when the rest were still trying to size him up.

"I am still here, if you need to talk," Kingston said before the door swung open.

Then she was standing there, and he couldn't think, much less speak. Surrounded by big, white snowflakes, some of which landed in her hair, making it glisten and sparkle, Jessenia glided inside. Sharing the same space with her was about as real as shit got. Far as he was concerned, it was heaven.

"Wow! You sure did a lot of work in just a few hours," she studied the room almost as if she could see it filled with plants.

"We're Shifters," Kingston winked at the tiny woman, and Furio's Stallion snorted angrily.

Damn beast was possessive as fuck over his *piccolina*. Had been ever since he'd first laid eyes on that messy bun. She always wore her curly chestnut locks that way. They framed her heart shaped face and made those crazy pink lips even more kissable in his humble opinion.

Mincha! How he wanted her. Furio didn't want to blink. Afraid she'd disappear in the time it took to close and open his eyes again, he stood completely still and stared.

Shit. He was an idiot, but she was perfect. Tempting and beautiful, cheeks pink from the cold, eyes sparkling like amber crystals, and smelling for all the world like the best damn thing he ever scented. And she was all his, even if the sassy female didn't know it.

Mine.

FOUR

Jessenia Banks, the gorgeous curvy little kitchen Witch that he nicknamed *piccolina*, was his one true and fated mate. Only, she didn't know it.

Had no clue, in fact. And why didn't she know it? That was actually kinda complicated. His Stallion snorted, and he could feel the animal's criticism down to his bones.

Okay, fine. Maybe it wasn't complicated. Maybe she didn't know a thing about it because he didn't have the fucking balls to tell her.

Shit. Sometimes being a Shifter sucked. He couldn't lie, not even to himself. The acrid stench that came with lies turned his stomach. It just wasn't an option for him.

Still, how could he tell that perfect, beautiful,

classy woman that she belonged with him? He was a fucking Neanderthal compared to her. From what he could tell, Jessenia was smart. Like super smart. When she wasn't cooking up a storm, she was producing videos for her website and writing articles. And when she wasn't doing that, she was reading. Like all the time. *For fun*.

Furio was not a big reader. Truth was, he'd been diagnosed with dyslexia after his parent's accident, which explained his bad grades. It was probably also the reason he'd always preferred to work with his hands.

Yeah. He was no good for her. Jessenia was better than him in so many ways. But knowing it still couldn't stop him from wanting her. He'd probably go to his grave wanting the beautiful Witch.

It didn't matter though. She hated his guts. Had basically told him to fuck off ever since he'd acted like an ass to Holley.

There it was. Another strike against him, in his campaign to impress the Witch and make her see what a catch he was.

Snort. As if. Furio wasn't even in the same category. Besides Jessenia's affection for Holley, which was obvious, she seemed completely immune to his charms. She spent all her time with Kingston's mate and her other BFF, Fergie.

He couldn't fault her there. Both women had wormed their way into his heart as well. Storm's mate was feisty and fun to be with. And Holley, well, she was amazing. And she was good for Kingston, which meant the world to him.

He owed the Dragon so much. Especially his loyalty. Furio's initial reaction to his Alpha's claiming Holley as his mate shamed both his human and Stallion sides. But he couldn't turn back time, no matter how much he wanted to.

The past was the past, and though he would never forget Neela or how good she'd been to him, he understood the Dragons' relationship was not what he'd thought. The revelation that Kingston had been honoring Edgar, willingly giving his own freedom to fulfill his fallen brother's dying wish, had been a shock.

Furio could only try to understand that kind of bond. Without a family of his own, it was hard as hell. The Guardians of Chaos were the closest thing he had to family. So, yeah, it had taken him some time, but he now could say he was genuinely happy that his Alpha had found and claimed his fated mate. A state he envied the man.

"Is Holley alright?" Kingston's voice broke

through Furio's silent monologue as Jessenia looked around the greenhouse.

"What? Oh, yes, I'm sorry," she replied and smiled. "She's fine, but she wanted me to remind you that her appointment is for three. It's two-thirty now."

"Is it? Shit. Furio, can you finish in here?" Kingston wiped his hands on his jeans and hauled his ass out the door before Furio could do more than nod in response.

"I am on it, bro," he returned, attempting to cover up the awkwardness he felt being alone with her.

"Wow, this is awesome," she spun around in a circle as she took in the empty space.

As far as greenhouses went, it was small, but empty like this, it appeared larger. She was smiling widely, like she couldn't help herself as she walked the length of the room, and he was powerless to do anything but watch.

"It's, uh, kinda small," he said inanely, "Just a simple thirty by fifteen-foot rectangle made of steel and glass."

Simple alright, but with her inside, it was his new favorite place. He swallowed down his nerves and waited for her to respond.

"Well, I think it's great! What's this over here?" she pointed up, and Furio took the opportunity to wipe his suddenly sweaty palms on the front of his shirt.

"Oh, that's a gutter system. It'll catch rainwater."

"Oh?"

"Yeah, it will repurpose rainwater and melting snow to benefit the plants once this place is filled. We're gonna put in a whole hydroponics garden on this side, with an overflow drainage system to prevent flooding. Some raised plots over there, and a rust-free, wire-shelving system in the back. There's going to be a furnace in the center, to heat the space in winter," he explained, watching greedily for signs of approval.

Fuck, he was like a kid again. Waiting for his teachers to notice when he did something right. He only hoped he didn't lash out and embarrass himself like he used to when praise proved beyond him. But he did not need to worry. He didn't want her praise, not exactly. He just wanted to be with her. Like this.

His Stallion nodded his great equine head in approval. Yes. Being with her was good. A soothing balm for his soul.

"Really? That sounds so amazing," her eyes twinkled in her excitement, "Holley will love it."

"It's not just for Holley," he murmured, the could've cursed himself when she slowly turned to face him.

"It's not?"

"Nah," he shook his head, "uh, anyone can use it."

"Yeah?"

"Yeah, like, you know, for herbs for cooking maybe, or potions," he shrugged.

Mincha! He sounded like a fucking moron. But what could he say? She was so pretty, he could hardly maintain a coherent thought.

Those big brown eyes were his undoing. Not to mention those soft-looking, wild curls framing her face. His pants were growing tight around his suddenly hard cock, but he could not look away.

Furio wanted to cuddle her close and nuzzle the flesh beneath her ear. To breath in that fresh, earthy *basilico* scent that clung to her.

He loved basil. It was his favorite herb. That she should smell like that one thing above all others made his Stallion whinny and stomp like a racehorse about to bolt right out of the gate.

Fuck, he would run a thousand miles just to get a whiff of her. And that thought alone kept his hands firmly stuck in his pockets. Furio knew if he even came close to her, all bets were off. The fragile truce that existed between them was too precious to break.

The hold he had on the metaphorical reins that held his Stallion back was precarious at best. He heard the smile in her voice as she asked intelligent questions about the design, and he basked in it. Furio was only too happy to stay with her, to explain anything she wanted to know about the construct of the small building.

"How do you know so much about all this?" she asked.

"What? Construction?"

"Yeah," she shrugged.

He felt his cheeks heat up as he rushed to think of an explanation. Fuck it. Might as well go with the truth.

"It was one of the things I learned back at St. Christopher's," he sucked in a breath.

Shit. He hadn't meant to let that slip out first.

"St. Chrisopher's over in Montville?"

Her eyes widened, and he turned around roughly. The last thing he wanted was her pity. Why the fuck had he ever said that? He could have kicked himself, but his animal snorted.

The beast reminded him he had nothing to be ashamed of. His past couldn't be helped, but his future could. And if he were lucky, she would be in it.

"I think that's great," she continued.

"What? That I grew up in an orphanage?"

He was being a dick. He knew it, but he couldn't

help it. Shit. It was the last thing he wanted. Seemed whenever he was around the woman, Furio couldn't help but make an ass of himself.

"Furio, I didn't mean to trivialize or poke fun at you. I don't know what you went through. I don't really know anything about you but—"

"No, you don't know," he gritted his teeth, "but whatever, right? Not all of us have perfect lives. We can't all have loads of friends, family, that kind of shit, right? Whatever."

The feel of Jessenia's small hand on his arm brought his head whipping around to the side. When did she walk across the room? Shit. He was really out of it if this little female could sneak up on him.

"Hey, I didn't mean it like that, Furio," she said his name with a slight accent that made his heart thud steadily inside his chest, "You know, I didn't have a perfect family either. My parents, well my mother, had denied her heritage for a long time. When I found out I had magic, it was a complete shock. She and my dad hated that I wanted to embrace my powers."

"What?" he asked, not bothering to hide his surprise.

His Stallion snorted. Right then, he wanted to find her parents and knock their heads together. How could anyone not be thrilled to have this gifted, beautiful Witch in their lives?

"Yeah, we still don't talk much. I mean," she shrugged a little self-consciously.

Furio sucked in a breath. He had to make fists with his hands to stop from reaching out to touch her. It wasn't his place. He'd tried that once, and she'd refused him. Maybe she just didn't like him. What the fuck did he know?

Now and then he thought he saw a spark of interest, but it was always fleeting. Wishful thinking, he guessed. Either way, she was talking now, and he wanted to hear more. So he nodded, encouraging her to go on.

"I learned about cooking and healing potions from my grandmother. My parents were horrified. Eventually, I went to live with her. They were just not that interested in me once I embraced my supernatural heritage. Granny was exceptional, but she was older. I was lonely."

"Shit, Jess," he got the words out barely above a whisper.

"Don't be. I pretty much gave up on them by the time I reached high school, and I guess I haven't spoken to them in years. Fergie was my only friend after that."

"I'm sorry," he frowned down at her, and he meant it.

No one should treat her that way. She was a gift. A fucking treasure. She deserved so much better.

We can give her everything she needs. Be her family. Her home. His Stallion pushed the thoughts at him, but he ignored the beast. Jessenia deserved better than him.

"Anyway," she swallowed.

"My mother and father died in a car crash. It's how I wound up at St. Christopher's," he confessed his past to her like it was some sin he carried.

He knew better. He really did, but deep down, he'd always felt as if he were being judged whenever people discovered the truth about his family. He'd had distant cousins, but no one who was willing to take on a tough as nails teen with a chip on his shoulder.

"Oh, Furio, I am so sorry," Jessenia stepped forward and impulsively gave him a hug.

The hard, brief contact set his entire body aflame, and it was all he could do not to return the embrace tenfold. As it was, she'd let go before he could even react.

"This really looks good. I think it's going to be great," she said, her brown eyes taking in the place once more, and he could see her excitement.

Hell, it was all over her now. Radiating off of her curvy little form in waves that seemed to wrap around him, making his Stallion whinny and his cock hard. He licked his lips and moved closer, crowding her.

She didn't flinch when he invaded her space, in fact, she seemed to lean into him. As if seeking his heat. Maybe she was. It was fifteen degrees outside, and the wind was whipping against the glass panes of the greenhouse.

"I should get back," her voice was low, but he had excellent hearing.

"Yeah," he agreed, "you should."

But still, his hands came up to grip her waist. Furio tugged her towards him until her lush body was flush against his hard one. If not for that hug she'd given him, he would never have dared such a bold move.

It was too late to close the floodgates now. Need pulsed through him, and he took in a deep breath. Sucking air greedily into his lungs, swallowing down Jessenia's fresh basil scent. It tickled his senses, teased him with promises of passion and joy, and before he could stop himself, he lowered his head.

"Furio," she whispered his name, but she was pulling him closer too.

The action meant something. It just had to, right?

He felt the growl build up inside his chest, and his lips came crashing down onto hers.

Holding on to his self-control by a thread, Furio claimed Jessenia's mouth with all the pent-up passion he'd been saving for her for months now. The world seemed to tilt on its axis, and fuck if he didn't hear the tide turn from all the way out there, deep in the Pine Barrens.

Kissing Jessenia was addictive, and yet it wasn't what he'd been meaning to do. Their shared kiss was not the soft, fairytale whisper he'd wanted to give her. It wasn't patient, or calm, or kind. No, it was like him, rough around the edges, demanding, and a little unrestrained.

They collided like two opposing forces, and the result was a phenomenon unlike any other. Like light and dark, refined and raw, soft and hard. She was his perfect counterpart. As if she'd been waiting for this moment too, she sighed and melted into him.

Jessenia's throat vibrated with her moan as she accepted his kiss, and even more astounding, kissed him back. Furio's body hummed with anticipation and barely restrained power as he continued to test and tease her silken lips.

Encouraged by the not so small fact she hadn't slapped his face, he pushed his tongue inside the hot cavern of her mouth. Testing, tasting, pushing his advantage until he felt the tiny pricks of her nails digging into the flesh of his shoulders. But still, she was not pushing him away. That fact had his blood singing in his veins. If anything, his *piccolina* was dragging him even closer.

"Come here," he growled, lifting her up until she wrapped her legs around his waist.

He held on to her, cupping the round globes of her perfect peach of an ass as he plundered her mouth. She tasted better than he could've ever imagined. Like sunshine and sin. A dangerous mix for sure. One he was sure to crave again and again.

"Mine," the word slipped from his lips as she slowed the kiss.

Big brown eyes bore into his, and Jessenia suddenly pushed against his hold. Reluctantly, he let her go. But he was helpless to stop the shiver that went through him as she slid down his body until her booted feet hit the floor.

"I, uh, I should get back," she was a little unsteady on her feet, but declined his outstretched hand.

That hurt a lot admittedly, but Furio remained still. He might not understand everything that just happened, but he instinctively knew she needed space. In fact, it was a great idea.

Watching from the doorway until she was safely tucked away inside the Keep, he turned and paced up and down until he stood at the back of the greenhouse. She'd been so excited about it. He was determined to stay up all night if he had to, just to finish the damn thing. But first things first, he thought with a sigh.

Furio stripped off his clothing and stepped outside. The sun had set, but that happened early this time of year, and it couldn't have been later than three or four. Fuck it, he thought and began to run, transforming into his Stallion mid-stride.

It was not something every Shifter could accomplish, but it was one trick he'd learned early on. Storm always said it must be a trait unique to Horse Shifters, but he wasn't sure the Wolf wasn't simply jealous. That would be funny, he thought. There was no need for envy among them. Each Guardian had their own talents and specialties.

In fact, he'd never begrudged any of the members of his group their abilities. The only time he felt that green-eyed monster, and he didn't mean himself, was when he watched Storm or Kingston with their mates. Egros, Byram and Elena didn't get it. He'd met his mate, and the fact he didn't have her was driving him mad.

The kiss had been promising, but something

shifted just at the end. Fuck all if he knew what had happened. One thing he understood was Furio needed this. To run, to stretch his long legs, and work out the pent-up passion bubbling inside of him.

True, he'd rather do that between the sheets with his mate, but she needed time and space. It might kill him, but he would give it to her.

Neigh. His Stallion whinnied furiously at the thought. Death was not an option. Not when he had a mate to claim, protect, and cherish. And he would. Just as soon as he figured out how to convince her to take him on.

Mine.

FIVE

"Wait," Fergie stalked after Jessenia with her mouth full of gooey chocolate from the fresh baked muffin she'd taken out of the oven minutes ago.

She'd been up all night long, tossing and turning. Ever since she'd kissed that long-haired pain in her ass. What the hell was that, anyway?

He'd picked her up like she weighed nothing and took her mouth as if he'd owned it. Then he'd said something. One word which had sent her straight to the library for some research.

Mine. He'd said *mine.* She scoured the ancient reference books documenting Shifter behavior in the old Keep's amazing library, and the result was disturbing. Not unwelcomed per se, but it shook her to her core.

"Jess," Fergie interrupted her train of thought as she busied herself cleaning bowls and loading the dishwasher, "You guys kissed? For real?"

Her BFF squeaked loudly, and Jessenia covered her ears. Dang Wolf Shifter vocal cords. They were going to be the death of her.

"Shhh! Do you want everyone to hear you?" she grumbled.

"Sorry," Fergie giggled, straightening her dark purple blouse as she did so, "Besides, it ain't like it's a big secret. You and *Mr. Fast and Furio-us* have not been exactly unnoticeable. And I see you made carrot cake again."

"For real?" she asked, ignoring the carrot cake remark.

Okay. So, she knew he liked it. He wasn't the only one, right? Shit. She picked up the cake and tossed it in the trash.

"Hey! What gives?"

"Nothing. Just answer the question."

"Fine. Yeah, for real you guys might as well be wearing a sign! *Sheesh*. But anyway, did you, see what I did there? *Mr. Fast and Furio-us?*" she snorted.

"Yes, Fergie, very clever," Jessenia rolled her eyes, "But what do you mean we aren't unnoticeable?"

"Girl, those big brown puppy eyes of yours follow him around like all the dang time."

"What? *Nuh uh.*"

"Yeah huh," Fergie said, confirming Jessenia's worst fears.

Great. So, it turned out her whole *if-I-ignore-these-feelings-they-will-go-away* plan didn't not only fail, but everyone, including the object of her affection, was in on it.

WTF. Was the whole world out to get her? Or just the supernatural one? Ugh.

"Why didn't you tell me it was obvious?" she demanded and cursed under her breath.

"Because Jess, you know how you are," Fergie said.

"What the heck kind of an answer is that? How am I?"

"Well, for one thing, you and a certain *Italian Stallion* have got like so much sexual tension between you, I'm surprised you can even see two feet in front of you."

"OMG! No, you did not just say that? Like, do you mean he knows? He's like known this whole time?"

This time, Jessenia was the one who squeaked.

Dropping her head into her arms, she leaned on the island in the middle of the kitchen. Crap. How was she going to face him?

"Hey," Fergie leaned closer, but Jessenia was too shocked to answer.

Was it that obvious? Did everyone know she had the hots for the Stallion? OMG. Did Fergie just call him the *Italian Stallion*? That was it.

Jessenia was going to kill Fergie, but it would have to wait. Her shoe inclined friend was still going strong. Her brows furrowed as she waited to hear what the redhead was going to blurt next.

"Between us besties, is he really, you know, *hung like a horse*?" Fergie reached out to snag another muffin, but Jessenia had reached the end of her rope.

Even best friends had boundaries, and Fergie had just crossed hers. Enough was enough. Jessenia straightened and picked up the wooden spoon she'd used to mix the batter, then she whacked Fergie right on her ass with the thing.

"Ow! Oh my God! Jess, how could you?" she hissed, "There was still batter on that, and now my pants are dirty."

"Boo hoo! The Keep will wash them. Now, what else do you know about all this between me and Furio? I spent all night trying to find out anything, but those old books need to update their indexes," she stomped her foot on the tiled floor. Not very effective considering she wore her favorite lime green Crocs at the moment.

"Ouch. My butt still hurts," Fergie whined.

"Serves you right," Jessenia pursed her lips, "Now, no more penis references before coffee, and I said those were for *later*. Now, tell me what you meant about knowing how things were between me and Furio?"

"Jess, I didn't mean anything," Fergie pouted, but she was so not getting another muffin until she explained herself, "I just meant you always do this when you like a guy. You get down on yourself and start acting like you aren't good enough for him. I don't want to see you go through that again. Besides, he's a Shifter."

"What? I do not, and so what, your guy is a Shifter," Jessenia frowned.

She started plucking still warm muffins from their pans and stacking the chocolate chip and banana nut goodies into two separate baskets with a little more vigor than anticipated. The result was one or two muffin casualties. *Sigh.*

"Actually, you do, Jess," Fergie insisted gently, "but if what you said about your kiss is true," she grinned widely, "I think this time you don't have to worry about all that."

"What are you talking about?"

"He said 'mine' right? When he kissed you?" Fergie asked.

"So?" Jessenia had thought the whole monosyllabic word was weird at the end of their kiss, but the truth was, she was kind of into it.

The whole growly, possessive thing he had going on during their heated exchange made her panties soaked with desire. In fact, the whole thing had filled her with torturous anticipation. She'd half expected him to hunt her down in her bedroom that night.

Okay, so it was more like she'd wished for that. Waking up extra early the next morning under the guise of baking fresh muffins had not resulted in catching a glimpse of the handsome Stallion. Much to her dismay.

"Well," Fergie said while she poured a second cup of fresh brewed Columbian roast, "Shifters only say that when they meet their mates."

The sound of the muffin tin hitting the tiled floor rang throughout the room like a bullet being fired from close range.

"Excuse me?" Jessenia's heart began to pound, and

that bubbly, zippy little feeling that was her usual magic went a little bit haywire inside of her.

"I said, it means you're probably his mate," Fergie's eyes went wide, and she heard her friend's hesitation.

"And how long does it take for a Shifter to realize someone is his or her mate?" she asked far too casually.

"Uh, immediately?" Fergie winced.

"I see," Jessenia said between gritted teeth.

She turned around and picked up the tin from the floor. Stacking the empty bakeware in a pile, she hardly registered the sounds of footsteps running towards them.

In fact, it was a full minute before she stopped what she was doing and looked to see three pairs of curious eyes on her. One bright green pair seemed a little tense. Maybe agitated was a better way to describe them. To her, those eyes were of particular interest.

"Mates? We're mates? And you didn't think to tell me?"

"Uh—" Furio opened and closed his mouth a few times, but Jessenia was so not having that.

He was wearing a pair of sweats and a tank top, typical sparing gear. Similar to what the other two Guardians had on. They must have started in the training room early that morning. Too early for her to have caught them when she started baking.

"Well, Furio? Is that true?"

"Jessenia, I, I mean," he swallowed then narrowed his eyes at her and the other people in the room seemed to fade away, "Yes. You're my mate."

"When?" she asked, "When did you know?"

"Um, I think we should go now," Fergie grabbed Storm's arm, tugging her mate out of the line of fire. *Smart*, she thought with a frown as she squared off in front of *him*. Anger and confusion warred within her. Was there something wrong with her? Did he think she wasn't good enough for him?

"Jessenia, we should talk," he said.

"When did you know?" she repeated.

"Everything okay here? Good, I am going to just go back to my room," Elena's pink gaze flashed between the angry kitchen Witch, and the confused Stallion.

Jessenia felt her anger rise. When that happened, her powers tended to go wonky, but she did not give a shit. A dozen nameless emotions batted up against the shield she'd constructed around her heart long ago to protect herself, the foremost of which was hurt.

Why hadn't he told her? Was he ashamed? She was only a kitchen Witch. She was not clever like Fergie, nor was she a powerful practitioner like Holley. The

Guardians' mates were kickass, but maybe she didn't measure up.

"Let me explain," he tried to reason, but she was not in the mood.

"Were you ever going to tell me?"

"Jessenia," he called her name in a plaintive, husky whisper that went straight to her core.

But she ignored her body's cry for attention. She was too angry for that. Hell, she was pissed off, and rightly so.

"How long have you known?"

"That you're my mate?" he asked, and she wanted to whack him over the head with the wooden spoon that was still in her hand.

"Yes," she growled between gritted teeth, "How long?"

"Since the first time I saw you," he finally confessed, and the world seemed to go still.

Silence. Deafening silence pounded against her. Then, it was a roaring tidal wave. No longer a still rock, her whole world was hurtling through space and time breaking records and barriers like an out-of-control asteroid.

Fucking hell. She needed a grip. Her magic sizzled and sparked. Angry as she was, it was a miracle she didn't burn the place down. But she was just a little kitchen Witch. Not dangerous, not important, and apparently not mate material.

"Well, isn't this great!"

Okay. Jessenia was full on screaming now. She paced back and forth along the tiled floor to try and regain her composure, but it was too much. All her life she'd been made to feel as if she were not good enough by the people who should have treasured her the most.

Her own parents denied her existence. She was nothing but a disappointment to them. A thorn in their sides. She knew Witches did not always have mates. But the truth was, after Fergie, *a normal*, had met her own fated mate, Jessenia wished for one of her own.

Someone who would truly want her. As is, no returns or exchanges. A mate of her very own to treasure and love. Someone to talk to and experience life with. A real friend. A soulmate. That was her secret dream, and she'd never been more ashamed of it than right now.

Ever since she'd met the Guardians, *Furio in particular*, Jessenia had to admit a certain affinity for the Stallion.

Fine. She'd been hot and bothered since she'd laid eyes on him. With his long chestnut hair, dark green eyes, straight nose, and impossibly gorgeous body, how was she supposed to resist?

She'd managed to keep her distance, barely. Downplaying her attraction and hiding her response to him for months now. But then yesterday afternoon, he'd kissed her. And like a complete idiot, she'd started to hope that maybe something could develop between them. Something more.

She had no idea his fervently whispered "mine" was a confession of sorts. When she'd confided in Fergie, she was hoping to glean some knowledge about how starting a relationship with a Shifter.

Her bestie had an in with Shifters that even as a supernatural Jessenia had not been privy too. She had no idea his gravelly voice was anything more than simply sexy when he'd uttered *mine* after they'd kissed.

Okay, so maybe she'd hoped it meant what it meant. But and this was a big fat horse's ass of a *but*, she'd been unaware that Shifters could tell their mates at first sniff. Once confirmed, it was something she could not un-know.

"So, what? You figured I wasn't good enough for you, so you just ignored it? You ignored me?"

"Jessenia, please listen. I swear, that is not why I didn't tell you," he stepped towards her, but she was still raw.

Her power jumped out at him, stopping him midstride. She was breathing heavily. Anger seeped from her pores.

"I don't believe you," she hissed, and her magic flared.

She could see him straining against it, trying to move towards her. Crap. She didn't know what was happening. Had never had her magic react like that.

She was just a kitchen Witch. Nothing to write home about. Her magic allowed her to create healing salves and potions from common ingredients found in the average kitchen and some not so common herbs and things. That was all.

And no, she did not use eye of newt, fuck you very much. Those kinds of stereotypes really pissed her off. As did lies of any kind, even omission. Still, her magic was not offensive, meaning it was not actively aggressive or used for fighting. But maybe she would have to change her mind about that, she thought as her powers lashed out with her hurt.

Jessenia could not believe she'd spent weeks, no, make that months, secretly pining for the long-haired jerk! She was his mate, for fuck's sake! His mate, only he did not want her. Humiliation threatened to send her to her knees, but she held on to her anger instead.

Of course, that led to her powers zapping him

again, which was not this kitchen Witch's intention at all. She was a healer. Only right then, she didn't feel like helping. Like, not at all.

"Ow! Fuck. Please, Jessenia," he begged.

Furio was sucking in air rapidly, but her magic continued to bind him. Anger and hurt made her blind to his pain. She felt like a total idiot. How could she be so stupid? She was a fool for believing in that kiss! She'd built castles on one insignificant meeting of lips.

Only a sad and desperate woman would do such a thing. She gritted her teeth as those words filled her brain. She'd wanted happily ever after. Instead, she got a reluctant mate. Hell! Of course, love would not be easy for her.

It never was.

Six

Anger and humiliation, along with a healthy dose of contempt, self and otherwise, made Jessenia feel like a powder keg ready to blow.

She'd been fighting her attraction to him to save her pride, and the very moment she'd let her guard down, things went to shit.

"I made a mistake," he grunted.

"Why? Why did you lie to me?"

"No lie," he tried to respond.

But she was too angry to hear him. Furio had known the entire time what she was to him. He knew from the moment he'd met her in that coffee shop when she'd been worried about Fergie's safety that she was his mate. He just didn't want her.

When Storm had turned out to be Fergie's fated mate, Jessenia had been in awe of their connection. Immediate, instantaneous, powerful, and mutual. There was nothing like it in the entire universe.

So yeah, she was happy for her friend, and a little envious. Okay. A lot envious. How could she not be? Having a fated mate was like getting a gift from the universe itself.

Your very own guaranteed-to-love-you-warts-and-all significant other to be yours for all time. Who didn't want one of those?

Shit. Her hurt was tangible now, and her magic was acting as an extension of that pain and anguish. No, she didn't want to hear anymore.

"Give me a second," he gasped, but she was not listening.

She couldn't. Not when tears threatened to spill any moment.

"Have to explain," Furio struggled against the invisible ropes of her power that held him hostage.

No matter how hard he tried, he couldn't break them. That fact salvaged whatever pride she had left. Or it would have. But then she took a good look at him.

"Oh my God!" Fergie came running towards her,

but her magic had created some sort of barrier between the kitchen and the rest of the Keep.

"Jessenia! You have to stop," she yelled, but Jessenia was not paying any attention to her former roommate.

Her eyes were on Furio, and they widened in horror as his face turned a terrible shade of red. She was doing that to him. The realization froze her.

Her magic was making it impossible for him to move. No, it was making it impossible for the man *to breathe*. She whimpered, and clapped a hand over her mouth.

"Oh shit," she closed her eyes, trying to pull back her wayward powers.

Utter horror at what she'd almost done damn near paralyzed her, but she forced herself to focus. It took a moment, but she finally got herself under control. Stunned at what she'd almost done, she sank to the floor and placed both palms on the cold tile.

Jessenia's magic had always ever been a benevolent force. Well, except for that one time, but that was not her fault. She was too young to understand what she was doing. Besides, her mother had ignored that part of her heritage, so she'd had virtually no control of her magic.

That was about the time she'd started lessons with

her grandmother. Even so, a kitchen Witch should not be able to do what she'd almost done. Her mind raced with possible scenarios and what-ifs. Sweat beaded on her brow, and her mouth went dry.

Heart pounding, she could hardly face herself, never mind him. She'd almost killed him! Remorse threatened to choke her as her eyes burned with tears. She would never want to hurt anyone, much less the object of her affections.

Not really, anyway. He might've deserved a thwack on the head, but he definitely didn't deserve to be suffocated by her magic. What the heck was happening to her?

Her body trembled in response to the adrenaline, and her eyes flashed to where Furio fell to his knees gasping for air. Her heart squeezed and she felt sick to her stomach. Magic was not supposed to be used to harm. It went against everything she'd ever believed in.

She turned to stand, needed to leave, to run from the room, but something stopped her. Looking down, she saw his hand wrapped around her ankle. Even though he still struggled for breath, Furio kept a firm hold.

Shit. She couldn't exactly kick him off and run away, now could she? Seconds away from a full-on panic attack, she tried to gently step out of his hold, but the Stallion was too strong.

Oh fuck. What did I almost do?

Embarrassment rose inside her like a vicious bitch of a wind. The kind she saw every February and March in the Garden State. She hated the way it stung her face and made her eyes tear. Only now, it was more like her own outburst that was causing her to want to howl and cry like a banshee.

How could she be so emotional over a guy she kissed once? Just once. But she was, and that was that. Shame and unease caused her to tremble and shake.

He meant so much more to her than *just a guy*. Witches could not always tell their mates the way Shifters could, but she'd recognized Furio from the start. Deep down inside, her soul had kindled in appreciation of his every time she'd looked into his forest-colored eyes.

When he was angry or excited, they glittered like emeralds. But now as he sought to regain his composure, they were dark and cold like the pine trees standing alone, out there in the snow-covered woods.

Shit. She'd really messed up. Even Shifters were under no obligation to claim their mates. What was a mate, really? Just some person, a stranger really. Someone the Fates randomly decided on.

In fact, it was pretty messed up now that she thought about it. Imagine not having a choice about whom to love? Who to be with? Imagine not having any control over your own physical reaction to that person? Maybe she was wrong to be envious of what Fergie had.

At the very least, she'd overreacted. It wasn't even Furio's fault she was caught up in this. If anything, he tried to spare her by not telling her she was his mate.

"I, I have to go," she pulled against his hold, but the Stallion's grip was strong.

"No," he said in his rough-sounding voice, "You got it wrong, *piccolina*. I swear to you."

"No, I was wrong. I was stupid," she sniffed loudly, "I, uh, don't blame you for not wanting me. And I know I sound like an idiot and I acted like a bad person, but I'm not, I swear I didn't mean to hurt you. But, uh, I don't feel sorry for myself either. Not really. I mean, it's not fair to you. Shifters can't pick and choose like the rest of us can, I guess. Look, just let me go."

"No!" he said roughly, squeezing her ankle between his long fingers, "I ain't lyin' to you. Never that. I was stupid. Me. Not you. Never you."

"You don't have to say that."

"Jessenia, just promise you will listen, okay?" he

cleared his throat, waiting for her nod, "I'm gonna let go. Promise not to bolt?"

"Yes," Jessenia replied, frozen to the spot.

She couldn't have moved even if she wanted to. Not with him still touching her. As Furio pulled himself up off the ground, his hand never left her. It inched up her leg to her hip, her waist, and finally, her face.

"You got it so wrong, *piccolina*," he grunted, "I want you all right. Let me show you how much," his big hands captured her face, and he pulled her closer.

Eyes wide, she had no time to do anything but react to his blatant display. Raw masculine power exuded from him, unlike anything she'd ever seen.

He was always the joker, the carefree one. Or he had been until Kingston mated Holley. Furio's response to the news that the Witch was his Alpha's fated mate had been less than what she'd expected of him.

But still, she understood it was hurt that drove his actions. Hell, she'd wanted to be the one to soothe him, but all she could do was watch as his harsh words put a wedge between himself and the other Guardians.

She'd seen it all and sympathized with him. But ultimately, she was happy for the Diamond Dragon and for Holley. Overcoming a variety of obstacles, they'd both faced trials during their long lifetimes, and then finding one another was a miracle. Incredible and totally awesome, to be honest. Jessenia was in awe of them both individually and as a mated pair.

The love between them was evident in every passing glance and seemingly casual touch. Kingston's hardened exterior shell had begun to crack and thaw with his mate's careful attentions.

Furio had none of the hostility and anger that so many of his brethren carried within themselves. Or, he hadn't when she'd first met him. He'd been the easy-going one, the clown, but not for months now.

This show of dominance was so unlike the Furio she knew, but it struck a chord within her. Like some ultra-secret feminine part of, buried deep down inside, under all the women's lib beliefs she held dear to her heart, was suddenly stoked to life.

Her skin grew warm as she melted into his taller, wider frame. Furio growled against her lips, wrapping his arms tightly around her body. His soft mouth brushed over hers once, then twice. Insistent, yet tender in his exploration. He licked the seam of her lips, pushing his tongue inside. Searching for more, tasting her very essence, and Jessenia was a goner.

No one had ever kissed her quite like that. It was like the man had a personalized map to her heart and knew exactly how to get there. Well, he knew how to kiss at any rate. Like her every own dream come true.

Towering over her like a pinnacle of physical perfection, Furio kissed, *and kissed*, and kissed her some more. Jessenia was powerless to do anything except react. She heard the others in the periphery, moving away to give the privacy, but she didn't care.

All she wanted was for this kiss to never end. Jessenia ran her hands over his shoulders and down his back, moaning softly as she returned his passion with everything she had.

Hidden desires, secret longings, whispers only lovers would share, all of it and more came rushing forward as their tongues tangled and hearts thudded against each other. He was gorgeous. All long limbs and wiry muscles, demonstrating his speed and strength.

She loved the way he felt pressed against her. All hard and hot, like her own personal furnace. He smelled incredible, too. Fresh air and cool streams, like the perfect spring day. The kind she longed for, especially now in the dead of winter. New Jersey was notorious for freezing temperatures and endless snows of February as it gave way to March.

But *he* made her feel warm everywhere. He was the promised sunshine of warm days to come, and she longed to bask in his rays. And she would. As long as he never stopped kissing her.

Sigh. His lips warmed hers, caressing the plump mounds until she was limbless. Using him for strength, she moaned as he slowed his silent exploration. Nibbling on her lower lip, his nose brushed against her cheek, and he pressed his forehead gently to hers. Jessenia had to work to slow her breathing, but it was impossible.

Or so it seemed. She wanted him so damn bad. Her sex throbbed, nipples ached, and heart squeezed. And yet, she couldn't help but feel slightly betrayed. She was his mate, and he'd known it all along. Why had he waited so long?

"Jessenia," he whispered her name.

She closed her eyes against the wave of emotion that threatened to send her to her knees. How could she still feel like this?

"That was, uh, nice," she cleared her throat and forced herself out of his embrace.

She almost half-hoped he'd refuse to let go, but he dropped his hands, and allowed her the space she felt she needed. It hurt, she wasn't going to lie to herself.

"Nice? That was more than nice," he frowned.

"Furio," she said his name, savoring it on her lips before pushing the rest of her thoughts through her lips, "you must have had a reason for not wanting to claim me. I guess I will never understand it, but I respect it. Truth is, I don't want to be with someone who has to work himself up to wanting me."

"But that's not it at all. Jessenia? Jessenia!"

He called her name, but she was already walking down the hall to the small bedroom she'd claimed as her own.

She'd stay in there all day if she had to, if only to avoid him. Maybe it was time to move on, she thought and fought against the hurt that rose inside.

This was always supposed to be temporary, she told herself and wiped the tears as she dug out her laptop and began to scroll for a rental.

SEVEN

"Well, what did you expect?" Storm slapped Furio in the back of the head.

Normally, he'd have tackled the shit out of the Wolf, but he didn't even have the strength to hit the fucker back. She'd walked away from him. Called him on his bullshit and walked away.

Yeah, he'd fucked this up. And it looked like there was no going back.

"Fuck man, it hurts," the Stallion rubbed the spot on his chest right over his heart.

The muscle was trying to kill him, or at least that was how it felt, how he felt. Strangled and suffocating at the same time. He tried to breathe, but his lungs refused to expand. Damn it, she refused him. Walked away from him.

Shit, shit, shit!

Rejection sucked in general, but being rejected by his fated mate? That was a whole new level of hurt. How did that even happen? He thought mates were supposed to fall in love and live happily ever after, like all the storybooks said.

Well, obviously Furio had been somewhat misinformed. Though, he knew beyond reasonable doubt, he was the cause of all this fuckery. He'd been an asshole for waiting to tell her. Stupid self-doubt. It ate at him, and now his *piccolina* had the short end of the stick.

"It can't be too late, *cump*," Storm shrugged.

"Fuck man, I don't know. Kingston? What about you?" he implored his Alpha.

"Look," the older Dragon said, "the women are all together in Jessenia's bedroom now. I am sure you are the topic of discussion."

"Yeah man, I gotta tell you, from Fergie's texts, it ain't looking good for you," Storm added.

"Fuck," Furio slumped forward, holding his head in his hands.

"Look, Furio, you've always had a difficult time expressing yourself," Kingston addressed him, and his tone held none of the Alpha powers Furio knew were at his fingertips.

This was just a couple of men talking, and for that, he was grateful. Besides, he needed all the advice he could get.

"For a Stallion Shifter, I always thought you were very firmly grounded," Byram said, "None of that aloofness your brethren seem to have inherited, and I liked that about you Furio, I always have," his cool voice only served to confuse him all the more.

"Brethren? You know others like me?"

"Well, not Italian Draft Horses, per se, but I am aware of other Equine Shifters. Jed Thorntree is one. He lives in a little town called Valentine. That's in Texas," the Vampire added, and his Stallion was piqued though now was not really the time.

"So, about Jessenia? How do I get her to forgive me?" he asked, feeling for all the world like the biggest idiot.

"So, what Byram here means, is you should have no problem expressing yourself to your mate," Egros, the only male Witch in the entire Keep piped in.

"Yeah, but you Witches don't have mates like we do," he gestured between himself and the other Shifters in the room, "You don't understand the call."

"Look, Witches may not be able to identify our fated mates by scent like you all do, but we are supernaturals too. We have fated mates, they are just revealed to us in different ways. Jessenia is a kitchen Witch, so her powers work differently from mine, anyway."

"What's that mean, bro? You tryin' to say my mate isn't powerful?" he growled on the offensive.

"No, man, not at all," Egos raised his hands up to ward off the attack Furio was dying to hurl his way.

Dammit. Now he was losing his shit for no reason at all. The guys were just trying to help him.

"Furio, that's exactly what we are trying to say. That rage is the beast inside of you. He wants his mate," Kingston grinned, obviously enjoying the man's discomfiture, "He's pushing you to claim her, yes?"

"Yes," Furio barely got the word out between gritted teeth.

"I see," he shrugged, "Well, first, you need to woo her."

"I need to *what* her?"

"Not what," Byram grinned along with Kingston "*woo.*"

"And how the fuck do I *woo* her? I don't even know what that is, bro," Furio stood up, and paced.

This was so not helping. He was not some ancient Dragon or suave Vampire. He didn't know shit about fuck when it came to wooing women.

When he'd had an itch in the past, all he really had

to do was point and the females would line up to fill his bed.

It wasn't conceit, merely fact. Especially where human women were concerned. Shifters were simply attractive to them. So yeah, he never had to work for sex before. But this, this wasn't sex. This was his mate.

He didn't want to fuck her. Okay, yeah, he did want to fuck her. But it wasn't just fucking. It was something else. A deep-seated, primal instinct that was making his Stallion wild with need.

She was his *fated mate,* or she would be. If he could just get her to listen.

"Look, *cump,* you know I got you, right?" Storm placed his hands on Furio's shoulders, "I wouldn't steer you wrong. What you need to do is flatter her, buy her things, take her places. I recommend shoes—"

"No! Not everyone has a shoe fetish, Storm," Kingston shook his head, "But ice cream can be a good way to bond," he said fondly.

"It's four degrees out," Egros pointed out.

"What about music or a movie?"

"We ain't in high school," he growled in frustration, "No, she deserved something else. Something, special."

"Then I guess, you already know what to do," Kingston nodded.

"Yeah," he said, and walked out of his Alpha's crowded office.

"Hey, Keep," he addressed the home where the Guardians had dwelled for decades, "I know you're listening, and I need your help."

The Keep had a habit of providing for the Guardians on what seemed to be an as-needed basis. Well, Furio sure as fuck needed help right then. He just hoped the Keep would provide.

Working on the greenhouse with Kingston and seeing Jessenia's reaction to it had given him an inkling of what his sassy little kitchen Witch might like. Maybe if he could break through that protective wall he'd helped erect around her heart, he could convince her he was sorry.

Plan in place, he set off towards his suite of rooms on the western side of the manse. The old building was more like a castle in a fairy tale than anything he'd ever seen growing up. Some days, he still couldn't believe he was there at all.

Him. Furio Do Luca, an orphan without a penny to his name, was a Guardian of Chaos. The elite group of supernaturals were renowned for their selfless dedication to the preservation of the freedom of magic for the entire paranormal world.

He'd been assigned to Kingston's group some three

decades ago, but he was a Shifter and a Guardian. He did not age the same way normals did, and it showed in his unlined face and still dark hair. But he was still the youngest of their group. Having left the care of St, Christopher's for the Keep at seventeen years old, this was the only home he'd ever known outside of school.

Kingston had been a father-figure of sorts, a friend for sure, and as good an Alpha as he could have ever hoped for. Stallion Shifters were not commonplace, especially in New Jersey, but he was at home in the pine barrens and swamps of the Garden State.

Restless and antsy, his animal had been in a constant state of awareness ever since she'd walked into his life. Jessenia deserved a far better mate than him. But she was his, and he would prove himself worthy. It was all he could do. Fuck that. It was what he had to do, or he might as well just lay down and die. And he was not ready to do that. Die for her, yes. But give up? Fuck no.

"Ah," he grinned, clapping his hands as the door to his room opened before him, "I can make this will work."

The spirits that dwelled deep within the manse were called the *manetuwak* by Holley, but he would probably just continue to refer to the collective as *the Keep*. It simplified things.

Most of the time he would rather be outside burning off steam with a good, hard run, but this project was special. He'd never had a real home, but he wanted one now. *With her.*

He knew he'd messed up big time, and he had a lot to prove. He wasn't like the others. Not debonair or whatever the fuck, but he was just right for his little *piccolina.*

Just need a little spit and polish, he thought with a wide smile. And he would show his future mate just how much she meant to him.

Yes, his Stallion whinnied, *mine.*

EIGHT

The sound of yelling and feet stomping through the halls brought Furio out of his work-induced daydreaming.

His mind often drifted while he cut wood, hammered nails, and put together the perfect second floor loft for his *piccolina*. Jessenia was a Witch, and he had his suspicions the title kitchen was going to be dropped after her powers had kicked his ass earlier that week.

It had been days since he'd seen her, but he knew she was still there. Could catch her fresh basil scent in the halls. And okay, so maybe he'd been spying on her from afar. He couldn't help it.

Now that he had publicly announced she belonged to him, his Stallion was more possessive than ever. The beast wanted her claimed, and he did not understand how building a loft was going to achieve that.

But Furio knew better. At least, he thought he did. Sure, he could seduce her. And that thought humbled him, but he did not want her to feel tricked in any way.

This was a labor of love, and he hoped to achieve one thing only with it. And that was her happiness. Provided she accepted him as mate, Furio would get the chance to make her happy for a very long time. Something he looked forward to with relish.

If not, well, he didn't want to think about it. In fact, he couldn't. His Stallion would not allow him to entertain thoughts of failure, though he supposed at the very least he could move out of the room. Give it to her since it only made sense if she was living there. But he was really fucking hoping he would not have to.

When he looked up, he wasn't at all surprised to see over a dozen hours had passed since he last checked. He was tired, but curious. No one ever ran around the hallways in the Keep. It was too dangerous. The corridors could and would continue forever if you didn't have a clear destination in mind.

Designed that way to keep intruders and burglars busy for hours or sometimes longer, until one of the Guardians returned to free them or send them on their way to the local Enforcers. Spells and similar wards and enchantments were used to protect the ancient castle and all who lived there.

Kinda cool. Furio had been doing some reading about the place. It was slow-going because of his dyslexia, but he wanted to know more about it before he'd started his project. Understanding the fundamentals of the magic used to create the Keep was important. Good thing Holley was there. He'd sought her out in his efforts to win Jessenia and she'd recommended the book. Even helped make it more accessible by bespelling a pair of glasses to help correct his dyslexia.

"A dyslexic brain is not a broken brain," the sassy Witch had told him firmly, *"It should have been identified by your teachers when you were young. But no worries, I have just the thing."*

For the first time ever, Furio laughed about his hidden problem. He'd accepted the glasses and promised to seek her out should he have any more trouble.

All Shifters had inherent powers that allowed them to share their bodies and souls with an animal half, but most, like him, were wary of actual magic. The kind of magic Jessenia had used to nearly suffocate him was scary as fuck. But at the time, he'd deserved an ass whopping.

More yelling sounded in the halls, and he knew he had to see what was up. He stood and wiped his hands on his jeans, grabbing a flannel along the way. Comfortable with his nudity didn't mean running around naked. His Stallion had been pretty fucking picky about that lately as well. He wanted one person's eyes on him, and until he had her, he'd prefer Furio to stay buttoned up.

Mincha. He rolled his eyes and shrugged the shirt on, snagging the vegan leather thong he used to keep his hair back from the dresser. He opened his door, and damn near bowled Storm over in the process.

"Shit," he grimaced, "You okay? What's goin' on?"

"It's Holley," he said, and for the first time in memory, the Wolf Shifter looked scared.

"Something is wrong with the young," he whispered, as if saying the thing aloud would make it true.

"Fuck," Furio cursed.

He felt as if someone punched him right in the gut. Shifter pregnancies were fragile and dangerous at best. Holley was a Witch, but her mate was Dragon. If any supernatural had a low birth rates, it was surely those rare, fantastical beasts.

"Come on," Storm slapped him on the arm, "Kingston wants us to meet him in his study."

A few seconds later, and they were inside the

familiar room where Kingston conducted most of the business side to his Guardian duties. The man looked haggard and as scared as Furio had ever seen him.

"Where is she?" Byram whispered, moving next to their leader.

"In our bedroom," he grunted, "Jessenia, Fergie, and Elena are helping her into bed."

"What happened?" Furio whispered, but in a room of Shifters and other supes, that was kinda pointless.

"Shhh," Storm scolded, and the look he gave him would've turned a lesser man to stone.

As it was, Furio shook it off. It might not be his place to speak up, asking about their Alpha's mate, but fuck it. Even after the way he'd responded to Kingston's mating, he cared dammit.

"Why is he here?" Egros asked.

Maybe he didn't have a right. Maybe he didn't even deserve to be in that room with the rest of the Guardians, but he would support his Alpha. Despite his past actions, he was still a Guardian. *Always.*

"Quiet," Byram hissed, "This is not about any of you," he said and watched his leader turn back around to face them.

Someday he would earn their trust back. He would prove his worth, and his loyalty to their group of Guardians. He'd thought he was forgiven, but Shifters were pretty dang serious when it came to mates. His trespasses were severe, and he might not ever gain back the same regard he'd had prior to his stupidity.

It's your own damn fault, he reminded himself, and kept his mouth shut for the duration.

No, they weren't all privy to his past. They did not all know about how he came to be there. The way Kingston had picked him up from the orphanage, and the way Neela had welcomed the teenaged Shifter with the chip on his shoulder the size of Morris County.

He'd seen the she-Dragon as a mother figure. And yeah, he'd felt betrayed when he'd learned the truth with the rest of them. But they wouldn't know about that either. He wasn't some pansy-ass motherfucker who needed to explain his feelings with them.

No fucking way. His Stallion snorted, taking offense at the suggestion. He did his best to placate the beast. Yes, it pained him to think he'd lost his place with them, but he'd made his bed, now he'd lie in it.

What choice was there? Furio had no use for whining. He would face what he had coming to him like a man. But he still cared, dammit. Whether they believed him or not, he cared about Holley, Kingston, and their young.

"Holley woke up to some spotting and cramps," the Dragon explained between gritted teeth,

This was difficult for him to say. Fuck, it was difficult to hear. Holley was not only new to their circle, but she'd been in some kind of magical suspension for centuries. None of them knew what that meant or how it would affect her pregnancy. Still, Furio's heart wrenched at the words his Alpha spoke.

"She is worried, we both are. Egros called a healer, but he will not be here for at least a day," he ran a hand over his face.

The tension in the air was thick and heavy. No one moved, or even breathed. Suddenly, the sound of the bedroom door cracking open had everyone turning. Without seeing, he knew instinctively who was there.

Furio's heart began to thud inside his chest. It was Jessenia. She looked worried. Her normally jovial expression was replaced by something else. Fear, empathy, and determination.

"She is resting now," Jessenia said to Kingston.

Her eyes swept the room and landed on him for a moment. She took a deep, calming breath as she approached the room full of powerful Guardians. And still her gaze came back to his, seeming to take strength in his presence.

Fuck. That felt good, he realized. He nodded

slightly, hoping to reassure her. Her eyes widened, but she looked away far too soon. As if catching herself.

"Thank you," Kingston nodded, barely holding on to his control, "What else can we do for her? Do you know of anything?"

"Actually, that's why I left the bedroom just now. You see, Holley, and I were talking about some temporary remedies that might work. Things to help sustain a Shifter pregnancy. I know of at least one tea that could help. She agrees it might, but the ingredients can only be gathered at certain times," she hesitated, "and under certain conditions."

"I will do anything," Kingston said, "just tell me."

"You can't, Kingston. You have to stay here, with her. Only a woman can gather what I need to make this tea."

"So, Elena then?" the Dragon asked.

"No." Jessenia licked her lips, and Furio watched the byplay with more than passing interest. "I have to be the one."

"I can't ask you to put yourself at risk." The Dragon shook his head, and Furio felt relief rush through him.

He was smart enough to keep his fucking mouth shut, but it was a near thing. The idea of her being in harm's way sent his Stallion into a rage. The Loyalists had been quiet lately, but that was nothing to go by. They could be plotting something. No, she was better off inside the Keep. But his relief was short-lived.

"Don't worry," she said, and nodded at his Alpha. "I can and will do this."

Fucking hell. His Stallion whinnied, stomping his feet with his ears pressed back tight against his head. Agitated was not exactly the word to describe how his animal felt. Angry as fuck fit better. And yet, he knew if he said one word, he would damage whatever truce they'd had going over the last few days.

"Okay," Kingston said in the background. "But what are the special circumstances?"

Jessenia looked around the room. The tart scent of her embarrassment reached Furio. He frowned as others stared openly at the little kitchen Witch. Egros cleared his throat. Clearly, the guy had some idea, but he simply averted his gaze when Furio stared at him in question. What the hell was going on? He wondered, anxiety starting to rise.

"Well, the remedy requires ingredients gathered from the forest. Bark from a mature Black Cherry tree, to be exact. It can only be harvested under the light of the full moon by a female Witch. Preferably the one who plans to brew the healing tea," she said and hesitated again.

The scent of her embarrassment set his Stallion on edge. But his curiosity was also truly piqued. What was she hiding exactly?

"Tonight, is the full moon, and it's already eleven o'clock. I have to leave soon to find the right tree. I have to do it before midnight, so I can harvest at the exact time the clock strikes the hour."

"I know where a Black Cherry tree stands, I can fly you there," Kingston replied.

Furio's chest tightened, and an ugly green-eyed monster started reading his head. But before he could protest, Jessenia shook her head.

Thank fuck.

"No, I have to walk." The pretty kitchen Witch said and shook her head. "It's part of the sacrifice required to balance the spell. And yes, Holley told me you'd both seen one a few months ago, I know where to go."

"It's too dangerous," Furio said aloud.

He received matching glares from everyone in the office. But the Stallion didn't give a fuck. Jessenia was precious to him. He had to say something.

"I will be fine," she hissed in his direction.

"She is right," Egros added.

Kingston's head swiveled to where the male Witch stood. And everyone else's did too. Only Furio remained unmoved. His eyes remained fixed on the pair of rich brown beauties that were currently attempting to drive daggers through him.

Shit.

"Of course, I'm right," she snapped, then took a deep breath before continuing. "I'm only a kitchen Witch, but I know my stuff, okay? I have to do this alone."

"There's no only about it—" Furio tried, realizing his mistake.

"Enough," Kingston interrupted and nodded sharply. "Look Jessenia, I appreciate what you are trying to do. Holley is my life. If anything were to happen to her, I don't know what—"

"It will be okay, Kingston," Byram said and nodded, his belief in the Jessenia evident. "The little kitchen Witch knows her stuff."

The seemingly casual remark made Furio both growl and gnash his teeth. Byram grinned slightly. Well, fuck. The Vampire seemed delighted at his response, which made his Stallion even more pissed. The beast snorted in warning.

Then Jessenia moved, and his attention was fully on her. She exhaled and straightened her shoulders. Giving him one scathing look before leaving the room.

Byram's smile grew wider, and he bowed at

Jessenia as she passed him. Furio snorted again. Out loud. He didn't like the Vampire's overly familiar grin. He liked even less that it had been directed towards his mate.

Fuck. She wasn't his yet. He had to remember that. But he could not stop himself from caring about her. Something was definitely up, and he needed to find out what.

Following her path along the corridor, he kept his destination in mind. Trying to catch up with the surprisingly fleet of foot Witch was not all that difficult. He was a Stallion, after all. Keeping her in mind was not difficult either.

Jessenia. Mine. Mate.

Yes, that part was easy enough, but once confronted with her closed bedroom door, Furio started to sweat. He didn't have time to think about what to do or say.

Mincha! Furio's Stallion butted against his skin. His animal wanted out, wanted her, but he reined him in tightly. Wiping his suddenly damp palms on his jeans, he stood up straight the second he heard the knob click. The door opened, and the scent of sweet, fresh picked basil tickled his senses.

There she was. His gorgeous *piccolina*. Delightfully flushed and wearing a floor length hooded cloak. Wait, what? Had he missed something? Was Halloween twice this year? Eyes roving over the thin black garment, his lips pursed tightly when they came to her bare feet.

"What are you doing here?" she asked, and he detected a familiar note of annoyance in her voice.

Shit. Choosing to ignore it, he decided to go with the obvious. He gestured to her clothes with his hands.

"What are you wearing?"

Cocking his head to the side, he realized that was the wrong question. The right one would have been, what wasn't she wearing?

"Nothing," she said, "and don't try to stop me."

Her face burned a brighter shade of red as she stepped forward, pushing past him in the process.

"Wait, Jess," he said.

He wanted to try to explain. To offer his help. But she was moving so dang quickly. Like she couldn't even stand to be in the same space as him.

Shit. That was his own damn fault. He should just let her go. Was resolved to do just that, but his hand shot out as if of its own accord, and he stopped her.

"Furio!" She gasped.

That's when he noticed a flash of pale skin where the two sides of the long, black garment suddenly parted. The fuck?

"You're naked!" he shouted.

Cursing roundly, he moved fast. Had to block her from view since he heard footsteps sneaking up on them, and fast.

"Uh, what's going on here?" Fergie asked, her arm looped through Storm's.

The couple was probably headed towards the kitchen. Looking for snacks, he hazarded a guess. But Furio was beyond speech at the moment. He was growling loudly.

The angry sound reverberated through his chest as his Stallion stomped and snorted. The beast was tearing him up on the inside.

"Knock it off, Furio," she said, but he stepped closer.

Blocking her entirely with his tall, wide frame, he was about a second from freaking out. Well, what was he supposed to do? His mate was naked in the hallway, and there were others present.

Her small hands pressed against his chest, and his animal whinnied. He wished like hell she was touching him for another reason, but he'd still take it. Dog that he was.

"Greetings everyone," Byram said.

Great, another fucking person joined them, and his Stallion was about to burst through his skin. The animal understood what was happening on a level best described as basic.

His mate was nude in the hallway where anyone could see her. And the suddenly murderous beast had one response.

Hell fucking no.

NINE

Jessenia closed her eyes as wave after wave of embarrassment, and humiliation threatened to drown her. She'd barely gotten out of Kingston's office with her secret, but here she was.

Butt ass naked in the hallway with the one freaking Guardian she'd been avoiding all week. Crap. She would so rather not have to explain this to him, of all people.

She'd been reading about Shifters and their mates. Understood a little better that like it or not, his animal was going to be like batshit crazy jealous over everything until they formally mated. And maybe even after.

Sigh. Some people got their kicks off of jealous significant others, but Jessenia had almost little to no experience with it. She just didn't inspire jealousy.

Hell, she was a mousy little kitchen Witch with a big mouth, a fat ass, and a love of bookish things. What could she say? She was average at best.

"Fucking perfect," he growled, pressing his nose to the crux of her neck.

She yelped at the press of his hard, *and yes, she meant hard*, and hot, *oh boy, very, very hot, like smokin' hot* body against hers. The stone wall was cold, but she hardly felt it from the inferno coming off him.

"Um, guys? You need to keep walking or *Mr. Ed* here is gonna go apeshit," Jessenia nodded at Storm and Fergie, who she knew was about to protest.

"But—"

Fergie yelped. *Sigh.* Luckily, Storm bent down and propped his mate over his shoulder, hustling her out of the hallway while she tried to get the situation under control.

"Mine," Furio growled again.

The word shouldn't have sent spikes of desire shooting straight to her core, but they did. *Oh yeah, they really did.* She could feel her needy sex throb and grow slick with want of him.

Great. Now she had to go traipsing through the forest with the female version of blue balls.

What the hell even was that? Blue ovaries? Blue nipples? Whatever. Fucking fabulous.

"No!" she scolded, "Bad horsey!"

"What?"

The slap to his ass seemed to prompt him to lift his head. He looked shocked, but also a tad bit interested. Dammit. That only turned her on even more.

"Listen, *Pony Boy*, I have to go," she pushed against his check.

"Pony boy?" he looked confused.

Oh well. She had to say something to shake him up. Poor guy was vibrating with emotion. He had the most big, hard, *oooh*, make that *very big and hard* body, pressed up against hers. His hands were on the wall behind her head and she was positive, he'd left a dent.

She shoved slightly and he moved back a step. Okay, so she immediately missed his incredible warmth and strength, but she wouldn't be admitting that aloud. Not anytime soon, anyway.

"I have to go," she said.

"You aren't wearing any clothes."

"That's right."

"Jessenia, why aren't you wearing clothes?"

He tried for calm. She could see it in the way he controlled his breathing, and she silently applauded the effort. Jessenia knew enough about Shifters now to understand this was tough on him.

Not that he deserved her consideration. After all, the man had lied to her. By omission, but still, it counted. The question in his dark green eyes was begging for a response, and she felt her resolve wavering.

Dang it. Jessenia always was a big softy at heart. She couldn't help herself. The way his jaw was clenched tight, and the furrows in his brow made her want to reach out and soothe his Stallion.

The nostrils at the end of his straight, Roman nose flared in his angst, and she clenched her fists lest she throw herself at him. Literally.

Fine. Maybe she should give him a break. Even if it was kinda nice seeing him all worked up over her. He was the one who'd been denying what they were to each other for freaking months now. Leaving her wondering why she wanted him so badly, and he hardly seemed interested.

"I am a Witch, Furio. You know that, right?"

"Yeah, but you usually wear clothes," he grunted.

"True," she said, and he did have a point, "Holley needs my help. Her baby is in distress, and only a special tea brewed from the bark of a Black Cherry tree can help her while we wait for the healer to come. In order to get the right magical benefits from the tree bark, I have to harvest it a certain way," she felt her face heat.

"You also have no shoes on," he frowned.

"Yep." She nodded. "No clothes, and no shoes. I can't wear them. At all. The cloak's just until I get outside."

"No," he growled.

"Yes."

"I don't like it," he tried again.

"Well, too bad for you," she scoffed.

"You'll freeze," Furio shook his head, causing his hair to ripple on either side of his face as it came loose from its tie, "and it's not safe."

"I'll be okay," she argued, somewhat fascinated by his glossy locks.

Honestly, Jessenia was frightened. Holley had been attacked just outside the Keep. Offner was gone now, that was true, but his followers were still at large.

The Loyalists had tried separating themselves from their former leader's radical fanaticism, but they were not exactly known for their fine judgement. Wanting to control magic was as unnatural as wanting to control the tides. It was just not the order of things. Magic was wild and wonderful. It could be used for bad, but in its most basic form it was a thing of beauty. But only if free.

The Guardians' creed came to mind, and she smiled, reciting the words in her brain. From chaos comes creation. Yes, indeed.

But she was not a Guardian. Nor was she a *conpar*. Not yet, maybe not ever. What if the Loyalists were watching them now? Shivers of fear raced down her spine, but she shook them off.

A naked kitchen Witch would be a sitting duck. But she was still going. Jessenia couldn't fail in her mission. Holley needed her, and besides, she was made of stronger stuff than anyone knew. Even her.

"I am going with you," he said, and for a moment gratitude flowed through her.

Jessenia wasn't a warrior, but she believed in the Guardians of Chaos. She supported their cause as her own. Deep inside her Witch's heart she knew without a doubt that fighting for the freedom of all magic was what she was supposed to do.

Even a kitchen Witch could turn the tide. She had more than enough self-respect to know that. It was like her grandmother always said, everyone had a role to play in this world.

Furio's expression booked no argument, so she nodded. Thankful he was going with her if for no other reason than to ensure the job got done without incident.

"Okay."

"You're saying yes?" he looked shocked.

She ignored him, putting one foot in front of the other. Jessenia managed to not fall on her face as she reached the back door. Before she could touch the handle, he was there.

Opening the door for her, one hand outstretched as if he wanted to place it on the small of her back but didn't dare touch. Regret welled up, but she pushed it away. Their story was not over yet.

The future could still be theirs, maybe if they were both willing to exchange in a little give and take. She stood still for a moment and tried to gain her courage. Her feet were frozen on the cold stone patio. It stretched only a dozen or so feet beyond the Keep, and after that, a thick blanket of white snow covered the ground.

"Are you sure about this?"

His question was quiet, low, like a whispering wind fleeting through her mind. Jessenia sucked in a deep breath and nodded. She cared very much about Holley and Kingston, about all of them. She would help. If she could, she would. Period.

"I am sure," she said, "They're my friends. I would do anything to help a friend."

With nothing to prove to anyone but herself, Jessenia inhaled one more cold fortifying breath. She knew her limitations as a Witch, but this was medicine she'd studied with her grandmother. This was a magic old as time itself.

Treatments normals now ignored in favor of big pharma. No one appreciated the sacrifice and creative forces that went into healing anymore. The first Witches were healers, midwives, that kind of thing.

But they were few and far between these days. Witches were the only species of supernatural that were ever well and truly outed throughout all of time. And no one was despised more, except maybe the Devil himself.

"You will let me walk with you the whole way? I'll keep you safe," the latter was more statement than question, but she found herself nodding at him.

He might have denied her in the beginning, but he was here now. His animal was pushing him hard, somehow, she could tell, but for whatever reason,

Jessenia was willing to take it. She did not want to do this alone.

"Okay," she said, "but you can't interfere. Promise?"

Her eyes bore into his, she saw the hesitation, the questions in the glittery green pools, but she wasn't about to address them. Their relationship was on rocky grounds as it was.

Maybe they could have a future. Somehow, some-way, but she couldn't rightly tell. Precognition wasn't one of her kitchen Witch's powers. Furio seemed to study her passively, and she let him. Pretty soon there would be nothing between them. Literally.

Jessenia had to fight her nerves to control the shaking of her limbs as she turned to face the path that led straight to the heart of the barrens. Her hands trembled as she undid the ties that held the cloak together.

Getting naked in front of a man, any man, was never easy for a woman like Jessenia. She knew she was cute, but that didn't mean self-consciousness aban-doned her at any given time during her life.

A realist, she knew all too well that being vertically challenged with average sized breasts, a bigger than she'd have liked butt, and a soft belly put her squarely in the *okay* range on the hotness meter. And she didn't even want to think about her thick thighs and other jiggly bits.

Sigh. The fact she'd been lusting after the man she was about to strip in front of, and not for any fun time reason, only made her more nervous. But it was too late to back out now.

Besides, Holley needed her, and she would not let her friend down. Jessenia sucked in some cold air and grabbed her metaphorical balls, then dropped the cloak. Ignoring his sharp intake of breath, she took the first step forward into the cold night.

"I'd say it's colder than a witch's titty, but that would be too self-deprecating even for me," she tried to make light of the situation, but was met with only silence.

A moment later she knew why. Jessenia turned her head to glance at her escort, only to be greeted by the sounds of cloth being ripped and torn. Next came the telltale cracking and stretching sounds of bones and muscles breaking and re-knitting.

Gasping at what she'd never realized was obviously a painful process, Jessenia stopped and stared in wonder. The air shimmered with green ethereal lights surrounding his body and whirling in a fury of activity. It was incredible, beautiful, and something Shifters rarely shared with anyone else except maybe in the heat of battle.

The lights dimmed, and he was there. Smelling like sunshine and spring breezes, even though it was near midnight and no more than twenty-degrees outside. Then Furio was standing beside her. Only, it wasn't him exactly.

It was his Stallion. The magnificent beast whinnied and shook his head, sending his glossy mane shimmering in the moonlight. She'd never seen his imposing steed before.

The Italian Draft Horse was an incredible animal. He was enormous, with a shiny white coat that looked like a bolt of glittery satin in the darkness. His mane and tail were both long and dark, like his own ebony locks.

Breathtaking and powerful, but not at all like the racehorses she'd seen on TV. She knew instinctively he was built for more than speed or entertainment. No, nothing so frivolous as that.

His beast was designed to conquer. A true warhorse. Nineteen hands high, and over eighteen-hundred pounds of pure muscle and strength. His enormous head nudged her, as if to say go, and she did. Shivering once she realized where she was and what she was doing.

"We better hustle," she said aloud, knowing he understood her even in this shape.

Furio kept pace beside her, blocking the wind from chilling her further with his enormous body. Who was she kidding? Temperatures were already dropping, but he gave off heat like a furnace and she was grateful though her toes were numb as she stepped carefully on the ice and snow.

A noise like an animal scurrying sounded to the left, and she turned her head. It was nothing, but it sent her heart racing, and she stood still for a moment too long. Furio whinnied.

"I guess it was nothing," she whispered and placed a hand on his back for her comfort more than his.

With only a thin, steel blade in one hand, and her other secure on his tall back, she ambled forward. The pine forest was dark and imposing. The moonlight glinted off the snow, creating shadows and an atmosphere more suited to a horror film than reality.

Her breath made cloudy white puffs in the air, and she tried not to tremble, but it was part of her sacrifice she knew. Magic demanded that from her, and she gave it freely. The least she could do to help her friends was take a walk through the snow.

Still, she was scared. Jessenia was so much more at home in the kitchen. Her magic practiced through cooking and baking with healing prayers, healthy wishes, love and positivity as her only intentions.

She wasn't going to deny her fear. That would negate her sacrifice all together and it might sully the magic. No, she acknowledged it, and that alone gave her strength and power.

It was a twenty minute walk from there to where the stand of Black Cherry trees stood, and she was more grateful by the second for his company. The woods at night were beautiful on one hand. Stark and silent, the trees towered above them, overwhelming in their magnitude.

Holley had described the path in detail, but it was so very different up close. With the heavy snowfalls just lately, Jessenia found herself up to her ankles in some places. The pain of the freezing ground shot through to her bones, but she knew it was all part of it. It was the price required by the universe for the ritual to work.

Biting back her discomfort, Jessenia gritted her teeth, refusing to give in to the cold. She kept on going, the gently snorts and chuffs from Furio's Stallion kept her mind from wandering too far.

Everything took on a sort of silvery luster beneath the enormous moon and its bright, glowing light. She was taken back by the pure beauty of her home state. She loved it there, never wanted to leave it.

New Jersey wasn't all concrete cities. It was mountains, forests, beaches, and trails. It was magic and moonlight. A hub of supernatural activity. And she was part of that world.

Even if she was just a kitchen Witch.

<h1 style="text-align:center">TEN</h1>

"There," Jessenia's whisper cut through the silence like the steel blade she carried in her grip.

In her excitement, she was not paying attention. Suddenly, she stumbled over some tangled tree roots the snow had hidden from her sight. The air hummed and shimmered with magic as Furio returned to his human form. His arms reached out to snag her before she could hit the cold ground, but she shook her head.

"No," she shouted, and braced herself for the fall.

"Fuck! Are you okay?" he reached for her again, but she shied away, and lifted herself off the cold snowy ground.

"Jessenia?"

"I'm fine," she breathed, and shook the snow off her skin.

She only thanked the gods she'd dropped the blade first. Otherwise, it might be embedded somewhere entirely uncomfortable. Like her very cold, very pink skin.

"You're freezing, *piccolina*," he growled, and something about the pet name he called her made her warm inside.

"It's okay," she got the words out between her chattering teeth, as she looked through the snow to find the blade.

Once in hand, she approached the tall Black Cherry. Well, shit. Of course, it was gigantic. And she, being herself, could barely reach a branch.

"Fucking hell," he grunted, but she ignored him, "it's not even midnight yet. You'll never make it if I don't get you warm."

"Can't," she shivered, "Have to sacrifice for the magic to work."

"You sacrifice too much, *piccolina*," he grunted.

Furio reached for her again, and this time, there was no stopping him. With one hand on her waist and the other on her neck, he pulled her forward into the circle of his arms.

Oh my.

He was like a furnace. Her body shivered in delight at the warmth of his touch. Smooth skin, rippling muscles, and that springtime scent were driving her mad. Anticipation flowed through her, making her weak with need to the point where she lifted her face, sighing in relief when he bent his head.

Furio whispered her name reverently, almost hopefully, then their lips met, and she could hardly think. Walls closed in on them until they were the only two beings in the universe.

Jessenia gave in to the moment. That kiss was a promise. She felt it as real as the soft stubble that graced his cheeks and chin. The steady pressure of his lips on hers was intoxicating.

She relaxed against him, opening her mouth just wide enough for his tongue to invade. Thrilling wasn't a word she'd ever used to describe a man, but it was how she felt in his arms.

He was that and more. He was adventure. He was comedy, safety, and desire. Tantalizing and captivating. Strong, willful, proud, and yet tender, giving, and so damn sweet.

She wanted more. She wanted it all. But did he truly want her? That was the real question. The evidence of his carnal interest was currently pressed against her belly, and she had no doubt the two of them would set the bed on fire.

At the moment, she knew it more a question of when rather than if. Jessenia moaned softly, but no other sounds except the beating of their hearts, and their racing pulses made it to her ears.

Everything seemed to fall away as she kissed him back. Her arms were pinned inside his embrace making her his prisoner in effect. But she was not afraid of him. She had never felt safer or more protected than with him.

Before she was ready, Furio ended the kiss. Pressing his forehead to hers, he breathed like it was something difficult. And she somehow realized, it was. He didn't want to let her go, and the knowledge of that warmed her like nothing else could.

"Feeling warmer?" he cut through her reverie, and she closed her eyes as the timber of his voice rolled through her like hands stroking her skin.

"Yeah." She nodded, and pressed her lips to his chastely once more.

"It's midnight, *piccolina*," he whispered.

Jessenia wanted to curse. Hell, she really wanted to stay right where she was, but she had a job to do.

Turning around to face the old cherry tree, Jessenia raised her arms high. Chanting the words

Holley taught her, she began to slice pieces of near-frozen bark from the trunk.

The wood was hard to cut through, but her knife was sharp and her aim accurate. Sometimes it paid to be a good cook. She hacked at the wood, collecting the bits in her palm.

Next, she moved to the branches nearest her, cursing herself for her own lack of height. Bark from the trunk and branches both were necessary.

"Climb on my back," Furio said from so close behind her, his breath tickled her neck.

"I d-don't know," her teeth chattered.

"I'll shift and kneel down. Climb on my back, *piccolina*, and you can reach the branch. Let me help you, let me help Holley. I think you've suffered enough for balance. Besides, I'm the one sacrificing my back to your ice cube feet," he joked.

His voice was so deep, and his words attractive. She knew they were meant to help, but Jessenia wasn't going to risk it. She was going to do this old school. And little did he know, but having him there was giving her the strength to do all this when all she wanted was to curl into a ball and let the cold overcome her.

"Just stay with me," she whispered back, "I can do this, I know I can."

"Of course, you can," he said, as if that was obvious.

Jessenia smiled then, and it hurt her poor, frozen face, but she couldn't help it. That was the Furio she'd grown so fond of. The one who stated the most outrageous things as if they were evident to all.

Jessenia jumped up and grabbed the end of the branch. Pulling it down with all her might, she ignored the sting of the frozen snow that fell and hit her naked skin. Struggling with the knife to whittle off more bits of bark and some twigs as well, she concentrated on the task at hand.

All the while, she was keenly aware of his eyes on her. Even as she'd chanted the spell Holley taught her, Jessenia knew her Stallion kept watch. Protecting her.

Once she'd collected enough, she turned to see Furio still standing on two feet. Uncaring of his own nudity, he simply waited. An imposing, yet steady presence that bulked her spirit.

His hair hung in a dark tangle down his back, and she wondered if he had any idea how good-looking he was. Of course, he probably did. But really, she found herself tongue tied.

He looked like he belonged to another time. With his chiseled features, cords of rippling muscles, tall frame, and naturally bronzed skin, he could have been a Spartan soldier, or a Roman legionnaire. Maybe a gladiator fighting lions with his bare hands.

"Are you finished?" he asked, looking at her curiously while she stared like some lovesick teen.

"You didn't shift?" she asked, shaking herself out of her own stupor.

"Nah, if you walk, I walk."

"But before you—" she started.

"Before my Stallion took over before I could control myself. It seemed better to allow him to have his way."

"I don't understand. Why couldn't he control himself?"

"Jessenia," he snorted as if it were obvious. "You're naked."

Like that explained everything. She looked down at her puckered nipples that tipped medium-sized breasts, the soft belly beneath them, wide hips, and the dark curls that covered her sex. Short legs and red, cold feet followed. Hardly beautiful, but he was staring like he couldn't get enough.

"So?"

"Do you even know how gorgeous you are? How much work I find myself having to do not to reach out and grab you right this fucking second?"

"Oh, come on. You're not a teenager, Furio, and I know my physical limitations."

"You really have no idea how drop-dead gorgeous you are right now?"

"I am not the first woman you've seen naked," she scoffed.

"Jessenia, you are the only woman that matters to me," Furio told her as the Keep came into view. "When are you going to believe me when I tell you that I want you? I always want you. You're my fated mate, and even if you weren't, *piccolina*, I would still want you."

Her heart was pounding in her chest as his emerald green eyes bore down into hers. Before she could utter a single reply, two things happened.

First, a group of men dressed in black leapt out at them from the shadows, and second, Furio kissed her hard and fast, before pushing her towards the Keep.

"Jessenia! Run!"

Eleven

Bespelled iron shackles bit into his wrists, but Furio refused to utter a sound as the group of Loyalists shoved him into his cell.

"Fucking Guardian filth!"

"Look at this bastard! Thinks he can tell us what to do!"

"Traitor to your kind!"

"Get in there before we turn you into glue!"

He'd heard shit like that all his life, and it was easy enough to shake off. The back of his head still throbbed from the blitz attack, but he did what he had to do to keep their focus on him. He'd almost gone fucking nuts thinking about what they would do to Jessenia if they caught her.

His Stallion raged at him, battling against the

group of Shifters until he saw his mate haul her sweet little ass out of there. Thank fuck. The group of armed-to-the-teeth Loyalist fuckers had been so focused on getting him secured, she'd flitted right through their trap.

He should have known better. Should've been paying attention, but that was pretty difficult when his mate was parading around in the freezing cold in her birthday suit. And what a suit it was.

Mincha! He could die a happy man right then, having seen the heaven he would surely find one day in her sweet embrace.

No fucking way. His Stallion snorted and stomped. The animal within him was in no way, shape or form going to allow him to even entertain thoughts of death. Not when his *piccolina* was out there needing him.

She might be pissed off at him for being a jerk, but she was his. And now they both knew it. Furio couldn't exactly blame her for being pissed at him, and he would readily accept it and apologize every day of his life forever now that he knew she wanted him too.

Fucking a. The sassy little kitchen Witch had shown him how much with the sweet, desperate way she'd returned his kiss. Both kisses.

Rrrr. His Stallion growled and snorted. The beast

wanted out. He wanted to find her. Now. Was pissed as hell Furio hadn't claimed her when in all the months he'd known her.

Restraint was hard for a guy like him, but for her, he would wait forever. And he'd prove it too as soon as he got the fuck out of this mess. She was worth it. Hell, she was worth everything. Furio closed his eyes, mumbling a quick prayer for her safety. There were some things that were simply ingrained in a man.

Growing up in a Catholic orphanage meant praying came naturally to him despite everything he disagreed with about organized religion. He always felt a certain peace come over him whenever he spoke to God, or the gods, and yes, he prayed to both.

It was all the same to him. And he would continue to pray to any and all if they would just make sure *she* was safe. It was incredible, and a little crazy, to think how fucking stupid he'd been to deny his feelings.

But he understood now that he loved her. Had since the day they met. He should kick himself in the head for delaying claiming the beautiful female. Stupid self-pity. It didn't matter if he thought he was worth it, she did and that was all that mattered.

Besides, Furio was a good man. He would work his ass off to deserve her. Now that he'd had a small taste, he wanted more. Hell, he wanted it all. His Jessenia was sassy as fuck.

Bellissima, molto bellissima. So fucking beautiful. Rrrr.

Watching her cut a path through the snow, her gorgeous womanly shape had him so hard he could barely stand up straight. But it was more than her body that enticed the beast. Hell, he loved every inch of her inside and out. Especially the way her big brown eyes lightened to amber when he kissed her.

She had such a big, beautiful heart. Pure gold was how he'd describe her to anyone who asked. Even the damp, dark cell he was currently chained to couldn't dim his feelings for the woman.

The reality of his situation sucked, but it was temporary. Hell fucking yeah, it was. Unlike his feelings for his *piccolina*. He would get out, and he would go to her. Claim her as his own.

Yes, his Stallion stomped in approval. The beast was desperate to give his mark to the woman. She his true and fated mate. Her and no other.

Shit. He had it bad, but that fact only made him grin wider. He loved everything about her. He could admit it now. Well, to himself anyway. This crazy thing he felt was more than just fate, it was love. And she thought he was upset about it, that he wouldn't choose her freely.

His fault, he knew. But he would make it up to her. If it took the rest of his life. For months he'd watched her. Learned everything he could about the little kitchen Witch.

She was honest and bright, practical, and silly too. Her laughter was the best damn sound he'd ever heard. Rich and earthy, like the wonderful concoctions she crafted in the kitchen.

She was one hell of a cook, and yeah, he'd noticed her dishes taking on a much more vegetarian aspect since she'd moved in. Hope blossomed at the realization she'd been doing that for him. Just another reason to survive whatever these fuckers had in store for him.

In all her interactions with the Guardians, Fergie, and Holley too, Jessenia proved to be kind and loving. She gave everything one hundred and ten percent. Look how she'd volunteered to walk naked through the forest in the middle of the night in February to gather the ingredients needed for a magical tea to help protect Holley and Kingston's pregnancy.

In-fucking-credible. Pride flowed through him at her selfless act. But fuck, he shouldn't have let his guard down. Furio should have shifted to his Stallion and ran her sweet ass home.

He couldn't help the thrill that raced through him at the thought of her mounted on his Stallion's broad back. She'd hug his sides with her thighs and tug on his mane while he whisked her through the pines and snow-covered forest.

Even better, he thought of his sexy little *piccolina* astride his naked body, taking him deep inside her sweet body, while he took every care to ensure her pleasure and satisfaction.

Only yesterday, he would've doubted her desire for him, but today he knew better. He was ready to admit it and accept it. Hell, there was no denying it now. Need had sweetened her scent when he'd had the feisty little kitchen Witch wrapped up in his arms.

Just thinking about it made his cock hard and thick. He reached down and pinched himself, not wanting to be vulnerable considering where he was. A hard-on was damn inconvenient in these surroundings.

Mincha! He needed to find a way out. Needed to get back to her. To make sure she was safe.

Jessenia, his Stallion whispered inside his mind's eye. He wished like hell for fiftieth time that hour, that he'd claimed her already. Maybe then he would know for sure if she was alright.

No, that was no way to think. She was safe.

She had to be.

Twelve

"Help!" Jessenia's voice rang through the kitchen as she used the back entrance to enter the Keep.

"What is it?" Byram came hurling into the room.

Thank goodness for his super-speed, she thought inanely. The movie star good looks of the Vampire would have caught her off guard once upon a time, but she knew him well enough by now. He was not for her. He was a friend. That was all.

Unmoved by his chiseled features and handsome face, she reached out as her frozen, stiff limbs met with the tiled floor. Byram stalled a moment, probably shocked at her nudity, and she fell to her knees.

"Jessenia!" he shouted.

Jessenia did not have time to worry about the Vampire, not when Furio was in danger. Stupid, stubborn Stallion. She closed her eyes as panic threatened to overwhelm her.

No, that was so not happening. She had to save him! Shaking from head to toe, she was grateful when Byram grabbed the tablecloth, wrapping it around her shoulders. He placed his hands on her arms, and she shied away from his touch, but recognized it as perfunctory.

Byram was only trying to help, she told her magic repeatedly. But it was as if the powers inside her refused the logic. That had never happened before, and she forced them to heed her will. She didn't want to hurt him.

"Ouch," he gritted his teeth when her powers shocked him.

"S-sorry," she mumbled between her chattering teeth.

He could help Furio, she told herself. That fact alone seemed to reassure her powers. Byram used his grip to help her stand, adjusting the cloth to preserve her modesty while he guided her to a chair.

"What happened? Jessenia?" he shook her shoulder gently.

Fuck, didn't he know she was trying hard not to

zap his ass? Her powers started to swirl and pulse, angry at his touch. She did not want his hands on her. They were wrong. *He* was wrong.

"Apologies," he bowed his head, and the Vampire smartly stepped away from her.

She dropped the Black Cherry tree bark she still had clutched in her palm on the table. Egros and Kingston had come running into the kitchen by then, followed by Storm and Fergie.

"Oh my God!" Fergie dropped to her knees by Jessenia's side, "Honey, are you alright?"

"W-we were amb-b-bushed. Please, we h-have to h-help F-Furio," she was shaking too hard to speak clearly, but they got the gist.

The moment they understood what she'd been trying desperately to convey, they started to make plans.

"I can't stay here," Kingston rubbed his face, "I have to help. Egros, can you and Jessenia make the tea for Holley?"

She knew it was difficult for the Dragon to leave his mate. But he assured her she was resting well and easy.

"Yes," Egros said and nodded, "Holley explained it all to me before she fell asleep," the male Witch began to gather other ingredients, and set them in a pot of boiling water to steep.

"Okay." Kingston was pointing to the place where Jessenia said they'd met with the enemy on an old map. "They must have taken him to the old hunter's cabin. Place is in ruins," he growled.

"G-get me clothes," she turned to Fergie, who nodded and ran down the hall to her room.

"No, you can't come with us. You aren't a Guardian, and besides, he'd want you here," Storm said.

The look she flashed him as Fergie came back and held up a blanket so she could pull on a pair of leggings and top must've been more powerful than she'd thought.

The Wolf raised his hands in surrender and averted his gaze. Good. Last thing she wanted to do was freak out on her bestie's man, but she'd had enough of people telling her what she could and could not do.

First, Furio had made the decision to delay telling her she was his fated mate without any input at all. And now these fuckers thought they were leaving without her to save her man.

Hell no.

He'd sacrificed his own escape for her sake. She knew that, even though he would never admit to committing such a selfless act. But that was Furio. He never wanted praise. Despite his seemingly cocky attitude, he was shy about being in the limelight.

Something she understood all too well. Her vlog allowed her to connect with people, but it also held them at bay. She had all the power in that scenario. One click, and the connection could be severed.

But that wasn't the case with a mate, was it? No. It couldn't be that way. She would have to give up some of her power, her control. But the rewards, oh the rewards, would be worth it.

She only had to look at Fergie to understand that mating Storm was the most important decision her best friend had ever made. Truthfully, this was the happiest she had ever seen her. Even happier than during Nordstrom Rack's last shoe sale. And yes, Jessenia was thrilled for her, but she wanted some of that for herself.

With Furio. Images of her Stallion flitted through her mind. The thousand different ways he tried to tell her how he felt over the past few months, but she was too stubborn to see. He always held doors for her. Stole too many little glances to count. Whenever they went into town, he made sure she walked on the inside of the street.

He always took out the trash when she was

finished cooking, and she'd caught him loading the dishwasher once or twice. He cared. And not just for her. But for every single one of them.

"Okay, you aren't getting rid of me. That Stallion is *my mate.* He put himself in danger to save *my butt,* so first," she grumbled, "we are rescuing his stubborn ass. Then, I'm going to kick it. And afterwards, I am going to claim him. Anyone have any objections?"

By the time she was finished, she was breathless. Green sparks seemed to shoot from her hands, and she was trembling, but not with cold. It was more like her powers were energized because they had a new purpose.

Find her mate and save his ass so she could kick it for putting her through this. Then maybe she could kiss it all better.

Yup. Solid plan.

"No problem here," Fergie grinned, elbowing Storm, who simply nodded his agreement.

Though Jessenia noticed, his eyebrows had somehow disappeared into his hairline.

"Sounds fair enough," Byram grinned.

"About time, little Witch," Elena smirked, "But how about I stay behind with Holley and Egros? That all right, Alpha?"

Kingston nodded at the Panther Shifter and closed

his eyes. Probably communicating with his mate, Jessenia thought as she pulled on the heavy fleece Fergie had grabbed for her.

Next, she donned thick socks and waterproof boots. Finally, clothed and warm, she was ready. Kingston finished up discussing their plan of attack, and she listened intently. Her magic sparked at the opportunity to rescue her mate. Furio had been gone too long.

"Jessenia, can Egros do this?" Kingston turned and asked.

She saw the plea in his eyes but knew only the truth would do. The male Witch was not her biggest fan, and yet, he was honest and true to them all. He took his role as Guardian very seriously, and she admired the trait even if she didn't exactly like the man.

"Yes," she answered, after swallowing her surprise.

Egros was powerful, and he'd been a Guardian for decades. Surely, the Diamond Dragon trusted him. But that he should ask her, a mere kitchen Witch, meant a lot to Jessenia.

"Of course, he can do this. Egros, you good?" she asked, turning to watch as he measured out ingredients.

"I have everything I need," he stated in his usual quiet voice.

"Good. Let it steep for no more than ninety minutes. Then have her drink one full cup. You can save the rest for later. It will ease her discomfort and fortify her."

"Yes, I have been researching supernatural pregnancies," he told the room at large, "Seemed prudent in light of all the mates we seem to be acquiring just lately," he grinned, "Anyway, Dragonlings require triple the amount of nutrients, magical and natural, as other pregnancies. She simply needs more nourishment if you ask me, but I will check with the healer. He will be here on the hour."

"Makes sense." She smiled, surprised that the usually standoffish Witch had done so much work without telling anyone.

But that was Egros. Quiet and reliable. She looked forward to discussing more about his portals, after they used one to get them closer to the spot where Furio was more than likely being held.

He spoke with Kingston another minute, probably reassuring the Alpha of the Guardians that his mate would be okay.

"Are we ready?" Kingston asked.

Jessenia's heart thudded inside her chest. Now that

she knew without a doubt that Furio was her mate, she wanted him more with every minute. Their relationship had developed slower than was usual for Shifter mates over the past few months, but it did not stop the rush of feelings that flooded her the moment the proverbial cat was out of the bag.

Her powers pulsed and hummed, as if seeking him out among those nearest. It missed him. Wanted him. Needed him. Now. But even then, she understood what it meant for Kingston to leave his own mate behind.

"Are you sure you want to go? He will understand if you stay with Holley," Jessenia began, but Kingston was already shaking his head.

"Furio is one of our own," he said in a gruff voice, "Holley has taken each of my Guardians, and their mates, under her wing. She will never forgive me if I let anything happen to him," he grinned, "Besides, Holley has everything she needs now, starting with that tea. Thank you for risking your life to get it," he said, eyes flashing with his Diamond Dragon.

"Okay," she swallowed hard, "Let's go get him."

Thirteen

Dammit. Running into these fuckers was just about the worst luck he'd ever had. And that was saying something.

Furio had had no choice. He growled as he strained against the cuffs. He'd needed to protect her. So, he practically offered himself up on a silver platter. Their group was made up of three Gila Shifters and two Rhinos. It was those big ass bastards that had finally taken him down.

Sure, he could've outrun them, but he wasn't willing to risk them getting to her. The precious moments it would have taken him to shift might have been too long to get her out safely.

So instead of trying, he'd slammed his lips to hers then shoved her in direction of the Keep with instructions to run. They'd been close enough for her to make it. And he'd made sure those fuckers' eyes were trained on him.

Five to one were just the kind of odds he liked, but he'd been distracted with thoughts of his mate. And they'd gotten him, eventually. Of course, he got his licks in too. Even now one big Rhino fuck was glaring at him through one almost closed eye, and a series of bruises and broken facial bones.

Furio grinned at the asshole. And the resounding growl only made him laugh. Fuck them and their efforts, he'd delivered one hell of a kick to that fucker's face if he did say so himself.

But now, they were not interested in fighting fairly. The sons of bitches were using magic. That sucked ass as far as he was concerned. Furio was more a fisticuffs kinda guy.

Judging from the glyphs and inky dark tendrils coming out of the thing, he figured it was dark magic. The bastards were up to no good, and the stink of lizard told him those freaks were remnants of the Gila Shifters who'd been in Offner's thrall.

"Is that the right spell?" one hissed.

Furio's Stallion whinnied in response. Horses were not predatory animals. Squashing his fight or flight instinct was difficult, but over the years he'd honed the fight part of his natural abilities.

Used in battle for thousands of years, his Stallion was genetically prone to stand his ground and stare the enemy in the eye. He never ran from a fight anymore. His beast more than able to engage with these assholes. Hell, he was ready for a rematch now.

Rrrr. The Stallion agreed.

"Shut up!"

The bastard threw something at the bars of the cell and the resounding ringing had him covering his ears.

Fucking dickhead.

He was too stupid to know it would hurt his brethren as well. The sound of someone punching the idiot's lights out was satisfying. He only wished it was him doing the honors.

"What is it you idiots think you're doing, anyway? You know I'm a Guardian, right? My team will come for me," he interrupted their little meeting, with his gravelly voice echoing in the small brick space.

Furio needed to identify where he was, to devise a plan, and that meant getting the morons to talk. He'd been knocked out with that blow to the head, but he knew he hadn't traveled very far. The scent told him he was still there, in the pine barrens.

For some reason, it was his experience that bad

guys loved bullshitting about themselves. It was like they couldn't help it. Braggards and fools, the lot of them.

Standing up in his cell, he found he had to crouch because of the chains binding him. But as long as they were distracted, he could check for weakness in the links.

"I don't think so, *horse-breath*," a Shifter wearing black jeans and a gray thermal shirt laughed as he spat the words in Furio's direction, "You're on everyone's shit list, aren't you? They don't give a fuck about you."

"The fuck you say, dick lips?" he growled, but the words hurt.

"We've been watching you all for weeks. They avoid you like the fucking plague. You've pissed off your Alpha. Tried to come between him and his mate. They all hate you now," he sneered.

"You know nothing about us," Furio returned.

"I know enough," the one holding the grimoire turned to him, "Offner was single-minded, but he was right about the ley lines beneath that old castle. Once we get our hands on that plump Witch you were with, we can use her to gain control of it. You see, we have a plan," he remarked with the familiar fatal hubris of bad guys everywhere.

Dickheads, all of them, his Stallion thought with a whinny.

Still, there was that little seed of doubt threatening to plant itself inside of him. Were his Guardian brethren still mad at him for what he'd done? How he'd acted?

"No," he said aloud.

"No? Ha! As if you have a choice," the *soon-to-have- a horseshoe-shaped-dent-in-the-side-of-his-head-motherfucker* licked his lips.

He approached Furio's cell with all the cocksure mannerisms of a man who did not know he had moments to live. All this talk of Jessenia was making his animal eager for battle.

Horses might be vegetarians, but they were murderous sons of bitches when pushed. And this bastard had pushed him far enough.

"I saw your little whore Witch running on her chubby legs. Her bare-ass and tits jiggled with every step she took through those woods. Makes my dick hard just thinking about it. Don't worry, I'll have my cock buried in her cunt soon enough. You can bet on that, and with this grimoire, I will control her, and all magic. That's right, *me*!"

"Yeah? And just who the fuck are you?"

"What? You don't know me? I was Offner's right

hand," he spat as he talked, but Furio managed not to blink.

"Sorry, you Lizard fuckers all smell the same to me."

"Well, when your friends come and find you dying, tell them it was me! Tell them that I, *Brian Thomas*, killed you!"

Furio grinned and reached through the bars of his cell, gripping Brian Thomas' neck in his hands while his buddies hollered and jumped out of the way as a ferociously loud roar sounded outside.

But they were not quick enough. Furio held onto the sonofabitch who'd threatened his mate, squeezing his neck until the man's eyes bugged out of his head.

He let go, Tossing the man's lifeless body to the ground, just in time to see *Brian* disappear under the crumbling brick and wood that gave way under a certain Diamond Dragon's massive stream of flame.

"What the?!" the Rhino Furio had kicked in the face yelped as more flames hit him right on the ass.

"Yes!" Furio laughed and rattled the cage he was in.

"Hey, Fur, you good?" yelled Storm.

The Stallion nodded, he'd never been so happy to see his friends in his life. But his joy was short-lived as the sounds of a certain kitchen Witch's bellow of rage met his ears.

"Jessenia!" he growled.

She was there? What the fuck!

His Stallion reared up inside of him. The idea that she might be injured or hurt in any way freaked him out completely. Beast and man both agreed, her safety was tantamount. His eyes glowed green, tinting everything in the same ethereal light. Or was that just his hands?

He whinnied aloud, pulling on the magicked cuffs they'd used to imprison him. Furio heard the Loyalists' crying out in pain, but it was not enough. He wanted them all to die just for thinking of hurting her.

Those fuckers deserved everything they got. Plotting against the supernatural world earned them a motherfucking beatdown. Plotting to hurt his mate? That earned them a death sentence.

Right then, he needed one thing and one thing only. To get to his mate. Snapping the chains with one last tug, he turned around and threw a mean back-kick towards the iron bars.

Shifting only his leg to his Stallion's powerful one, he barely grunted as the clang of his hoof breaking through the magicked metal echoed. It was music to his ears.

Once out of the cell, he saw his mate being manhandled by two Gila Shifters, and his vison went from green to red. Without even thinking about it, Furio shifted from his human shape to his enormous Stallion faster than he'd ever managed before. Only something was different.

"Holy shit, Furio," Storm yelled from where he was wrestling with one of those huge, horn-sprouting Rhino bastards, "You have wings, bro!"

Furio snorted as newfound powers blazed through him. Fucking hell. It was exactly how Storm and Kingston had both described the extra boost of energy, strength, and magic that had come from just meeting their fated mates.

In the wild, horses had almost three-hundred-sixty-degree vision. He was used to that. But it was what he saw with that vison that made him snort loudly.

Two enormous, diaphanous wings that appeared to be made of fiery green smoke were protruding from his back. Now that was not something he'd ever seen before. He shook his great equine head from side to side but stopped when a scream of pain reached his sensitive ears.

It was her. His mate needed him. Momentary panic at his new wings aside, he crashed across the room and into the bastard who'd been holding her. Stomping him into goo, he lashed out with his back leg and delivered a punishing kick that sent the other

Lizard Shifter crashing into what remained of the outer wall of the building. He stomped on that bastard next, growling and snorting in his anger.

"Furio?" Jessenia's voice broke through his murderous anger, and he turned his head to see her smiling at him.

Without delay, he kneeled beside her, grateful when he saw understanding in her amber orbs. Thank fuck. He hardly felt it as she grabbed his mane in her tiny fists and vaulted onto his back.

Furio whinnied as joy flowed through him at having her gentle, reassuring weight resting on him. Heat from her core warmed him and he snorted. His entire body shook with need. He needed to get her home, in his room, in his bed, now.

Turning to see the rest of the Guardians had rounded up those Loyalist assholes, he whinnied once more to get someone's attention. Of course, the Wolf would be the one to turn to him, a wide, knowing grin on the fucker's face.

"Go claim your mate, *cump*," Storm called out, "We got this."

That was all the okay he needed to take off. His heart thundered like thousand revved up engines and when he snorted, he swore he saw the same fiery green smoke his wings were made of stream from his nostrils.

"Take me home," Jessenia's plaintive whisper sped him into action.

Using strength and muscles he didn't even know he had, Furio galloped to the nearest Dragon-made exit. He propelled forward, faster than ever. For a moment, he was scared she'd fall off, but her thighs squeezed him tight. The sound of her laughter peeling out even as she pulled on his mane and hugged his neck close to her chest was exhilarating.

Fuck, it wasn't just his legs. It was those fiery wings pushing them forward. They were not flying exactly, but he sure as fuck wasn't just running either. This was a speed he'd never achieved before, but he couldn't stop even if he wanted to. Not yet. Not until she was safe.

The cold forest air hit his face like a sharp slap, but he didn't care. The urge to protect his mate, to get her away from danger, was the driving him hard. There was also the primal desire to have her, to mark her as his own once and for all that had him pushing speed limits.

. . .

He hardly noticed how far he ran, he just knew he needed to get her away from the bastards who'd chained him before they dared touch his precious female. By the time he slowed down, he saw shadows emerge from the tall pines like long, needlelike spikes across the thick white snow that covered the forest floor.

Furio halted and whinnied, snorting furiously. Ears back, he used his supernaturally enhanced senses to scout for danger. They were safe. For now. Thank fuck.

"Easy, easy," she leaned forward, and the reassuring pressure of his sweet Jessenia's slight weight on his back caught his attention.

"We're okay," she crooned, "I'm okay now. You did good, *Pony Boy.*"

Furio looked around through his Stallion's eyes. Somehow, he'd brought them home to the Keep. Swirls of smoky green magic surrounded him, blinding him. Furio blinked to regain his vision.

One minute he was a Stallion with his mate on his back, the next he was a man, and Jessenia was in his arms. Exactly where she belonged. He recognized that as the only truth he needed.

"We gotta talk about this Pony Boy, nonsense," he said with a grin and arched his brow.

"Oh yeah," she sassed back, "What about it?"

"I'm not a boy, *piccolina*, I'm a Stallion."

"That might be true," she squinted, "But I am not calling you that in bed."

. . .

Heat flashed through their shared humor, and for one moment all he thought was how absolutely crazy he was about her. There was no denying it. No cure for it either. Even if there was, he wouldn't want it.

She was perfect. Curvy and gorgeous with her soft brown curls and deep eyes that bore into his. Something had shifted between them. Some wonderful and magical thing had changed the atmosphere that existed between the two as they faced off in the chilled February morning.

His chest was heaving with the effort it took not to jump her right then and there. But he knew, oh yes, he knew. She was ready for him to claim her. And he was not going to wait another second.

"Mine," he growled and mashed his mouth to hers.

Fourteen

"Mine," his voice echoed deep within her, and Jessenia felt the truth of it down to her marrow.

Her tongue swept inside of his mouth, tasting every inch of her magnificent Stallion. She was greedy for him, wanted all of him with every last inch of her.

He must have felt the same. The evidence was long, hot, and hard pressed against her stomach through the fleece she wore.

Fuck, he was naked, she realized. His whole beautiful body was on display, and her powers reacted predictably.

"Mmm," he murmured, refusing to end the kiss even though she'd zapped him just a tad on his rear end.

What could she say? She'd been waiting months to get her hands on his luscious glutes. But she didn't mean to toast them!

At least, not yet. She tried to pull back, to keep from harming him, but Furio didn't seem willing to end the kiss despite her finicky magic.

"Mine," he growled roughly. The single syllable wreaked havoc on her.

Holy hell. She trembled and went still all at the same time. Jessenia had no idea how he managed to pull that off. All she knew was that the tiny sparks of arousal that had been dancing along her spine had turned into an all-consuming, towering inferno of need.

That and more, she thought, always so much more where he was concerned. Her sex moistened, readying for his invasion, and she moaned in anticipation.

"Want you," she admitted against his lips, loving the rumble that seemed to grow inside of him as she finally gave voice to her feelings.

"Bed," he said and nodded. "Now!"

With that he lifted her in his arms and those crazy beautiful, green wings that had magically appeared on his Stallion's form, seemed to wrap around them both, spirting them down the corridor to his room.

By the time he carried her to his door, the thing

opened as if by magic. Jessenia smiled around her mouthful of his very clever tongue. The Keep approved, or so it would seem, she thought.

The magical manse was known for tending to its Guardians and their mates' every need. And she needed this, wanted it with every bit of her. Finally, she was going to lay claim to her Stallion.

"Mine," he breathed the word, laying her out on the bed like something prized and precious.

Her face flamed, but she pushed her embarrassment away. This was Furio. Her Furio. She bit her lip, and he peeled away the layers of clothing she'd worn to protect herself against the cold. She'd done things in the last few days she would have never imagined herself capable of.

He gave her the strength to see it through, she thought with wonder. His belief in her was everything. Hell, she rushed into battle and fought to get him back.

As if sensing her thoughts, Furio cupped her cheeks and kissed her forehead, her cheeks, her chin, and her mouth. Softly though. Gently, too. And not nearly long enough, she thought greedily, even as he pressed his forehead to hers.

"Thank you," he said in a voice rough with

emotion, "for coming to get me, but you have to promise to never do that again."

"No," she shook her head and tugged his head back down to hers when he tried to move away, "I won't promise that. I will always come for you, Furio."

"Jess," he shook his head, eyes glittering down at her.

"Always. If I am yours, then that makes you mine too," she stated baldly, "Now, are you going to claim me, or what?"

The taunt was just enough to push him over the edge. Furio growled as the thin hold he had over his self-control snapped.

"Yes," she moaned as her Stallion took the neckline of her sweater, the only article of clothing left on her body, and tore the thing off her.

He stood up between her splayed legs that were hanging off his bed, appraising her with his glittering green eyes. She watched, breathlessly as his gaze seemed to devour her.

Jessenia was not an exhibitionist. Short and curvy, she'd been the nerdy girl in high school. The one who clung to her comfortable sweats and flannels, hiding her chubby body from the mean girls and judgmental jocks.

Fergie was her only real friend from her childhood,

and though she was also a curvy girl, the woman owned that shit. But Jessenia wasn't a dorky teenager anymore, and she'd learned to be comfortable in her own skin.

Even so, no one had ever looked at her quite like that. Her pussy grew wetter under his steady green stare. She loved his eyes, loved them on her. Her breast swelled, nipples hardened, all in preparation for him. Only him.

Sex had never been like this. No, this was magic at its best, she thought as her powers reflexively reached out to stroke his skin. She felt it inside of her, as if she was touching him with her hands. His eyes widened, and he growled, leaning into the ethereal touch and licking his plump lips.

Jessenia followed the move with her eyes, desperate to do so with her tongue. Her breath came in short, quick bursts, but Furio shook his head. He wasn't budging until he'd looked his fill.

She could neither talk nor could she look away. Everything was contingent on his next move. It seemed like eons passed, but it was more like seconds until those limitless green pools met her searching stare.

"Ah, *piccolina*, you are so beautiful," he said, and reached out with trembling hands to touch her, "So perfect."

Jessenia closed her eyes and allowed herself to simply feel as he learned her body with his deliciously rough, callused fingers. His fingertips grazed her hair, cheeks, her lips, the slope of her neck until they rested on her chest above where she wanted him so badly.

"What is it, *piccolina*?"

"Touch me," she begged, unashamed as her hips flexed of their own accord, and her back arched, searching for more from him.

"I am touching you," he leaned on the bed, continuing the slow steady stroke of his hands across her clavicle.

"More, Furio, please," she arched again, gasping as he traced her nipples with light feathery, barely there touches.

"Like this?" he asked.

Jessenia shook her head. Eyes closed, she whimpered in need. He was driving her nuts, but when she reached out to take control, he clamped his other hand around her wrists and held them against the mattress above her head.

"Uh uh," he grunted, "I have been waiting months to touch you, *piccolina*. It's my turn."

"Then do it," she said, frustration making her angry, "Touch me, and stop fucking around."

"It's never fucking around with you," he grinned

and finally, cupped one hand around her aching bud, "Your breasts are gorgeous," he growled over her harsh moan.

"They're small," she answered and moaned as he skimmed his heated palms over each hardened nubbin.

He growled and lightened his touches, carefully molding the soft, plump flesh of her breasts, and she whimpered at the loss of friction. For a bigger woman, her breasts were decidedly average-sized. She'd often wondered if that was a blessing or curse, but the way he was petting them and praising her, she had to believe the former.

"They're perfect," he corrected, bending his head to take one inside his hot mouth, "I love your pink, dusky nipples," he sucked her hard, then released her bud with a soft pop, "Love the way they feel and taste in my mouth."

He growled and bent his head again, suckling one breast then the other. She writhed beneath his attentions. Gasping as the pleasure heightened, and not-so-secretly reveling in the fact that no matter what, he did not let up. Not for a minute.

She felt moisture pool between her legs, and her pussy throbbed. Empty. Needy. Fuck, she wanted him so bad. Never like this, she thought.

Her mouth opened, and she whimpered against

the constant pressure of his mouth on her sensitive nipples. The tugging sensation sent waves of pleasure rolling through her. She was slick and ready for him, but he took his time.

Damn him, she winced as his teeth grazed her nipple causing her to hiss.

Love him, her magic corrected.

Fine. She loved him. And she wanted to show him. Tugging on his hold, she whimpered when he let go of her wrists. Still, Furio was not about to be rushed. She tugged on his head, but he just growled and licked and tasted her skin, whispering all the things he was going to do to her between his hot kisses.

"Furio," she tugged on his hair as he hovered over her, attempting to push him where she wanted him most.

"So impatient," he grinned at her.

"Please."

"Don't worry, *piccolina,* I have everything you need."

Her desire was almost painful now. Spreading her legs wide as he slid down her body, Jessenia flexed her hips, rubbing her mound on his hardened abs.

The friction made her hiss, and he growled in response. The sexy sound reverberated through to her soul, and she gasped.

Furio used his long, slick tongue to lick his way down her chest, giving one last tug on each nipple before sliding further down. She cringed slightly as he reached her soft belly, her arms reflexively moving to cover herself, but he would have none of that.

"Mine," his voice had somehow gotten even deeper, and she whimpered in need, "never hide from me, baby. You are beautiful, perfect. Made for me."

"Yes!" She nodded, accepting his words as truth.

Her magic pulsed, as if agreeing with him. She'd learned the hard way to trust her powers, and she didn't want to make the same mistakes here.

Jessenia knew she belonged with him. He was hers as much as she was his. If he said he wanted her the way she was, then he did. And the result of that knowledge was instantaneous. A wave of heat flooded her, her pussy clenching on air, needy for him.

"Need you," she moaned.

Honesty was like breathing to the Guardians, as far as she could tell. She knew Shifters could scent lies, so most of them avoided it, but it was not the same with Witches. They could lie, hell they had to. For centuries, lying about their magic kept them alive. But there would be no lies between them. Not even ones of omission. Not anymore.

"Gonna give you what you need. First, I gotta taste

you, mate," he slid down further, nipping her hip with his blunt-edged teeth.

Furio's rough hands found her thighs, pushing her legs open even wider. He teased the sensitive flesh with his fingertips. Tracing circles up her thighs till he was parting her outer lips.

Her body was so aroused, even that tiny flitting gesture had her moaning. She gasped at the sensations that rushed through her as she leaned on her elbows and watched him stare at her needy sex.

"Furio," she whined his name, flexing her hips to entice him closer.

Okay, so she was a total slut for the man. She couldn't help it. Her whole body was wound tight. Like she'd been waiting for his touch for an eternity. Maybe she had.

"Ah, *piccolina*, you smell so fucking good. Gonna taste even better," he growled, and finally, his oh-so-flexible and talented lips found her core.

Holy shit. Jessenia's gasp echoed in the room. Was that a Horse thing? She could only wonder as he buried his face between her legs. His thick fingers dug into her thighs as he expertly nibbled her sensitive flesh, and she wanted them buried deep inside her.

But she was not content to be idle. No, she was no bystander. Fuck that. Jessenia swiveled her hips, grinding her pussy into his face. She moaned aloud when he finally pressed one thick digit into her sopping wet heat.

Thank fuck, she thought, as he began to move. Curling his finger and stroking in short, upwards motions, he found that perfect spot deep inside that incited a husky, deep moan to eke out from her parted lips.

"More," she begged, and he gave it to her.

Adding another finger as his tongue curled around her clit in times with his deep strokes. More heat pooled as his fingers still caressed her walls. All the while, Furio continued to lick and nibble her sensitive nubbin until she thought she was going to explode.

Jessenia wound her hands through his long, thick locks. Holding him where she wanted him, she rocked her hips, chasing her pleasure.

"Come for me," Furio commanded, then he sucked on the tiny swollen nub. *Hard.*

Jessenia's mouth opened wide, and she yelled as she rode his hand and mouth. Explosions of pleasure went off, starting inside and working their way throughout her entire body.

Wave after wave of ecstasy flowed through her. She threw her head back and yelled his name, claiming the utter joy he'd gifted her in this, their shared passion.

"Mine," she said, tugging his hair until he moved up her body, so their faces were close together.

Then she kissed him. Tasting herself on his lips, Jessenia moaned around his tongue as her hands smoothed over his muscled back until she reached his ass. She continued to pet and stroke him until she found his thick cock, placing his head at her soaked entrance.

"Make me yours," she said, noting the fire in his emerald gaze.

"Mine," he growled and pushed deep inside.

Finally.

FIFTEEN

Furio was in heaven. There was no other way to describe the absolute bliss of finally sinking into his mate's tight, hot body. Months of banked down desire came rushing forward as he pressed deeper.

Careful to make sure he did not hurt his *piccolina*, he couldn't stop until every inch of his cock was buried deep inside her slick pussy.

Sweet unobliterated heaven, he thought again, growling her name between tight lips.

"Jessenia. Mine."

Mate, he grunted and settled his big body between her splayed thighs. She was so small, so perfect. Her tight sheath stretched around him, caressing him like a velvet vise. Her body cradled his, so soft and warm, the perfect foil for his hardness.

She was his now, and he was never letting go. She had to know that. Once she allowed him, *him* with all his faults and rough edges, to sink into her, that was it.

"Mate," he said against her mouth, before claiming her lips.

He pulled out slowly, then pushed in again, groaning in pleasure as he buried himself to the hilt. Giving her a moment to adjust to his length and girth, he hissed when his *piccolina* wiggled impatiently. Drawing a smile from his lips, even as he refused to give hers up.

No way. He had every intention of continuing to claim those plump, pink lips of hers. Furio wanted to kiss her, and kiss her, and keep on kissing her until he was drunk with it. After months of denying himself, he couldn't seem to stop.

"Don't stop then," she returned, "I want to kiss you too."

Her tongue tangled with his, and he felt the pleasure she felt when she was kissing him back. It made his soul sing with joy. He wasn't sure if he'd spoken aloud, or if she'd simply read his mind. It didn't matter. He wasn't going to stop. Not until they were both too boneless to move.

Being inside Jessenia was like every dream he'd had in the months since he'd met her coming true all at once. She was so beautiful and so fucking responsive.

Her body was more than welcoming. Every plunge and withdrawal, flex and swivel was in time with his. Every time he pushed his cock deep, he felt her channel tighten and stroke him perfectly.

She lifted her hips to meet his with just the right amount of pressure, the perfect pace. Like she was made for him.

Yes, he supposed, she was made for him. His one true and fated mate. His perfect match in every way. And fuck it, he could admit it now. He loved her. Would show her how he felt now with his body. And he did.

Arching his back, he swiveled his hips, grinding his pubis into her as she moaned his name. Her nails scored his back as she lifted to meet his thrusts. Every nerve ending aflame, Furio damn near burst apart as joy and wonder filled him.

He reached between them with his hand, tapping her clit in time with his thrusts. Her pussy tightened, and his balls drew close to his body with the need to come.

"Come for me," he growled, mashing his lips to hers before sliding down to her neck.

"Furio," she ground out his name, caught in a soundless scream, her back arched.

He opened his mouth and sucked on that sensitive spot just under her ear that he noticed earlier. Faster and harder, he made love to his sweet mate.

Thrust, withdraw, thrust, swivel, swivel, grind, tap, tap, tap. His own need to come, the desire to fill her with his seed was damn near overwhelming. He wanted her bearing his mate mark. Wanted her to belong to him in every way. And she would. As soon as she came.

He worked harder. Had to. His Stallion whinnied. The beast wanted him to claim her already, but he wouldn't, not until he brought her to orgasm. The Stallion snorted at him, demanding he get on with it already.

Fucking hell. He couldn't think. Her sweet, hot body was molded to his. Furio was never so fucking grateful in his entire life. Jessenia was in his bed, with him, and as he sank balls deep into her honeyed pussy over and over again.

"Perfect, mate," he praised his *piccolina*, thanking the heavens she'd chosen him.

"Close," she moaned, and his balls tightened again with the need to explode.

Her words seemed to pull something loose. Whatever restraint he'd been holding onto, and he roared with need. Lifting her legs to his shoulders until she was practically bent in half.

"Come, *piccolina*. Gonna claim you, but you gotta come for me. That's good," he growled as her sex squeezed him tighter, "S'very good."

Thank fuck. He felt her walls tighten as he increased his tempo. Hands gripping her thighs, lips locked around her neck, Furio's movements took on a wild, positively feral pace.

Passion built, straining, bulging, threatening to drown him, until finally she screamed his name. Arching beneath him, mouth open as her sex continued to squeeze and suck his cock, milking him for all he was worth, Furio opened his mouth and bit down.

A Stallion's bite differed from that of other Shifters. He knew he had to be careful. Without fangs to cut and sink into her skin, his mark would be created by far more blunted incisors that would essentially pinch rather than slice through her skin.

Powerful, but painful if not done correctly. And he would never want to hurt her, which is why timing was key.

Furio's orgasm rushed forward as hers reached its

pinnacle. Without delay, he bit down on her skin, marking and claiming her as his own for all time.

Bodies straining against each other, slick with sex and sweat. He roared against her throat as her pussy continued to grip and squeeze him. He filled her with his seed, marking her with his cum as surely as he marked her with his bite.

Heaven, he thought again. She was heaven in his arms.

"Mine," he grunted when they were nothing more than a sweaty tangle of limbs.

"I love you," she said. Her small hands reached up to cup his face, and she lifted her sweet mouth to his.

"I love you too, *piccolina*." Furio smiled through the tears that pricked his eyes.

Rolling over until she was astride his hips, Furio gripped her thick thighs.

"Love you so much," he growled, kissing her lips, loving how her eyes went all amber and wide once she realized his cock was hard again, and still buried inside her sheath.

"Can you?"

"I'm a Shifter," he said and lifted her hips.

"You're a Stallion," she corrected, taking the reins and slamming her body back down on his shaft.

"I'm your Stallion," he said.

"Good, cause I want to ride," she moaned into his mouth, pushing on his chest until he lay flat beneath her.

Fuck, she was glorious. Her curly hair hung in wild disarray as she continued to make love to him. And it was loving. Always would be.

"Mate," he reached for her, and together they made it to heights he'd never imagined.

Through it all, Furio kissed her. He was still kissing her, hours later when they'd managed to make love across his room from the bed, to the floor, the sofa, his gaming chair, and the brand-new loft he'd been working on with the Keep just for her.

"I can't believe you built this for me," she said from her position on top of him, which was quickly becoming his favorite if he did say so himself.

"I love you," he shrugged, "want you happy."

"You make me happy," she grinned, "This is just cake."

"Speaking of cake," he said, and she groaned.

"I knew you just wanted me for my carrot cake," she started, then collapsed in a fit of giggles under his tickle-assault tactics.

"No, baby, I wanted you for this," he dropped his head and kissed her again.

"Mm," she sighed, "I love you, but if you want to do this again, I need food."

"Food? Why didn't you say so?"

He pulled her up and carried her to the shower. Yes, he was more than pleased to find she liked the skylight and mini greenhouse he'd built on the new loft in his, *now their*, bedroom. He wanted to show her how happy he was, but first, she needed feeding.

Epilogue

"He built you a loft?"

"Yep," Jessenia was positively glowing.

She could feel happiness radiating from her pores. Yes, he'd bult her a loft in his room complete with an enormous skylight and row upon row of shelves for her herbs and organic lettuce.

Cooking was her passion, but both her edible recipes and her Witchy ones required fresh ingredients. The outdoor greenhouse would be a wonderful addition, undoubtedly. But this was her own bit of heaven.

Well, besides being with him. She sighed and ignored the gagging sounds coming from her best friend.

"So, you know you are sick, right? Getting hot and bothered over some shelves for your plants?"

"For my herbs, but anyway," she answered Fergie while she prepared a midnight snack for her and her mate, which included a fresh carrot cake for her lover, "you should talk. I heard you and Storm banging against the wall after your latest shoe delivery arrived last week."

"What? Do you know how long I've been waiting for those slouchy *Manolo Blahnik* suede boots to come in red and in my size?" she blew a raspberry at Jessenia, who laughed and rolled her eyes while she added a handful of pignoli nuts to her pesto.

Thank goodness, the Keep had a way with the gas range and ovens. *A magical way.*

She'd no more than tossed ingredients together than the ovens magicked them ready. Dessert was iced and on the tray. The pasta was finished, and she was just waiting on the garlic bread.

"Holy crap! I admit that smells better than my sandwiches, but me and my boo need the meats," Fergie sniffed and frowned, "So, you are going vegetarian, huh?"

"Not really," Jessenia shrugged, "I just wanted pasta."

She hadn't thought about it, but the idea of not

eating meat wasn't exactly repulsive. Either way, she knew Furio had no preference. He just wanted her happy. And wasn't that awesome?

Sappy sigh.

"You know, Jess, I wanted you to know I was chatting with everyone tonight and, well, they all love Furio here. No one is mad at him, least of all Holley."

Fergie reached out and took Jessenia's hand. Tugging the woman in for a hug, she wiped her eyes and smiled.

"Good," she said, "Because he loves all of you too. We both do."

"Good," Fergie cleared her throat, "Families fight, and you're both our family. You know that, right?"

Jessenia's heart damn near burst, but she just nodded. Both women hastily wiped their faces. After years of knowing each other, making bald statements like that were cause for a little emotion. She wasn't uncomfortable with it, but it would definitely keep.

"You ready?" Storm came into the kitchen and took the tray of ham sandwiches Fergie had grabbed from the fridge for the two of them, "Wassup Jess?"

"Hey," she said and smiled, looking behind him for her mate. "Where is Furio?"

Two arms wrapped around her from behind, and her pulse sped up. She recognized him immediately by scent, touch, and the pulsing matebond that connected them. Sighing happily, she returned his embrace. Loving how he always wanted to snuggle and touch her. Needing that connection herself.

"Mate," he whispered and kissed the spot on her neck that bore her mark.

She shivered in response. That spot would always be a source of arousal and pleasure for her. She somehow knew that, just like she knew how much he truly loved her. It was something to do with their matebond, she realized.

As a Witch, he'd managed to convince her to drop the whole kitchen thing since her powers were proving more badassed by the minute. She understood the matebond they shared was deeply steeped in magic.

Even so, she'd never have imagined such a powerful connection with another being. But Furio truly was made just for her.

"How's Kingston and Holley?" she asked him, knowing full well where he'd gone while she insisted on preparing a meal for them.

"Good," he said, "The tea helped, and he said to tell you the healer wants to talk to you, but I told him in the morning."

"Okay." She nodded. "I can do that tomorrow. I want to check in on her, anyway."

She was so thankful the other Witch had been looked at by an ancient healer, and that her tea had helped. But she was also glad they would have the rest of the night alone.

"Hey yo, cump," Storm nodded at her mate, "We sparring in the morning?"

"You know it," Furio answered, and she could tell he was happy.

Life at the Keep was definitely moving forward. And that was a good thing. They all needed that. The Keep and the Guardians and mates who dwelled there were connected in a way that most people would never understand. Jessenia's heart swelled with pride and feeling when she thought that she was officially a part of that now. Because of him. Her mate.

"Catch you two later," Fergie giggled after Storm whispered in her ear.

They waved their farewells and took off down the hall.

"Come on," Furio took the covered tray from her hands, and together they walked to their bedroom.

"So, I smell pasta," he grinned, trying to guess what she'd made them.

"Yep, pesto," she returned knowing full well it was his favorite, "and for dessert."

"Carrot cake?" he looked so dang hopeful.

"Yes," she cleared her throat.

"I don't need carrot cake, *piccolina*, or pesto, or anything else. You know that, right?"

"I know," she grinned, "I just like cooking."

"And you are great at it, but I love you for so much more than that," Furio placed the tray on the small table in front of the sofa by the television.

Grabbing her hips, he pulled her flush against him, and pressed his forehead to hers. She loved it when he did that. It was like he just wanted to breathe her in, to be still for a moment in a world that was sometimes too crazy and loud, moving too fast to understand. But this here, with him, this was her anchor. He was her strength, her hearth, her home.

"Mate," she whispered the word.

Testing it on her lips, she liked how it felt, but it was too important not to simply shout it. She did not want to break the peace of the moment or the magic she'd felt being with him.

"Hearing you say that does things to me," he confessed, "You have no idea. You are everything to me, *piccolina*," his voice was rough, and she opened her eyes to see his glittering down at her.

"Are you sure?" she asked, finally giving voice to her greatest fear.

"Oh Jess, I choose you, always. Willingly, willfully,

fated mate or not, you are the only one I want. Forever. Mine," he cupped her face in his hands, and pressed his hard body against hers.

Then he bent down and took her mouth in a kiss that pushed away any lingering doubts she'd had. This was as real as it got.

Furio was her Stallion. Her mate. Her shield against harm, now and forever. Food forgotten, they tore clothes off each other in their need to connect.

Joy and pure bliss pulsed through their matebond, and Jessenia moaned with happiness as he entered her in one, perfectly executed thrust. Coming together with him was a soul-deep connection she craved, like oxygen.

When she was with him, everything else fell away. He was her love, her life, and she was so ready to embrace that. To be his mate in every way.

When they were finally spent, hours later, Furio nuzzled her neck, kissed her mate mark, and together they slept wrapped in the warmth of the bed they'd made and unmade together. And they would do it again tomorrow, and all the other tomorrows they got on this Earth together.

"I love you," she said.

"I love you too," he affirmed, "Always, *piccolina*."

.   .   .

The end.

Did you enjoy this story? Grab the next Guardians of Chaos book here! The entire series is now available.

Don't forget to tell me how you liked this story by leaving your honest review! No pressure. 🙂
A review can be one or two brief sentences where you simply state whether you enjoyed the story and would recommend it to someone! It is an enormous help to authors and the best way for us to reach larger audiences so we can keep writing the stories you love!
Thank you so much!
Xoxo!
Del mare alla stella,
C.D. Gorri

PANTHER SHIELD

GUARDIANS OF CHAOS 4

BLURB

She's a fierce Panther Shifter fighting to preserve the freedom of all magic. He's a normal with a target on his back. Will she risk it all for him?

Elena Soussa is the only female Guardian of Chaos in her group. A Panther Shifter, she is a loner by nature, but ever since the members of her crew started meeting their mates and gaining new powers, her curiosity has been piqued.

When she finds a normal cornered by the enemy, she is compelled to save the ridiculously handsome man, but to do so means violating the Guardians' code.

He is not her problem, but her inner she-Cat sure
wants him to be.

Will Elena risk it all for one man's life?

GUARDIANS OF CHAOS PLEDGE

I am the watcher in the storm.
I am the iron shield.
I protect against those who seek to control the wild nature
of magic.
I am the guardian of chaos.
To thrive, we must be free.
From chaos comes creation.

PROLOGUE

Elena grunted. She ducked the fierce blow coming from behind her.

Yes, her father was one hell of a fighter, but he'd taught his only daughter well. Too well. She'd been noticed for her antics at school, and on the varsity basketball team. One of the only females to reach six feet in height, she'd been a shoe in for the position as starting point guard since she'd been a freshman.

But this wasn't a basketball game. This was training with her dad, and Anthony Soussa took no prisoners. He was one tough SOB, and his little girl was a chip off the old block.

Elena fell into a defensive stance, gritting her teeth with the effort it took not to shift into her stealthy and more powerful Panther counterpart. That simply was not an option out in the streets where too many normals could witness such a supernatural feat.

That was why all the hand-to-hand combat training. She had to rely on her human body to get the job done. A Shifter was faster, stronger, and deadlier than any normal. Elena knew that by heart. But relying on her animal side could prove fatal, as it had for her late mother.

A police officer stationed in the rough city of Newark, New Jersey, Jasmine Soussa had been killed when a routine traffic stop turned deadly. The normals, group of hotheaded, low level drug dealers, had panicked and gunned down the female in broad daylight when Elena had been just four years old.

Unable to shift to her sleek Panther because of the number of humans in the area, Elena's mother had taken nine bullets to the chest and abdomen before succumbing to her injuries. It had been a horrible tragedy and had even made the papers. To this day Elena hated the sound of bagpipes and could still hear them playing in her head whenever she thought of that rainy Autumn morning when they'd buried her mother.

Jasmine's husband and Elena's father, Sergeant

Anthony Soussa, swore from that day on he would do everything in his power to see their only daughter grow up strong and fierce. But he'd accomplished much more than an increased sense of self-preservation in his child.

By the time Elena turned seventeen, she was the deadliest Panther in the small group of like Shifters that roamed the city of Newark. They were their own task force, and it was her dealings with thugs, supernatural and not, that got her noticed by one of the most elite forces in all of the supernatural world. The Guardians of Chaos.

She'd thought the legendary group of supernaturals was nothing more than a myth. The same thing went for Dragons and Vampires. That was, until she met one of each waiting for her after the brief high school graduation ceremony that had come and gone with no notice from her dad. Anthony Soussa had too much on his plate to worry about mundane human celebrations, so she'd been alone when they'd approached.

The Vampire had looked at her with impassive eyes, and the Diamond Dragon had merely sized her up. After their introduction, they'd explained who they were and what they wanted.

"You're unique, Elena, but your antics will get you noticed by the normals, eventually. Let us put your substantial skills to better use. Help us defend magic. Help us keep it free for all beings. What do you say?" Byram, the Vampire, spoke first.

"Do I get to kick ass?"

"Fuck yeah," Kingston, the Dragon and Alpha of the group, replied.

"Then I'm in."

Elena had needed no time to think it over. She'd agreed to join them on the spot. Of course, she had yet to tell her father, and that was scary enough. Anthony Soussa swore his daughter would be tough, but he didn't want her anywhere near law enforcement, normal or not. And what were the Guardians if not supernatural cops?

He would never agree to it. Her father had already given too much to keep the people of the world safe, or so he always said. But this was her life and her choice. Elena stood up, accepting the bottle of water her father held out to her.

"Good match," he said, drinking from his own bottle. "But watch your reaction times, Elena. You seemed a bit off today."

"Dad? I have to talk to you," she called to him just as someone knocked on the front door.

"One moment," he replied, and turned to see who had come visiting their small

Shit.

They were early.

"Hello Mr. Soussa, we're here to collect Elena..."

And the rest was history.

"Elena, we've been through this," Egros turned to her, his eyes changing from blue to green to silver as his anger flared.

"I know, Eg, but there has to be something else you can give me to stop my stupid heat cycle!"

"You're just delaying the inevitable. You are a Panther Shifter, big cats go into heat once they reach adulthood. As you continue to deny yours, it will only get stronger and more frequent every time it comes upon you," he added.

The male Witch closed the alchemy book he'd been reading and slammed it on his desk. He'd been working with Jessenia, Furio's mate and a kitchen Witch, as well as Holley, another talented Witch mated to their group Alpha, on finding a way to stop the symptoms of Elena's heat cycle. But so far, nothing. The results of their inquiries and experiments were not good.

It always amazed her the rest of the supernatural world hadn't banded together, but most ignored the plights of their females. Pregnancy rates were notoriously low for supernaturals and there was no rush to deny what little chance they had at reproducing.

Regardless of how unfair it was to the females involved. Elena growled angrily. She was no one's fucking handmaiden. And she would not be forced to copulate and reproduce. It was barbaric!

Holley had concocted a potion made of several wild herbs she'd found growing near the Keep, and so far, so good, but the effects were wearing off at an alarming rate. Instead of her heat hitting her once a quarter, it was more like every month for the past year. Looked like Egos' grim predictions were right.

Fury flooded her system, threatening to force a shift, but Elena was in control. Always. She reined in her inner kitty, pushed the snarling she-Cat back, and counted to three before meeting Egros' curious stare.

This simply was not fair. She was a warrior, a fierce Panther Shifter, a true Guardian of Chaos. They were neck deep in this war with the Loyalists, and she did not have time for this shit. Elena had been training for this her entire life.

Hadn't she left her father and her home before she'd turned eighteen for this reason? To protect the world of magic at all costs. She was not cut out to be a mother. Hell, she didn't even have a prospect, much less a mate. Regardless of what tradition dictated, she wasn't getting knocked up by some stranger simply to preserve the species. Fuck that.

Elena had too much self-respect to be a damn incubator. If and when she had a cub, it would be on her terms. Not some biological imperative. Anger coursed through her, and she kicked at something on the floor, sending the box of whatever flying across the room.

"Hey! Those are my files, thank you very much," grumbled Egros.

"Sorry. Ugh," she moaned and sat down on a stool while he checked the data log on his computer.

While she waited, memories of her own mother crowded her brain. She recalled the sweet way she used to brush Elena's pale blonde hair and tie the laces on her patent leather shoes. Elena had loved her strong, fierce mother, especially all the attention the female gave to her only daughter.

As a child, she had been ultrafeminine. Pink was

her favorite color. She'd played dolls and pretended to be a mother with her own brood of beautiful babies. It was something she'd envisioned from a very young age, being a mother and having a mate, a family of her own.

The sudden violent death of her mother had put a stop to that kind of innocent daydreaming. Elena's warm and once happy home had instantly turned into a training dojo, and her once carefree father had become her brutally honest instructor.

It was a difficult change for a teenage girl, but she'd learned to cope. More than that. Elena had excelled at combat. She had a real feel for it and had spent years training, perfecting the skill set coveted by organizations such as the Guardians.

She'd been approached by the usual normal agencies, CIA, FBI, and a few black ops mercenary groups. But Elena was not interested in the petty wars of humankind.

She was a Shifter, and her place was serving the supernatural world. Kingston Baldric, the Alpha of their group of Guardians, had offered her the job, and she'd never looked back.

Where else could she use all of her power, speed, and the fierceness of her Panther to get the job accomplished? The Guardians of Chaos were more than her employers, they were her family. But this business with her heat was getting in the way.

What started out as a way for her father to work out his grief and protect his daughter had turned into a way of life for the she-Cat. Elena had truly learned to love the deadly beauty and grace that accompanied her many mixed martial arts trainings.

She was an expert with several black belts in varying degrees, having studied combat with masters the world over. Neela, the late wife of their leader and Alpha, Kingston Baldric, was one of her mentors.

It had been difficult for Elena to accept Holley as his mate, but after she'd learned the circumstances of his first mating to Neela, the Panther Shifter understood and respected her Alpha even more. The complicated relationship he'd endured with the she-Dragon bespoke of a man of real honor and worth.

Holley was lucky to have him. Hell, he was lucky to have her, too. In fact, it seemed as if more and more of their group of Guardians were finding their mates these days. Pregnancies were running rampant too, with Holley nearly ready to give birth and Fergie announcing her own coming pups just the other day.

Elena was overjoyed for them, and yet, she felt sadness and grief, some guilt as well. She knew nothing like that would never happen for her. The Fates had not aligned to grant her a mate. Besides, she knew she was far from ready for cubs of her own.

Imagine finding her own Fated mate? Ha! That was only a dream for someone like her. Which is why the whole thing with her heat cycle was especially cruel.

Shifter males preferred human females, or even Witches, as they were nearly human. Shifter females, rare and precious, were typically coddled by whatever Pack, Clan, or Pride they belonged too. Elena had been none of those things.

Panthers were lone creatures, existing in smallish family groups, but no real Prides. She had no affiliations with any other group than the Guardians. Just the fact she'd chosen to hone her warrior's skills instead of finding someone suitable to impregnate her was enough to tell all males for miles and miles exactly where her priorities laid.

It was not with a potential mate or family. It was with the Guardians. She had no one else, and that was okay with her.

Keep telling yourself that.

Shut up!

Elena snarled at the snarky bitch inside her head.

Her inner kitty was getting rather nasty lately. The beast was antsy and restless. Just other ways to say horny, she scoffed derisively. Then Elena clutched her stomach as a wave of pain almost sent her crashing to the floor.

"Elena!" Egros rushed over and took her hand, but she pushed him aside, not wanting his touch.

In fact, her Panther hissed and growled. She was not having any of that Witch. He was a friend, but nothing more. Not now or ever.

"I'll be fine."

"You're not fine. Your heat is coming back already!"

"So, what? I'm supposed to stop being a Guardian, now? I'm just supposed to stay home barefoot and pregnant cause fucking biology? Bull shit," she snarled.

"Here. Try this, but I warn you it will not stop it," Egros said, ignoring her bad temper. He handed her a vial.

"This is the last of Holley's potion, but at the rate you are metabolizing the herbs, it will wear off within a few hours."

"Thanks," she growled. Tossing back the bitter tasting shot of potion with a hiss of displeasure.

"I could always, you know, *help*."

Egros' voice was so low she almost missed it, but Elena was a Shifter with supernaturally enhanced hearing. The fact she could sense his lust made her beast growl angrily. The she-Cat would not have him. She wouldn't even think about letting him touch her.

Odd. Her reaction was so strong, but Elena thought about his offer, or at least pretended to. She shook her head. For a while now, she'd suspected the male Witch of having some sort of crush on her. But the cold hard truth of it was Elena did not reciprocate his feelings.to

"No," she replied, and shook her head. "That would not be wise, Egros, and you know it."

"I know, El. But I mean, you need me, and I am here. I can't bear to think of you in pain—"

"No. I will be fine."

Elena walked out of the new potions room the Keep had magically whipped up for the now three resident witches and turned down the ever changing hallway. She shook her head, mindful of her destination, and walked until she stood before her door.

"Shit," she whispered, and walked into her sitting room.

Each Guardian had their own suite of rooms in the Keep, and hers was perhaps the largest aside from Kingston's, simply because she had been there the longest after Storm. Elena had been a Guardian almost fifty years now.

Shifters aged differently than normals, sometimes hardly if at all. Guardians were granted longevity in return for their dedication and service to all species, and, of course, magic itself. In all that time, she had eluded her heat cycle successfully. She closed her eyes and sunk down on the plush purple couch. The color was dark, almost black, and fabulously soft.

Despite being a rough and tumble warrior, Elena had to admit she liked her creature comforts. Sure, there was also a barre against one wall that she used for stretches and to strengthen her core and tonality. An old wing chun wooden dummy occupied one corner, and a ten-foot cat scratching post the other.

She really had to replace that thing, she thought with a frown. Her inner kitty sure did love keeping her claws nice and sharp. Elena rolled her shoulders and closed her eyes.

She only had precious few hours until the potion wore off, then her feline would be yowling and prowling for a male to sate her biological imperative to mate. Not to find her actual mate. Just mate. As in fuck.

Sigh.

Feeling all sorts of gnarly, she stood up and tore off

her clothing, opting for a quick shift and stretch in the warm rays of sunshine filtering through the enormous oval skylight before she had to do what needed to be done.

Elena welcomed the magic that transformed her nearly six feet of powerful woman to a sleek black Panther nearly triple her human weight. She didn't know how the Keep did it since the outside resembled a medieval castle, but she was grateful all the same.

Her inner kitty simply loved the sunshine. The idea of what she was about to do was both intriguing and somewhat nerve racking. She'd never been the type of woman who indulged in one night stands.

But she couldn't fight what was essentially her biological makeup. Elena was an unmated feline Shifter of the age to bear cubs, and her Panther was fully aware of that.

Kitty cat wanted a cub, whether she'd found her mate or not was irrelevant. And if she couldn't have that, she damn sure wanted to practice making one.

Fuck me. Elena thought, whipping her sleek tail back and forth while stretching in the sunshine.

Yes, please. Her feline pushed back at her.

Looked like she was going to need a few minutes with Fergie, Holley, and Jessenia before she went out. The three females were mated to Elena's fellow

Guardians and were as close to gal pals as she'd ever had.

They were pretty damn awesome. And Elena needed some advice. But first, she could take a little fortifying catnap, couldn't she?

Prrrrr.

Two

*D*ammit.

Logan slammed his hands on the stainless steel worktable of his makeshift lab. Having his own money came in handy when he'd left his cozy job with big pharma and decided to dive into his research on his own.

Logan Wells had been on the verge of a groundbreaking discovery when his own bosses had shut him down. He didn't need them. He had connections, wealth, and more degrees than he could count. But that would not help him now.

The sample was contaminated. It was the only thing that made sense.

Human cells did not regenerate at such an aggressive rate, nor with such fantastic results. If they could, minor injuries would require no attention. And what was thought of as major injuries, like those received in a motor vehicle accident, would be gone with nothing more than an aspirin, and a pat on the head.

No. Something was wrong. The blood sample he'd personally taken from the victim of the warehouse explosion, who'd still been miraculously alive when responders had attended the scene, up until about twenty minutes ago, could not be untainted.

When Logan had seen footage of the aftermath of the explosion downtown, he'd sincerely doubted there were any survivors. But the EMTs and hospital ER docs had assured him, the patient had come from the wreckage, and he'd survived all of two days with 99% of his body covered in burns, and broken bones and torn ligaments from the weight of the debris on his body.

The old, supposedly empty building had been devastated by the explosion. Some suspected terrorists or secret arms dealers testing their wares of being behind the blast. Terrible, but not his purview.

His sister would smack him upside the head for that callous thought, but Margo wasn't there and, far as he knew, his twin couldn't read his mind even if she were.

Twin. Ha ha.

He smirked, thinking about his sister. The female had brass balls the size of boulders. She was tough as they came, and he couldn't have been more proud of her.

Of course, Grandfather always hated when he'd called his father's bastard his twin. But it had nothing to do with the later patriarch of the Wells family.

Margo Sinclair Wells was born on the same day as Logan, just minutes apart, in the same hospital even. Must have been convenient for his dad to walk from one room holding his first born son and heir, down the hall to see his newborn daughter from a long-standing affair. Logan's mother was crushed by her husband's infidelity, but she stayed with him till the tragic end, and made damn sure he got to know his sister.

As far as Logan was concerned, he and Margo shared fathers, were born on the same day, and had ever since developed a long standing bond that was rare between siblings far as he could tell. She was his twin. Even if he was as pasty as his English ancestors, and she dark as her African ones. Twins. And fuck what anyone else thought.

Margo shared the same high intellect with her brother, and he'd often suspected her of having an eidetic memory. Not that she spoke of it. She'd thrown herself into law and fought hard to right the injustices that plagued the judicial system.

A bleeding heart, he'd often joked. But his sister was the youngest black female attorney to be courted for judgeship. She'd turned it down for a stint in the FBI, and as he understood from her last email, she was elbows deep in some European shit hole hunting down one of the masterminds on their most wanted list.

Margo was tough as nails, but she always cared about the people involved in a crime while Logan spent his time finding other ways to benefit humanity. Like with his research. The warehouse explosion was terrible, but useful, too. Or it would have been, had his sample not been fucked.

Dammit.

It wasn't that Logan did not care about heinous acts of violence symbolic of a depraved mind or grossly desensitized individual. More so that as a geneticist and biochemist on the edge of a breakthrough in his research that could possibly alleviate real human ailments that have plagued humankind for centuries, he simply did not have the time to care about hunting down criminals.

To his way of thinking, there were people born to certain jobs. Everyone had their place in the universe, and some were lucky enough to know what their place was. Like him. He was a scientist and someday his work could cure things like dementia, arthritis, high blood pressure, diabetes, and more. Wouldn't that be amazing?

Hell. He had the skill set. Logan had been courted by world renowned hospitals and big pharma, but after his first stint with a famous drug company, he'd learned his lesson.

That very first job, he'd been so young and bright eyed, eager to make a difference. Logan had discovered a way to tap into a person's bio-chemical makeup to help regulate one's need for medicine. His research was bought, sealed, and then locked away for good.

Defeated and forced to sign an NDA, Logan left the company and had been using his trust fund to live and to pay for his own experiments. Someday, he could help humankind. That was the promise he'd made to his grandfather, whom he was named after, on the man's deathbed. And it was the promise he'd made himself after he packed his desk and walked out on that old job.

He still remembered the impression Logan Wells I had made on him, an orphaned boy of just six, when he'd gone to live with the man. It was as if the giant silver haired version of the adult Logan would become had looked right into his soul.

"You'll do alright, lad. Aye, you will."

But was he really? Logan couldn't help but feel like a total fucking failure. He was thirty-five years old. No wife. No kids. No job. He had his research, but no one would touch him after he'd sued his former bosses. Life was pretty much screwed for him.

His cell went off and he looked down. Shit. He was late for his set.

"Fuck. Fuck. FUCK!" he growled and slammed the desk again.

Temper, temper, his grandfather would have said, but fuck it. Logan had grown up on the streets of Newark, money or not. He was a foul mouthed genius, and he knew it.

"It's fucking contaminated," he grumbled as he hauled ass out of the makeshift lab he'd assembled in the basement of his townhouse.

He didn't care for opulence. He cared for privacy. Owning his own townhouse gave him just enough. Logan grabbed the case holding his *Rickenbacker Fireglo* and ran to catch his Uber.

Playing bass at *Midnight's* on Thursdays was just one of Logan's creative outlets. Even science nerds needed to blow off steam now and then. Like most teens, he used that period of angst in his life to study music, try his hand at the whole garage band thing.

Unfortunately, at the time, rock and blues were out of style, and boy bands were all the rage. He and his pals had no chance of getting anywhere. So, he'd turned to more scientifical pursuits, thinking that road would be rewarding. Unfortunately, disappointment abounded.

"You're late," Rick Melon, the bouncer, stated as Logan passed him on his way to the stage.

It was a small night spot in downtown Newark, four blocks away from Newark Penn Station and across the street from a *Dinosaur Barbecue*. The *Prudential Center* where the New Jersey Devils hockey team played was another city block over.

Not the ideal spot for a rock bar, but *Midnight's* did surprisingly well. Logan barely noticed the snow on the ground as he ran from the Uber driver's nondescript sedan to the back door of the establishment.

He grabbed his glass of iced tea from Simone, one of the bartenders, and got on stage standing off to the side and between Elliot, the front man, who glared at him, Denise, ignored him as usual while she fiddled with her guitar, and Roger, the drummer, simply tipped his head. After another second, Elliot got over his pissy mood, and they started to play.

Logan was unsure how many hours had passed

while he poured his frustration into his music. He did, however, note the moment she walked in.

Holy fuck.

He'd seen beautiful women before. Plenty of them. Logan was rich, smart, not bad looking, and he played bass. Getting women had never been difficult for him. Especially not at that time in his life, when getting women to fill his bed was all that mattered.

She was different, though. Something about her had every eye, male and female alike, zeroed in on the miles of ivory skin revealed in the skimpy miniskirt and tank top. February in New Jersey meant snow and temperatures in the single digits, but this woman had no coat, no hat, no scarf. Just two scraps of fabric that barely covered her tight assets.

Wouldn't they look great on my floor?

He missed a note, staring as hard as he was, it was a wonder he didn't face plant right off the fucking stage. The lights were dark, but even in the glow of the dark blue lights, Logan could tell something was different about the female.

She looked to be casing the joint. Not to rob it. But for something. He licked his lips, keeping time with the song, but no longer feeling it as he watched her scanning for something. He didn't know why it interested him. Was uncertain why he should care what the pretty woman was looking for, but he did. A lot.

In fact, he held his breath until she stopped searching. His lungs burned with the need for oxygen, but Logan couldn't fucking move. It was like she'd cast some sort of spell on him. The song ended, thank fuck, and Elliot announced their break.

Good thing too. Logan had stopped playing a few bars before the song had finished. Elliot was next to him, chewing him out between gritted teeth, but Logan could not give two shits what the jerk was talking about.

Then her eyes landed on him, and suddenly, he could breathe again. He gulped in air greedily, watching, star struck, as she walked over to him. All grace and lithe, like a ballet, she glided across the dark room until she was standing right there. At the foot of the stage.

He did not want to blink, refused to miss even a moment of watching the gorgeous creature. The lighting was bad, the room too crowded, and fuck, he wasn't sure, but he thought her eyes were the color of bubble gum. Dark pink, otherworldly, and so fucking hot.

Logan swallowed. He ignored the approach of one of Midnight's regulars. A fellow scientist, the squat little man, chatted him up occasionally. He was older, used to work for some big pharma label. He was there every Thursday and smelled like beer and stale pretzels. A harmless guy, but Logan was suddenly furious with him for trying to snag his attention.

"Hey Dr. Wells, missed a few notes tonight, huh? You know I've been meaning to talk to you about your research—"

"Not now, Harry," he growled, actually fucking growled at the guy.

What the hell was wrong with him? Logan was neither aggressive nor rude, but right then, he was both. The female smirked, pink eyes flashing at him while she slinked her way across the dance floor.

She moved like a predator on the prowl with a singular focus that he thanked fuck seemed to be him. Logan had never experienced such a thrilling surge of desire for a woman, but his reaction was unmistakable. His cock ached, rock hard against the suddenly too abrasive material of his briefs and jeans.

He wanted the stranger. Could picture himself now buried to the hilt in her slick heat, or with his head between her long legs, licking her to ecstasy. Fuck him. When did he ever want that? To taste a woman so damn badly he was salivating for her?

Never, that was when. Never had Logan ever

wanted to drop to his knees and eat some pretty woman's pussy until she was panting for him, screaming his name, pulling his hair. Fuck yes. He pictured all that in the span of time it took to blink.

And she knew it. Somehow, he knew she could tell how much he wanted her. It was in the naughty sparkle in her incredible eyes, and the way her fair hair sparkled like silver starlight in the shitty blue lighting from the bar. It was in every single step she took in that too short skirt, and those killer fuck me boots.

"But Wells, I really think we should tal—"

Logan pushed Harry's hand off his shoulder, moving closer to the woman as she stepped directly into his space.

"Meet me in the alley in three minutes."

Her husky voice stroked along his skin like hands roaming his body, and damn it, he really wanted that. Her hands on his skin. Like now. She waited, he realized for an answer and found himself unable to speak. That kind of proposal was completely out of character for a guy like him, and yet, Logan found himself nodding his agreement.

The gorgeous woman grinned, biting her lower lip, she eyed him from head to toe like he was a tasty meal, and she couldn't wait to dive in. Fuck, he couldn't either. Then she turned to leave out the front, and he was pushing past poor Harry, grabbing the case for his bass, and putting away the thing while shrugging into his jacket.

"Hey man, we have another set!" Elliot yelled, but Logan ignored the band's front man and took off for the back door like a man possessed.

Squinting against the darkness, he ignored the cold, the sight of breath like smoke streaming from his nose and mouth, and scanned the dank alleyway for the woman. A sleek sports car pulled up and the passenger door opened.

"Well?" Her husky voice reached him, and Logan didn't think he just acted.

Another first for the usually careful scientist. He jumped into the car and slammed the door behind him. The woman grabbed him by his shirt and slammed her mouth to his.

"Address?" she asked on a whimper, and he rambled off his address to her, not thinking or even caring if she was going to rob him, beat him, whatever, as long as she kept kissing him.

And she did. Eyes on the road, she damn near pulled all six and a half feet of him across her lap while her tongue stroked his as she zipped in and out of traffic.

Logan was so fucking turned on he couldn't think

straight. Eyes like bubble gum, he realized that was what she tasted like too. Sweet like candy, but more than that. She was deep, refined, like a good bottle of wine, and he was so fucking thirsty.

She purred against him, and he licked his way to her neck and chest, tugging the skimpy material aside so he could suck one pert nipple into his mouth. His dick was so hard he almost came from the thrill alone.

Then she was pulling into a spot and throwing the sleek little vehicle into park. Logan moaned as she pulled his head up, forcing him to release her breast.

"Keys?" she asked, panting with need.

"Yeah," he said, reaching into his back pocket and handing them to her.

Then they were both groping and kissing each other as they moved up his stairs to his townhouse. Finally, they opened the door. He didn't care about finding the bed or couch. Hell, he couldn't think about anything other than touching her.

She pulled her top off, then went to work on his while he buried his head between her breasts. Her skin was white as alabaster, smooth and soft, and he couldn't get enough of it.

His hands inched downwards, finding her thighs in the tight little skirt. He crept under it, moaning again when he found she was bare beneath the tiny little bit of fabric.

"Fuck, that feels so good," she moaned, tossing her head back as he picked her up and pressed her against the wall.

Logan dropped to his knees, prepared to do anything for the beautiful goddess. He kissed her inner thighs, loving the tight pull of her fingers on his hair. Then he was there, kissing, licking, and sucking her tight little nubbin, relishing in the heat of her wet folds.

"You taste so good," he growled, pressing his tongue inside her.

The woman hissed and growled, a real wildcat, she pulled his hair until he had to look up.

"Ouch. What is it?"

"Need you in me. Now," she growled, and his dick went even harder.

Fumbling for a condom, he sheathed himself before pressing into her right there against the wall. There was no stopping the avalanche of feeling that damn near consumed him as he fucked the gorgeous creature against his living room wall. Muscles bunched, she wrapped her long legs around his hips, skirt bunched around her waist, nails scratching at his shoulders, and Logan pumped his hips furiously.

"Yes, fuck, yes," she groaned, head tossed back, pink eyes wide as he pistoned faster and harder.

Sweat droplets coated his brow and ecstasy teased his nerve endings, it was just there, so close so close. But he never was a selfish lover, and more than anything, he wanted to feel this woman come on his rigid cock, wanted to revel in every squeeze and flutter of her perfect pussy.

"Need," she moaned, squeezing him tighter.

"I have what you need," he growled the words in a mostly testosterone fueled reply.

Then he was reached between them, strumming her tight little nubbin, playing with her clit as his cock stroked along her walls. And then she was coming.

"Oh gods!" the beautiful stranger screamed, her walls gripping him so hard, he went cross-eyed for a moment, pumping two, three, four more times before chasing her right off the edge into untold bliss.

A couple of hours and three condoms later, Logan lay in a spent heap on the rug in front of the fireplace. The beautiful blonde woman curled into his side, dozing lightly after their sex marathon, not that he could blame her. He was tired too.

Deliciously exhausted, and totally, completely sated. Really, that was a first. He'd read about passion like he'd just experienced. The kind that burned bright like wildfire or supernovas.

Poets wrote about it, musicians paid homage to it in song and artists created paintings and sculptures, but he never expected to find it at *Midnight's*. And he didn't even know her name.

In the morning, he told himself. He'd ask her in the morning. Then he draped an arm across her stomach and spooned in close, ignoring his hard on in favor of sleep. The woman with the pink eyes sighed and snuggled closer, and Logan drifted off easily for the first time in years.

THREE

hat the hell?

Elena blinked awake suddenly. Where the hell was she? The room was immaculate. Like cleaning crew clean. Expensive furniture straight out of a catalog. As if the person who lived there had money but not a lot of time.

Made sense. She wasn't much of an interior decorator either, preferring comfort to label. Elena sat up and the person beside her snored, shifting slightly in his sleep.

Uh oh.

Suddenly, the events leading up to her waking in that strange place came flooding back, and with alarming clarity. Sated and unalarmed, her inner kitty purred as she gazed down at the human male she'd chosen earlier that night to see her through her heat.

Her first thought was that the strange man was just so pretty. Not effeminate, just beautiful. He mumbled something in his sleep, and she stilled, not wanting to wake him.

Okay.

So, what she really wanted was to avoid him altogether. Nothing more awkward than being caught sneaking out after doing the dirty. Guilt assailed her, but she pushed it away.

She had no cause for that now. There was nothing nefarious about this. Just some no-strings sex between consenting adults. Her she-Cat snarled, and pushed her to stay beside the sleeping male, but Elena shook it off.

Grrr.

She winced as she stood up, deliciously sore in places that had been neglected far too long. Her body missed the warmth from his the second she pulled away. He'd been so very big and tall, warm too.

She mourned the loss of his heat as she inched away from the little nest they'd made. He'd used a throw blanket and pillows from the nearby sofa to wrap around them as they'd spread out on the thick rug in front of the roaring fireplace.

Damn.

She'd had no intention of doing more than sating her heat and speeding away from the stranger. But the second he'd touched her, that notion had flown right out the window. Something had happened to Elena. Something that was beyond her control.

Mine.

Her inner kitty purred, pushing the thought into her head just as Elena caught herself almost brushing the dark hair that had spilled across his forehead away from his handsome face.

Shit.

She shrank back. Okay. Reality check. The man was cute. That much was true. But no way was he *hers.* Not in the sense her inner kitty meant.

Mate.

No.

Grrr.

Her Black Panther snarled angrily, but Elena ignored the frisky feline as she tugged on her top and skirt, ignoring the ridiculously high-heeled boots, then slipped outside. It was snowing, but she did not care a fig for the cold. She just had to get out of there, and fast.

She took the magical shortcuts the Guardians used to cross the distance between their home base and

Newark in a fraction of the time. Normally, that was for emergencies only, but she was feeling all shook up and out of sorts.

Back at the Keep, Elena straightened her shoulders and walked in through the side door by the kitchen. Holley and Jessenia's kitchen garden was snowed over, but she noticed lights on in the greenhouse. The resident Witches used it to grow special herbs for potions and cooking year round.

Hopefully, whoever was in there stayed in there. She didn't want questions about where she'd spent the last few hours. Elena was keenly aware she stank of sex and man, but she was reluctant to jump in the shower just yet.

Truth was, she liked his scent. That mix of rain, spice, and man sent tendrils of remembered passion spiraling through her core. Every look, every touch, every meeting of lips had been beyond her scope of experience.

She was no virgin, but she'd never been as sexually active as others of her kind. It was completely natural, all physical, but she admittedly had issues with control. As in, she needed to be the one in control.

It irked her that she was at the mercy of her heat cycle. Actually, pissed her off was more like it. It was a curse, and yet, had she not been desperate for an outlet, she might not have met him. The tall, beautiful musician who lived in a townhouse seemed to have some money, kissed like a god, and rocked her world well into the wee hours of the morning. Far longer than she'd ever imagined any human capable.

That was all she knew about him. And it was going to have to be enough.

Mine.

No.

Yesss.

She rolled her eyes and closed the door soundlessly behind her. This was not the first time she'd used a male to see her through her heat.

Her previous partners were always supes like her, not human, but Jessenia, Fergie, and Holley had all assured her this kind of hook up was acceptable in normal society.

Still, she felt strange leaving him like that. Her past partners had known the deal beforehand. They understood she was at the mercy of her hormones and knew there would be no ties. Of course, this heat cycle had snuck up on her, and she'd had no time to make that kind of arrangement.

Egros had offered to partner with her, but she knew the Witch was not altogether honest about his motives. Her fellow Guardian seemed to be hiding some feelings for Elena.

Guilt and remorse struck a chord within her, but she shook it off. Whatever crush the male had developed on her, it was not her responsibility. She in no way encouraged him, and he needed to get over it. The faster the better.

The cold, hard truth was, she simply did not feel the same. Now, if it were a tall handsome normal with stunning hazel eyes and just the right amount of shadow on his cheeks, then she might be inclined to reevaluate her feelings.

Dammit. She really should not be having those thoughts. Why, oh why, had she listened to Fergie and Jessenia's advice? She shook her head, replaying the women's comments in her ear.

"Humans have one night stands all the time," the kitchen Witch had said.

"This way you'll be in total control," Fergie added. *"Find someone cute, boink his brains out. Or better yet, make sure he boinks your brains out. Then come back home. Easy peasy,"* the redhead stated baldly.

Yeah. Real fucking easy, she thought with a frown. Her damn kitty thought the guy was her mate, and now the beast would not stop yowling and scratching at her insides. The pain of her heat cycle finally abated for now, but her she-Cat was positively furious at her.

"I can smell him on you."

Elena refused to jump or react in any way to Egros' voice, though it did catch her off guard. She turned slightly to see the Witch sitting at the counter, in the dark.

"It is none of your business, Eg," she replied.

Tension spiked between the two old friends, but Elena was so not going there with him. They were colleagues first, peers. He should respect her enough to know the limits of their relationship. More than that, she'd thought they were friends.

"A human? You went to a human over me?" His anger and hurt batted up against her like fists, and she stepped back in shock before holding her ground.

"Egros," Elena began, friendly yet firm. "Why would you say this to me? It has nothing to do with you. You are my friend and my colleague, but my personal life is not your business."

"And how can you say that to me," he asked, pointing at his chest. "I've tried my best to help you. I have been patient, waiting for you to notice me, but you chose a human? How could you do that to me?"

"What? It isn't about you at all! That's it, move

out of my way, Egros. I am not discussing this with you anymore," she growled, shoving her way past him.

"I care for you, Elena—"

"Stop. Please, just stop."

The male Witch frowned hard, lines creasing his forehead and around his mouth. He was hurt. She scented it, felt it even, and that saddened her. But she was not about to explain to him or anyone else what she decided to do with her body. It was not his business.

"Fine. Do what you like, Elena," he replied, and shoved off the wall, preparing to leave.

Shoulders slumped, she headed towards her room. *Dammit.* This was not going how she'd planned at all. With her heat eased, she planned to get right back into the swing of her work as a Guardian. And yet, here she was, confused and missing a man whose name she did not know, and managing to piss off one of her dearest friends.

Sad yowl.

FOUR

The days passed one by one, a long succession of the same old for an entire week. Day in and day out, she'd trained, fought bad guys, and came home bruised, but sound.

Elena should have rejoiced in the steady success that was her sworn duty as a Guardian, but she felt off. As if she were missing a huge chunk of herself. All was right with the world, but something was bugging her.

Try as she might to hide it, the others could tell. Her fellow Guardians gave her a wide berth. Egros especially. Her relationship with the male Witch was tense as ever, but they were able to work still, and that should have pleased her. But needless to say, it didn't.

It wasn't until a very pregnant Holley grabbed her hand and pulled her towards the private room the

Keep had designated just for the females in the house that Elena knew she could not deny her feelings anymore.

"Holley? What are you doing?"

"Shh, just wait," the little Witch growled as she passed her curious mate and some of the other males who were discussing tactics in the conference room.

Once they'd rounded the corner, a marvelous mahogany door emblazoned with the words *ladies only* in a glittering, scrawling script waited for them/ The door opened of its own accord, as it sometimes did by the spirits of the Keep.

Holley pulled Elena inside, something the Panther allowed for two reasons. One, the female was mated to their Alpha, whom she respected, and two, she held the tiny Witch in great esteem.

"Okay," Holley said, and turned to face her.

"What?"

"Now, I have had enough of that expression and your silence. Tell me, what is going on, El?" Holley asked, brows furrowed as she rubbed her small hands over her ever growing belly.

"Is it obvious?" Elena whispered, closing her eyes, and sitting down heavily on one of the plush chairs.

"Yes. It is."

The door opened and Jessenia and Fergie filed in

soon after. Both women took seats on the matching velvet chaise lounges the Keep had furnished for them.

The *Ladies' Room* was not a bathroom, despite the odd name. It was more like a replica of an enormous old-fashioned dressing room. The kind designed for boutiques in the 1950s equipped with a raised stage, excellent track lighting, with several full-length mirrors, and a running soundtrack that seemed to only play the *Rat Pack*.

It was done in pinks and golds. Completely girly, over the top frilly, and just plain lovely, it was the only place Elena indulged in her secret fascination with fashion. Everyone always expected her to be the consummate warrior. And she was fine with that for the most part, but Elena had other interests too.

Like the three females who sat now waiting for her to open up to them. It was strange and nice, actually. Elena never had girlfriends, but here she was with three of the best females she knew.

Fergie, a former normal turned Wolf by her mate with an extravagant obsession with shoes, Holley a Witch who'd been trapped by a madman and rescued by her fated mate who was also a total clotheshorse, and Jessenia, the tiny kitchen Witch who stole the heart of their resident Italian Stallion.

They were the best friends she'd ever had, but there

was so much unsaid. Things they could not possibly understand. Loneliness was portable, she supposed. Even in crowds.

Sighing, she raised her head and glanced around. This morose behavior had to stop. After all, these three women were waiting for her, not pushing her to confide in them. Maybe she was wrong about them not understanding.

Elena sighed as her eyes fell on a rack of clothes, she couldn't help but appreciate. They were just her speed. Tight pants, crop tops, the perfect fabric for battle or to hang around in. The Keep was learning her style and providing thusly. Not easy since at six feet of lean muscle, she was difficult to outfit.

Fergie always grumbled about her skinny ass, but it was just one of the perks of being a Panther. The gods knew she ate like a horse. *No offence, Furio*, she thought with a wicked grin as she picked a salmon canape off the tray Jessenia had brought in.

"Okay. I'll spill, but first, food. These are so good," she moaned in appreciation, and Jessenia practically glowed at the compliment.

"Wait till you try my peanut butter dream cookies for dessert!"

"OMG! Jess, what the hell are you tryin' to do to me? I'm already big as a house with this little cub growing inside me," Fergie fake-complained while munching on a canape in one hand and a cookie in the other.

"Well, my young dragonling and I are very pleased with your efforts," Holley said smiling around a cookie she'd snagged from the still covered dessert tray.

"You guys! Those are for after the canapes," Jess scolded. "And Fergie, you are not big as a house."

Jess paused, looked her BFF over, then opened her mouth again.

"Well, maybe your ass is a little bit bigger," she added.

"Oh yeah? Wait till that pony you keep riding knocks you up! We'll see whose ass is big then, heifer!" Fergie said, sticking her tongue out at her bestie.

"Dog breath!"

"Witch!"

After they'd exhausted their insults, both females burst out laughing. Holley rolled her eyes over the females' antics, gesturing to Elena that the two of them were nuts.

"Hey, did you ladies see what the Keep brought us?" Fergie giggled, wiping her mouth with a napkin, her fake fight with Jessenia already forgotten.

"Oh yeah, I so need this," Elena said, her pink gaze

roaming over the latest gowns and baubles the Keep had magically created.

"Hey, how do we know this stuff isn't stolen?" Fergie asked for the millionth time.

"Because that is not how the *manetuwak* work," Holley repeated.

It was the same reply she always gave her. Elena had worried at first too that magical thievery was the means by which the Keep was getting their wares. She couldn't help but admire the racks and racks of delightful goods, but refused to wear them until Holley explained they were mostly replicas from famous designer labels.

Magically whipped up to suit their whims. If any of the ladies could think it, the Keep could make it. Besides, that was how Elena had found herself in the skimpy little outfit she'd worn the night her heat cycle had forced her out on the prowl.

"Alright, now before these two started going at it, Elena, I'd asked you a question," Holley spoke up.

"Oh? You did?"

"Yes, I did. Now, don't you think it's time you told us what's the matter?"

Holley's eyes narrowed in concern. She rubbed her belly and waited patiently for Elena to answer. No one was more patient and inspired more confidence than Holley, but she was unsure how to proceed.

"Nothing," she replied, figuring she might as well try ignoring her current dilemma.

"I know you're our resident badass, but please, we are friends here and this is the *Ladies' Room*! It's our safe haven, El," Holley said, obviously not taking the hint.

"She's right. Talk to us," Fergie seconded with her mouth full, so it sounded more like *she's wight twalk two ush*.

"OMG. Swallow first, Fergie," Jess said, then snorted. "Bet you hear that a lot from Storm, eh?"

"Okay, easy," Elena began, wanting to break up the friendly spat before it got out of hand. Fergie had that look in her eye, the same one she'd had when she hid one of every pair of shoes Jessenia owned.

Sigh. She really had a serious shoe fetish. But all kidding aside, what could Elena say?

Oh, I'm just mooning over some one night stand who probably forgot about me the second he woke up.

Not very badass of her. In fact, she was so shocked by her own reactions, she had no idea what to say.

"It's nothing," Elena began, deciding to spare her friends her own idiocy.

"That's it, I call bullshit," Fergie said not bothering

to look up from the bowl of Jessenia's homemade mint cookie crunch ice cream she was currently munching on.

"Where did you get that ice cream? I hid that in the back of the freezer for Furio!"

"Yeah, well, finders keepers, beyotch," she snickered, and dove in.

The redhead had announced her pregnancy to the group of Guardians after her mate, Storm, had put Furio in a headlock for teasing her about eating more than usual one night at dinner.

True, she had quite the appetite, but she was a she-Wolf now, and Elena was sure that was pretty fucking ordinary. Still, males were always so dramatically protective of their mates' feelings.

Especially when their mates were expecting. Elena gasped at the sudden punch of pain she felt in her gut. Would she ever have a male of her own to worry over her that way? She didn't need anyone to defend her, but still. It might be nice.

Expecting a cub or pup was definitely cause for celebration. Elena unconsciously touched her own flat stomach, a gesture that did not go unnoticed by the other three women. She was frowning too. Hard.

Her heat cycle aside, Elena was not expecting a cub. And she would not be. Not for a very long while, if ever. The purpose of a feline Shifter's heat cycle was to ensure the survival of the species. Unlike other Shifters, felines did not always wait for their mates, fated or otherwise, before engaging in procreation.

And that was because of one simple fact. There were fewer feline Shifters than other subspecies, and therefore, evolution ensured procreation would not wait for increasingly rare matings to occur. Survival was key, and as always, nature found a way.

But Elena had always refused to be controlled by her evolutionary hormones. Her heat cycle was not now or ever going to control her life.

"Come on, El. We know something is up. You haven't been the same since you went out that night and came back many, *many* hours later," Holley said.

"Yeah, talk to us," Jessenia coaxed.

"And let us know if we have to cut someone's dick off. Cause we will," Fergie nodded, pointing her ice cream dripping spoon at her.

Elena snorted. She stood up, then sat down again, hard, on and empty chaise and stared at the three very different women. It was amazing they'd found each other, accepted one another, and formed this tremendous friendship. Even more amazing they insisted on including her regardless of how she protested and tried to resist.

"We are your girls, El. We got your back always. Don't you forget it." Fergie narrowed her eyes, and it was as if she was reading her thoughts and not for the first time, either.

"Spill," the redheaded she-Wolf insisted.

"You, uh, know I hooked up the other night, right?"

"Really? How was it?" Holley asked, eyes shining with glee.

"OMG! Holley, pregnancy has made you such a horn dog! Seriously though, did he make you come, right? Did he go down on you? Cause if he didn't, and that is the problem, we can straighten his ass out," Jessenia exclaimed.

"What? No!" Elena gasped.

"No, he did go down on you, or no, he didn't?" Fergie asked.

"Ladies! Please!" Elena yelled, and this time she was blushing. "Look, I met a guy, and everything was fine in the bed department, though we didn't really make it to the bed—"

"Woot Woot! So, what's his name?" Holley asked, swaying side to side on her feet, something she said eased the babe inside her belly.

"Oh. Um. I don't really know," Elena replied, ignoring the wide-eyed stares of the women.

"That's okay," Fergie said, nodding encouragingly. "She is a modern woman. This was a one night thing, right?"

"That's the thing though," Elena said, swallowing down her trepidation.

If she couldn't be honest with them, then their friendship was doomed. Might as well spill the beans.

"What is it, love?" Holley asked.

"My Panther kinda thinks he belongs to us, well, to *me*."

"Come again?" Holley asked.

"Damn straight she wants to come again," snorted Fergie.

"Shh. I think she's serious," Jessenia added.

"I am serious," Elena confessed. "I think the human I spent the night with might be my mate."

Mine.

FIVE

A pregnant hush settled over the *Ladies' Room.* Holley's eyes filled with unshed tears, presumably happy ones since a wide grin spread across her face. Jessenia blinked her eyes, then looked at the other two females before looking back at Elena. As for Fergie, the redhead stood up and placed her half-filled carton of ice cream on the floor.

Uh oh. That was serious. Elena exhaled, relieved at her impromptu confession, and anxious at their reactions. Her Panther seemed quite pleased that she'd at least admitted to the possibility of the pretty human belonging to them.

Heaven knew he was pretty. Tall and rodeo cowboy lean with wicked hazel eyes that burned with passion when he'd touched her, skilled lips, and talented hands. He was a work of fucking art. Literally.

Of course, Elena didn't know how to respond to the stunned silence that greeted her. The trio of females always had something to say, but now they looked as shocked as she felt.

Was it so unthinkable that she would have a male of her own? As it stood, she was not even sure about it. Not 100%. After all, it could all be some residual effect of all the fabulous fucking for all she knew, and she said as much.

"Elena, I am so happy for you," Holley grinned.

"Yeah. Congrats on the fab fucking," Fergie added.

"Fergie, you are so crude! Anyway, where'd you meet Mr. Wonderful?" Jess asked.

"Uh, I met him at that club with the good music by the train station. It's called *Midnight's*," Elena replied, relieved she knew the answer to that question.

"Does he work there?" the kitchen Witch continued her line of questioning, but Elena couldn't do more than shrug.

"I mean, not really. He was in the band—"

"OMG! You picked up a rocker? How cool! Was he tattooed? Did he have piercings? Did you use condoms? Those guys are usually whores,"

Fergie squealed, then slapped a hand over her mouth.

"Fergie!" Jessenia shook her head at her big-mouthed BFF.

"Um, sorry, about that last part," Fergie grimaced.

"Okayyyy. Well, no to the piercings. Yes, one tattoo. On his left side," she said, biting her lip as she recalled the beautiful ink that covered his body from right under his arm down his hip.

"What of?"

"Well," Elena blushed, remembering how she'd traced the ink with her hands, then lips.

Seemed like kismet now. So sleek and beautiful. Her one night stand man had a black panther tattooed down his side.

Of all the things in the world, she sighed, thinking about how warm and delicious his skin had tasted beneath her searching mouth. The second she'd spied the artwork, her inner kit had growled possessively at the sight. A truly magnificent piece, but more so, it had called to her beast.

"So, a panther, huh? And you somehow doubt he's yours?" Jessenia made a face like Elena was crazy and shook her head.

"It's the way he responded to me that was kind of scary, I guess."

"Like how?"

"Did he hurt you?' Fergie stood up, a snarl in her throat.

"No! Of course not," chided Elena. "It was like he was really into me. He kept kissing me and touching me, and I mean we came together again and again, and he never seemed to get tired. And yes, before you ask *Moms*, he wore protection. The thing is that doesn't happen very often. Not to me."

"But you're a knockout, El," Fergie said. "How can guys not want to take you home and bang you all night long? I mean, if I was a guy, I'd be all over that!"

"Uh, thanks?" Elena said, but it came out more question. Jessenia was patting Fergie's arm and shaking her head.

"What? I mean it. Look at her for fuck's sake."

"I hate to admit this," Holley began. "But Fergie has a point. What kind of guys have you been dating, Elena?""

"I haven't. Not lately, anyway. But I always choose supes to see me through my heat when the potions don't work. Typically, they are standoffish. I think I threaten them. And I never dated a normal."

"Never?"

"Nope. Never had time. I made my pledge to the Guardians when I was still a teenager."

"Wow. You were so young, El."

"No, it's cool. I love my job. But you know *why* I went out. Anyway, I don't know. My Panther might just be confusing my heat cycle with whatever hormones go off when you find your mate, right?" Elena asked, looking at the three stunned females.

As she tried talking it out, the more likely it seemed that the male she'd gone home with was just some guy who, while gifted in bed, *or against the wall and on the floor as it were*, was most likely not her fated mate. It was just good sex. Period.

"Only one way to tell for sure," Fergie said after a few long minutes had passed.

"What way?" Elena asked.

"Go see him."

"What? I can't do that!"

"Sure, you can. It's Thursday. He might be at the bar tonight, rocking out on his guitar."

"Bass."

"What?"

"He plays bass."

"I see," Fergie said, eyes twinkling. "Looks like you already know more about him than you think. You like him."

"I do not—"

"Do too. Suck it up, buttercup. Go see him."

"No, I—"

But the more she resisted, the more the ladies argued this was her only recourse. They were probably right. She needed to find out for herself if this was a fluke or not.

"First, you need to get changed," Fergie instructed, grabbing some things off the rack.

"No, I can just wear this," she said, gesturing towards her old jeans and tank top.

"She did not just say that. Please tell me she did not just say that," Fergie sighed dramatically.

"It's no use, El. Ever since *Little Miss Woof Woof* here has gotten herself knocked up, she's been crazier than ever," Jessenia mock whispered.

"*Shyaddap*," Fergie barked at her BFF, then turned to Elena.

"Sweetie, what you need is something that says fun, flirty, and up for fucking."

"I don't think—"

"Good! I never do," Fergie said, slapping Jessenia's hand when the woman agreed.

"Ooh, I know, I know. She needs something naughty!" Holley chimed in, and before she knew it, they'd started tossing items out at her and giving her orders to get dressed.

Scary bitches, for sure. But they were her scary

bitches.

"Guys, I look like some fetishy freak in this outfit."

"Uh uh. You look totally *hawt*," Fergie said, and winked.

Dammit. Despite all her protests, Elena found herself in a short plaid skirt and a fuzzy maroon sweater that brought out the unusual hue of her eyes. Paired with knee high leather boots, she had to admit she felt a little like a cosplayer.

At the same time, Elena's confidence sure was boosted. At least the heels were flat, not like the ones she'd worn last time.

Elena jumped in her metallic black 1966 Jaguar XJ13. She loved the sports car, and though, it was for personal use, it had all the bells and whistles.

Her Jaguar had been modified with such perks as bulletproof glass, reinforced body, supped up tires and shocks to withstand ridiculously high speeds, and other goodies to counter attacks from their enemies.

With what was left of the Loyalists in hiding, things had been rather quiet for the Guardians of late. Elena quickly cleared her mind of any such thoughts, as there were some who believed in superstition.

Like firefighters and law enforcement officers, their supernatural counterparts, the Enforcers and

Guardians of Chaos, rarely liked to mention quiet spells in their line of work.

Elena gunned the engine. She must have been nervous to be having such thoughts. Ridiculous. What did she have to worry about?

Confident that she had his interest, at least she did the other night, there was no reason for the human to ignore her. Surely this trip was not for no reason. And maybe, just maybe, he'd be up for another round or three?

Licking her lips, she pushed her sports car harder, making the trip in even less time than usual. Sure, her heat was over, but the truth was Elena's body tingled just thinking about the devastatingly handsome man.

With his dark hair so carelessly loose around his face, the man should have looked messy or just plain shaggy. But to her, he simply looked hot. He had the most gorgeous hazel green eyes flecked with gold, that if she didn't know better, Elena would have assumed made him part Big Cat Shifter. Tiger or maybe Leopard, but nope, he was all human.

His rodeo cowboy build meant long, powerful legs, a solid six pack for his abs, and nicely formed pecs. He had light swirls of dark hair on his chest, and she liked the feel of it against her skin. The man was the stuff her dreams were made of, and that was just his looks.

Never mind the fact he'd given her the best sex of her life. Hell, he'd made her see stars with that amazingly gifted body of his. But it was more than the sex that had her going back to *Midnight's*, that cold winter's evening.

Tingles of anticipation traveled up and down her spine at light speed. Maybe Fergie, Holley, and Jess were right about this. Maybe Elena should consider getting to know the human a little better. After all, if she was still thinking about him all this time later, he must be worth a second glance.

Mind made up, she squeezed her car into a tight little parking spot outside the bar, almost blocking the alley. Nerves threatened to assail her, but she took a fortifying breath, checked her face and hair, then got out of the car. And that was when she got a whiff of the unthinkable.

Blood. *His.*

"You're coming with us!"

Thwack! Crash!

"Fuck you-oof!"

"Should have come quietly," a dark, sinister voice snarled.

"I said, fuck you."

Her supernaturally enhanced hearing picked up on some of the heated exchange. The blows were hard enough to draw blood, and her she-Cat was beyond pissed having recognized the spicy tang of her male's life force.

The last sentence uttered was deep and raspy, the responding remark riddled with pain and familiar. Elena sniffed, trying to get a lead on what she was about to face.

Gila Shifters. Grrr. And from the sound of it, they had her man.

Mine.

Her Panther snarled loudly in her mind's eye, the beast ready to obliterate anyone or thing that harmed a hair on her mate's head. Mate? Fuck. She didn't have time to debate the rightness of the statement with her inner feline. He needed her.

That was her last thought before she took off running into the dark alley. She sent a text to the rest of the Guardians, before shoving her cell phone back in the pocket of her ridiculous skirt. Not waiting for a reply, she shoved off the short bomber jacket she wore and readied herself to face the enemy. Elena wasn't going to wait for back up. Not when he could be hurt.

"Stop resisting," Lizard breath hissed into her human's ear, but the man put up a fight.

"Look guys, I'm flattered by your interest, but I am involved with someone else."

Lip bloodied, her human grinned and shoved one foul Gila Shifter off of him. The Shifter recoiled angrily, while his body brought his hand back, ready to swing.

"Hey there, asshole," Elena said, having snuck up behind him, she held his wrist and spun him around to face her.

"I guess you're going first," she growled, then struck him hard in the solar plexus with her fist, followed by a roundhouse kick to his jaw.

"You!" Her human gasped, then turned to jump in front of her when another one of the Lizard men tossed a brick her way.

"No!" Elena yelled, as she watched him take the hit meant for her.

Anger coursed through her, and she snarled at the soon to be dead fuckers who'd touched her guy. Poor, beautiful, brave normal. She grabbed the Lizard who threw the brick and lifted him over her head, tossing him into two others who'd come out of the shadows.

While they scrambled to regroup, she lifted her normal up and lowered him behind some garbage cans to keep him out of harm's way. She heard them the second they identified her and turned to face the Loyalist scum.

"She's a Guardian! Get her!"

Offner was gone, but his supporters remained and the war to protect magic was always raging. Was Elena selfish for laying this all at his feet? She wondered, thinking of the human bleeding for her on the floor.

Shit. She couldn't do this now. The Gila Shifters were getting their venom ready, she could see it in the way their glands swelled, readying to release the poisonous secretions. Fight first, think later.

Roar!

SIX

ours earlier...

It had been a shitty week all around for Logan. After waking up delightfully exhausted and hopeful for maybe another bout of hot as fuck sex, he'd discovered the pink eyed vixen had run out on him.

As if that wasn't bad enough, he'd spent the whole weekend trying to run down the victim of the warehouse bombing's next of kin to see if he couldn't ask for a blood sample to rule out his impossible findings. But John Doe had not been claimed by anyone, so that was out.

Starting from scratch, Logan had put a few more samples from regular run of the mill blood donors through his tests to rule out whether something in his equipment was tainted. Those passed with flying colors, so it had to have been the sample. But for some reason, it bothered him.

Everything about the blood appeared normal. Except for one thing. A burn victim with that level of injury should have shown signs of acute blood loss and anemia. But that blood was not only normal. It was better than normal. Under his watchful eye he watched John Doe's blood cells regenerate like something out of a sci-fi flick.

Logan should have destroyed the samples, but he didn't. He'd held on to them even after Margo replied to his monthly email check in, with her standard *get rid of that bullshit and reevaluate your life* message.

She had little time for his insistence that sometimes things were simply inexplicable. Margo preferred cold hard facts. Still, he enjoyed hearing from his twin. It was like a balm for his wounded ego, though he wasn't even sure why he mentioned his one night stand.

Why are you wasting time on this woman? She's obviously some nympho groupie. Did you use a condom? I hope you did, brother of mine, otherwise I'd watch out for a letter from some lawyer demanding child support. Stay safe and always wear a hat on your little head!

Fucking Margo. Blunt as hell, but he loved her. As if that bit of humiliation wasn't enough, he was worried about showing up at *Midnight's* on Thursday. He'd pissed off Elliot by walking out on them last week, but the band's front man had swallowed his pride while the other members simply shrugged and high-fived Logan on his score.

She'd been hot alright. Unbelievably sexy and seductive as hell, but sweet and vulnerable, too. In a way that made his cock throb in need, and his heart thud with emotion. He tried to just smile and accept the joshing over the mega hot babe who'd rocked his world then left him high and dry. Well, he was not crying in his cereal exactly, but close enough.

Fuck.

He didn't even know her name. But there had been something about her from the very beginning that drew him to her like a moth to a flame. What the hell was all that about anyway? Logan Wells did not do starry-eyed lover very well.

He had women, sure. But his work was the thing. His research was the reason behind everything he did. Sometimes he went weeks without coming up for air, except for Thursday nights. That was when he always reserved a few hours to unwind and let his thoughts just flow through the notes he banged out on his bass.

But this female had him tied up in knots, for fuck's sake. He was seriously borderline pathetic.

The woman hadn't even bothered to give him her name. hell, she hadn't spoken more than five words to him, and those were mainly *yes* and *harder*. Not that he'd minded.

Still, a guy felt a little used after a week flew by and no call, no note, no nothing. Shit. He was a total pussy.

Growling to himself, he took an Uber to the club, his *Rickenbacker* in its case. Teaching himself to play bass had been the smartest thing Logan had done with his time between AP classes back in high school.

A person with his kind of scientifically geared brain needed creative outlets otherwise he'd implode. Found that out the hard way when one of his best professors from school had told him of his attempted suicide over the pressure of being enrolled in some of Princeton's most advanced classes and getting his first pubic hair.

High pressure indeed. Logan had listened when his professor advised him not to get lost in the science, to remember that he was human. Music did that for him. It allowed him to connect with other people when that was something that had been difficult for him his whole life.

Music had given him a reason to be seen by the cool kids. Made him appealing to women. Hell, it still got him laid. Frowning as he got out of the Uber, Logan pushed all thoughts of pink eyed seductresses from his mind. He was ready to play himself into oblivion.

Fess up, brother, you're looking for her.

No, he was not waiting for her to arrive. No, he did not scan the crowd repeatedly for a flash of pink eyes or long ivory legs in a sinfully short mini skirt.

Liar liar.

When the band halted for their break, Elliot had started to give him some shit about disappearing, but Logan was in no mood. He grabbed his tumbler of iced tea and headed to the alley for some cold but fresh air.

The atmosphere in the bar had gone stale, and he was counting the minutes till he could get his sorry ass home. What he needed was a few weeks uninterrupted in his lab. Then he could forget about pink eyed blondes who tasted like bubble gum and made him come so hard his eyes crossed.

He leaned against the brick wall, grateful it was winter, and he couldn't smell whatever usual suspects were undoubtedly fouling up the alley. Newark was known for being a grungy, rough and tumble city, but it was doing its best to clean shit up. Like downtown

Jersey City, Weehawken, and Hoboken had years earlier.

Still, perhaps he'd been foolish to wander outside despite Rick going on break. The burly bouncer was a good guy, quiet for the most part.

"So, Dr. Wells, about your research, I had some questions for you." Harry, one of the regulars at *Midnight*, stepped out of the shadows, startling Logan into almost dropping his glass.

"Geez, Harry, you almost gave me a heart attack," Logan replied, shaking his head.

This guy could not take a hint. When he'd first approached Logan and said he'd recognized him from work, he'd smiled and nodded. Hell, he'd responded politely to his inquiries about where Logan had gone after leaving big pharma, and what he'd been up to.

Typically, Logan did not discuss his current research projects with anyone. Especially, since he hadn't exactly acquired his samples on the up and up. Knowing a few first responders who needed extra cash was helpful in that respect. He was able to acquire samples after the fact, and never ever at someone's expense. His research was groundbreaking, or it could be, as long as he didn't violate his NDA.

"Sorry, Harry, I am not talking shop tonight," Logan replied and shook his head.

"I'm afraid Dr. Wells, you do not have a choice."

The man smiled, and for the first time Logan noticed something very strange about his eyes. The slime green color was off putting, but the vertical pupil and corresponding eyelids were downright weird.

A few more men with similar coloring and equally disturbing eyes came out of the shadows, bracketing Harry on either side. Logan began to think this was a really bad fucking idea.

"What do you want?" He placed the glass on the ground and braced himself for the impending skirmish.

Logan was not big on physical scuffles, but he knew when one was about to happen. He changed his stance, bringing his left shoulder up to block his face and his right side back.

Not the best athlete, he was always a damn good student. One of the first boxing lessons his grandfather had given him was on the correct way to stand. Elbows against his chest, chin down, ready to defend. It seemed wrong at first, but Grandfather had insisted.

"Elbows down against your chest. Protect your face. Never drop your hands. Put your body behind your punch."

The old bastard was good at two things, making money and boxing. And he'd taught Logan well. With his Orthodox stance perfected, he had maximum torque and leverage. He could hit harder and react faster. Logan had been taught well how to defend himself.

But still, he was worried. Outnumbered and in the dark, freezing alley, it was a long shot. Still, he wasn't going down without a fight.

"You're coming with us!"

One of the men said pointing a long, spindly finger at Logan. There was something off about these guys. They were all really tall, and from a six and a half foot man, that was saying something. Tall and fast too. They way they moved unnaturally quick, and, what the fuck? One of them was clinging to the far brick wall like a fucking spider!

"Come along. Don't fight us, *Wellssss*," Harry hissed.

Oh yeah. Something was totally fucked about the guy. Logan noticed his skin taking on a greenish hue. That was quickly followed by a foul odor permeating the cold air.

"No, go ahead. Fight *ussss*," another said, and before Logan could refuse, the second stepped forward and punched him in the gut, then the bastard spit right in his face.

Thwack! Spit! Punch! Kick!

Pain exploded throughout Logan's entire body. He doubled forward then back with each blow. The place where the fucker had hocked a loogie on him started to burn, and he did his best to wipe it off, spitting blood onto the ground.

Anger burned in his veins, and something else too. Was it guilt? No, regret, loss, sadness over not seeing the bubble gum eyed beauty once more. If only he could've met her again.

Dammit. Why the hell was he thinking about her at a time like this? Logan was getting his ass handed to him, and he was starting to feel very dizzy.

"Ready to come along quietly, now?" Harry asked.

"Fuuuck youuu-oof!" His speech was slurred, that wasn't good. Add in another blow to his chin, and he was looking at a probable concussion.

Logan's head snapped back. He was an okay boxer, but these guys were something else. No matter how many times he struck, they kept on coming. Like his blows were nothing to them.

It was a little emasculating, but he chalked it up to steroids or PCP, some drug or something. Fuck, when did they all start turning green?

There was no way he could take on those two by himself. The truth hurt sometimes. Even more than a punch to the stomach.

"Should have come quietly," one of the men he didn't know said in a dark, sinister voice.

"I said, fuck you." Logan sneered, spitting directly in the man's face, then using his booted foot to slam down hard on the man's instep, then he drove his fist into his stomach, and watched in horror as the man smiled revealing three inch long fangs oozing slime.

"What the fuck are you?" Logan gasped, but before anyone could answer, something sleek and fast ran into them.

"Hey there, asshole," a familiar voice said to the man attempting to hit him yet again.

Shit. She was there! His mystery beauty of the bubble gum eyes. But this was dangerous. No! He needed her gone.

"Stay back!" Logan yelled out towards where he thought the mystery woman was standing, earning him another punch from the man-thing nearest him.

His vision was hazy and for some reason he felt numb on the left side of his body, but he felt it when her pink gaze landed on him. He didn't know why she was there, but she was not happy.

That was obvious in the way she took in his condition from head to toe. He must have been pretty fucked up because whatever she saw, it clearly angered her. The woman turned, a snarl on her pretty mouth as she spun to face his two assailants.

Words were exchanged, and he was having a hell of a hard time following. Fear for her safety outweighed the pain he felt, and he tried once again to tell her to go. Shit. His voice was not obeying him.

From the corner of his eye, he saw one of Harry's green goons reach on the ground for something. Was it a brick? Horrified at the thought of anyone marring her beautiful skin, Logan tried his best to warn her.

"This isn't your concern," hissed one of the men.

"Really? And that's your call, tough guy?"

Before Logan could say anything, she moved into a crouching attack position like something from one of those old Kung Fu movies he enjoyed. Then she started to kick some serious ass, but not before the sneaky fucker with the brick inched closer. Finally, Logan launched himself in front of her with one final burst of adrenaline.

The brick made impact with the back of his skull and Logan had never felt such intense pain. The woman caught him as he stumbled, lowered him behind some garbage cans.

"Stay here," she whispered, touching the side of his face.

Shit. He couldn't just lie there, though. He had to

do something, but he was losing feeling in his body. Terrified and unable to move like he wanted, Logan tried to trace what had happened. None of the injuries he'd received could've made him paralyzed. No. It had to have been something in that goon's spit.

Fascinating. And also, pretty fucking impossible.

"She's a Guardian, you idiots!" Harry yelled, attempting to grab Logan from behind the trash cans.

He started to drag him down the alley, surprisingly strong for a short, stunted looking man, but Logan was not going anywhere without a fight. Mustering all his strength, he turned and grabbed for something, anything on the alley floor.

Finding his iced tea glass, he closed his bruised and somewhat numb fingers over the cold hard container and smashed it right over that fucker Harry's head. He listened for the man's stunned scream to make sure he'd hit him, then Logan scrambled away from the jackoff.

He needed to find his mystery woman and get her the hell out of there. What was she doing? Coming to his fucking rescue it seemed, and wasn't that emasculating?

Shit. He didn't give a fuck about that, and if he could have, he would have laughed. Right then though, he was pretty sure his vocal cords were slowly freezing, like he was paralyzed by something. Whatever odd chemical was in that spit, he concluded.

Logan was all for equal rights between the sexes, but he did not want her tangled up in whatever psychotic plan Harry had for kidnapping him. What was the weird man up to and who was behind the attack?

Probably some big pharmaceutical company or government agency. They were always after Logan for his research, but he'd walked away from that a long time ago. His left leg began to twitch and slow, and he cursed roughly.

As a biochemist he hoped some of that fucking spit was still on his clothes for later research, but again that was something he wasn't all too concerned with at the moment. He scanned for the woman with his one still working eye and watched in awe as she lifted up one of the attackers and tossed him into a brick wall.

Holy fucking shit.

The female was a total badass. If he wasn't worried sick over her getting injured because of him, he would so have a hard on right then. Not that he needed to worry. Apparently, she was a better fighter than those green fucking bozos.

And she looked hot doing it. Fuck. He really needed to rein in his crazy lust-filled thoughts where the stranger was concerned. He crawled to where the woman was beating the shit out of one of the other men.

Blood poured from a wound on her stomach and Logan saw red. He grabbed the foot of the tall stool Rick, *Midnight's* bouncer, usually sat on, and used all his remaining strength to lift it and bash it over another assailant's head. He might be down, but he refused to just watch while she fought for him.

More men came running down the alley. One with long hair streaming behind him while smoke appeared out of his nostrils. There was another dark-haired man, and he held some sort of glowing blue flashlight that exploded as he punched one of the attackers dead in the jaw.

Just when Logan thought he was about to pass out, he rolled onto his back. And that's when he knew the spit not only had a paralytic but some kind of hallucinogenic as well. With a mighty roar that seemed to shake the very alley, Logan's one good eye widened as he tried to make out the shape coming straight towards him from the sky.

No fucking way.

It was a Dragon. Not some lizard they threw the tag on to make it sound cooler. A real fucking Dragon. A huge mythological *knight in shining armor eating*

Dragon. And it was circling the sky above the alley behind *Midnight's*.

Some more green hued men joined the fray, and Logan wondered how these men all had the same genetic makeup that would grant that strange color scheme. He started to lose focus as more and more of his body went numb. Maybe this was all some kind of crazy trip, he wondered as another flash of fire came blasting out of the Dragon's maw.

"Stay down!"

The pink eyed beauty ordered, and he tried. Really, he did. But some fucker was creeping in on her and he had no choice but to try and protect her.

Swinging out with what remained of the stool, he caught the asshole in the back of the knees. The mystery woman growled, her head snapping back and gaze catching his. She grabbed the attacker as he tripped and slammed his head on the asphalt. He was down for now, but Logan had a feeling it wouldn't be for long.

"I said down," she snapped at Logan, crouching low in front of him in a defensive position.

Dizzy and out of sorts, Logan took a moment to appreciate her long, powerful build as she kicked some serious ass. Snarls and growls came from the remaining attackers. He was feeling weak and dizzy, and at this point, doubted he could lift any part of himself off the ground.

He'd wanted to see her again so badly. But like this? Shit. Not what he'd planned.

"Hey, are you okay?"

Her husky voice sounded so sweet and concerned as her bubble gum gaze found his eyes. Damn, was she beautiful. He wished he could speak or reach out for her, but Logan was too far gone.

Eyes closing, he went down for the count. But he could've sworn she held him and whispered to him, as she lifted him out of the alley.

"I got you."

SEVEN

"In my office now," growled Kingston.

The big Diamond Dragon, and Alpha of their group of Guardians, was used to being listened to. So, when Elena showed signs of hesitating, he turned to snarl angrily at her from the corridor of the Keep. Even had white smoke puffing out of his nostrils.

"My love, is there a reason you are going all Dragony in the hallway?"

"Holley," Kingston said, turning towards his fated mate with all the love he felt evident on his face.

"Nothing that concerns you, *conpar*. It's just Guardian business."

"I see," she replied, moving past him to enter the

infirmary where Elena was standing over the unconscious male she'd brought back with her.

"Elena, may I?" Holley smiled and gestured for her to move aside, but her inner kitty really was not cool with that idea.

"I promise not to hurt him, I merely want to check his wounds."

"Uh, yeah sure," she mumbled in response, but her she-Cat was growling softly, and there was nothing she could do to mask the sound.

Fuck.

The feline was possessive already, and all her suspicions about the human male and what he was to her started filling her head. Still, she felt like an idiot.

Holley was fully mated, pregnant, and in no way a threat. She grabbed her inner kitty by the ruff and pushed the beast back down. The normal looked pale and his vitals were not great. Worry and anxiety filled her till she thought she would choke on it.

Elena had never been so afraid, and that was positively galling. She'd always been a loner, a badass, a tough as fuck female. But here she was, practically in tears over one puny human!

Dammit. That wasn't fair. He'd been brave and protective. He'd come after her to try and fight the Gila Shifters, though he did not know what he was up against. He wanted to save her, even though she more than likely got him into this mess. And that was the real problem. Elena felt guilty.

Jessenia filed in soon after, along with Byram, the only Vampire in their group and the one with the most knowledge when it came to healing injuries.

"Elena, he will be okay. Go now with Kingston and the others, I will let you know if we need you," Holley spoke directly to her, voicing all of Elena's unspoken concerns while ignoring her own grumbling mate.

If anyone could handle the Dragon, it was the otherworldly Witch. To think Holley had been imprisoned behind the walls of the Keep for hundreds of years before Kingston had rescued her, boggled the she-Cat's mind. Holley was one of them now. A Guardian's *conpar* or most sacred fated mate. Elena not only respected her, but she loved the Witch too.

She looked into Holley's eyes and Elena gave in. The Witch would keep him safe. Even her Panther acknowledged he was in better hands with the two Witches and the Vampire, though she hissed a warning to all three as she left the room reluctantly.

Kingston stalked behind his desk and waited until all were present. Furio, Storm, the Dragon himself, Elena, and finally, Egros stood in the Alpha's office.

Her face remained impassive while Kingston rattled off the standard questions.

"Furio and Storm were tracking the Loyalists when we got your text," Kingston said in his Alpha voice. "What I want to know, is what were you doing there? You were not out on a mission tonight."

"No, I was not. I was there on personal business," she replied, noting with unease the four pairs of male eyes on her.

"So, you didn't know the Gilas would be there?"

"No, sir."

"Well, why the hell didn't you wait for backup?"

"They were attacking, sir."

"A normal? You risked exposure for a normal."

"Sir, I could not let them take him. They were trying to kidnap him maybe to use him as leverage to get to—"

"To get to who?"

"Me!" She yelled, startling herself and those in the room. No one had ever raised their voice to Kingston Baldric. Except now.

"Why?" The Dragon asked in a deceptively level tone.

"He and I...*we*, that is," she stuttered. "It is personal, sir.:

"Elena, you ignored our most basic instruction to

keep normals out of this war. You engaged in a supernatural battle with the human present. Then you brought him here when an emergency room would have sufficed. Why, Elena?" Kingston asked, his stance unbending.

"No, sir, he was hit with Gila venom. He needs our help. And the truth is, I was there to meet—"

"Who could be so important you risked outing our secrets?" Kingston glared at her as he spoke, his anger palpable.

"I'll tell you what she was doing," Egros interrupted, the Witch's eyes flashing angrily at her.

She stepped back, shocked by the emotion she saw there. Elena tried to gather her thoughts, but Egros was already moving forward. The male Witch was vibrating with anger, and while her heat was not exactly a secret, she could not believe he was about to share her personal matters with all of them.

"Eg, no—"

"She was in heat. The potions Holley and I have been making to manage it, are not cutting it anymore. Elena went to work through her heat cycle with some human," he spat the word as if it disgusted him, and that hurt worse than any blow.

"Egros, you have no right," she said, fighting the rage that threatened to spill over and consume her.

Egros was a Guardian, like her. Her friend, or so she had thought. How could he do this? Humiliation warred with fury, but she kept a tight rein on both.

"*I* have no right? You had no right. A human, El? A weak human over—"

"Over you? Is that what you were going to say? You were never in the running, Eg! Never!" She shouted the words cruelly, wishing she could take them back as soon as they'd slipped from her mouth.

The tension in the richly furnished room was thick and irritating. The Keep seemed to sense it, and the lights brightened for a moment, causing them all to step back and blink.

"That's enough!" Kingston roared.

"Yes, it is enough. I did what I had to do, Kingston. Punish me or not, it is your call, Alpha." She spoke directly to the Dragon, ignoring the other males in the room.

He blinked and paced, shrugging in his discomfort. She knew what he needed to ask and waited.

"So, you went through, uh, your heat with the human?"

"Yes, sir," she stated and turned to the Witch who was standing, eyes widened in shock as if he realized what he did. Maybe he had. Either way, it was too late.

"I made the mistake of thinking Egros was my friend and confided in him about my cycle—"

"Elena, I am your friend, but you risked a lot for this *normal*—"

"No. You risked our friendship by spilling details of my personal life in this conference room that is reserved for Guardian business. You had no right to tell anyone anything concerning me and my choices," she replied with quiet dignity.

Her heart was pounding, her inner feline scratching at her skin. The Panther wanted out. She was angry at Egros, annoyed with Kingston, ambivalent about the other two, but more than anything, she wanted to be in the infirmary.

With him.

"Elena, I am sorry about this. It is grossly unfair that a female should have her personal life under a microscope—"

"It should not matter that I am female, Kingston. None of the males here are subject to scrutiny when they fall into bed with someone," she replied through gritted teeth.

"I agree that Egros overstepped, but what you do as a Guardian has consequences," Kingston began, but she cut him off.

"Yes, he did. I am no different than any of you," she said, meeting each male's gaze in the closed space.

Never before had she felt such anger at her fellow Guardians, but this was bullshit. Shifters were notorious for guarding their females, but sometimes it could be a little claustrophobic. Not to mention hypocritical.

"Furio, Storm, and even you, Kingston, are guilty of going even farther than I have with this man. What I did for him, any of you would have done for your females!"

"Elena," Storm said, attempting to intercede.

"I'm not finished yet," Elena snapped, growling at the Wolf.

"None of you have any right to my private life or my personal matters. Even if I hadn't slept with him, this male is the victim of a Gila Shifter attack—"

"That he wouldn't have been involved in if not for you," Kingston replied.

"No. You are wrong. What I was doing there doesn't change the facts, Kingston. They were after him, not me."

"What?"

Eight

The Diamond Dragon's mouth fell open as he began to connect the dots Elena had been so desperately trying to arrange for him. Egros was a jealous fool, and she could forgive him that. But not if the Witch put her human in danger because of his own stupidity.

"You heard me," Elena said with slightly better control of her emotions.

"I didn't put him in danger. I *found* him in danger. Furthermore, I acted as any of you would have done, in the *victim's* best interest," she said, her voice getting stonier by the second.

"You brought a human here," Egros seethed, but a growl from Storm had the Witch zipping his lips tightly.

Though Fergie had changed to Wolf after he'd bitten her, Storm was still a little touchy about the whole human Shifter prejudice thing that, unfortunately, was very real. The Guardians protected magic for all, but Elena supposed she'd never really thought about how some of them felt about humans. Clearly, it was something they needed to discuss.

"Look, Kingston," she said, choosing to speak to her Alpha and not the group at large. "The man needed help, I brought him here. Anything that happened between us previously is none of your business."

"Elena, your heat cycle is personal, I agree, but—"

"No buts, Kingston. A Shifter's heat is painful, hell, it is downright unbearable if not sated. That is simple biology. But it doesn't make me less of a Guardian."

"Of course not, I only meant there are protocols—"

"Bullshit. Males go into something very similar to rut and it has never been acknowledged as a negative. Besides, none of you need time off when that happens. You simply fuck at will."

The men in the room winced and looked anywhere but at Elena. She had a point, and they knew it. It was chauvinistic at best to celebrate a male Guardian's prowess when his hormones demand he sate his lust between the sheets, and to want to force a female to take a leave of absence for the same damn thing. Fuck that.

"You chose a human—" Egros spat, barely able to control himself.

"Easy, man," Furio said to the furious Witch.

"Elena, I am not judging you, and I don't think any of us should," Storm added, eyes narrowing at Egros.

"We just want you safe is all," Furio, the only Stallion Shifter among them, added.

"Thank you for that," she said, and shook her head. "But I am a warrior, *a Guardian of Chaos*, just like you. The fact is, I don't have to explain myself to any of you."

"The hell you don't—"

"Egros enough! Everyone, out. Now!" Kingston commanded. "Except you, Elena."

The three males left the room, leaving with their concern, anger, and sorrow. Thank goodness. Their emotions had been batting up against her through their Guardians' bonds, and she wasn't sure how much more she could take.

Aside from her father, who'd all but disowned her when she left his house, Elena never had much family.

It was oddly humbling to feel so much emotion from their group. But at the same time, she resented their interference.

"Elena, I hope you understand, we are all just worried about you."

"Worried? Why? Because I fucked someone, Kingston?"

"No! I mean, yes. I mean, shit," he shook his head and sighed heavily. "It's just—"

"When have any of the men in this group asked me who they can fuck, Kingston? You included. I am not a virgin. And I wasn't one when I met him."

Kingston watched her intently. He was a great leader, and occasionally knew when to be quiet, and when to interfere. Like now. He simply waited for her to speak, and she figured she owed him that much.

"Look, I went back to see him, and he was already under attack. That is the truth."

"I never doubted you, Elena. But why did you go back?" His voice calm and even, she saw no reason to deny his question.

"Because I needed to wait till after my heat was fully over to see if my Cat was right. To see if—" She paused, stumbling over the words, too emotional to give voice to what she was thinking.

Kingston gestured to his large leather couch, and

she took direction, sitting down heavily. He poured them each three fingers of some old hard to read label of Scotch. After a few minutes, she sipped and allowed the smokey strong liquor to slide down her throat.

Shifters needed a lot of alcohol to get drunk. Even then, their metabolism burned through it rather quickly. It was the same conundrum that made the potions she was using to stave off her heat cycle becoming less and less effective.

"So," Kingston began, jogging her from her thoughts. "Come on, El, tell me why you really went back to that bar."

"I went back to see if my Panther was right," she replied, unable to lie to her Alpha. "To see, if he really is mine."

Kingston's shocked eyes met hers, and she couldn't be sure if that was happiness or shock on his face. The look swept across his features so briefly. Someone knocked on the office door, followed by a woman's voice.

"He's awake," Holley called before opening the door.

Elena sped past the pregnant Witch carefully and raced to the infirmary. The antiseptic smell was not unpleasant, and even better, was finding the same hauntingly familiar hazel eyes peeking up at her.

"Hi." Elena breathed the word, watching him for signs of pain or recognition.

He blinked slowly, pushing himself up, but wincing with pain as his hand reached up to touch the bandages on his head where he'd been whipped by one Gila Shifter's spiked tail. Holley had removed the poison and patched up the cuts, but he was human, after all, and healing would need time.

"Do you need help sitting up? A pillow? Water?"

"Your name."

"What?"

"I just need to know your name," the handsome stranger said as he lay back on his pillow.

His hair was tousled carelessly across his forehead, and his voice was hoarse and scratchy. But Elena never saw a better looking male in her entire life.

His shirt had been removed, and Elena's eyes flashed to the tattoo she knew was there but could barely see at present. The ink covering his side was big enough to wrap around the small of is back and some of his chest and abdomen too.

Elena's mouth watered just thinking about it. Entirely inappropriate considering how banged up he was. Still, she allowed her gaze to roam over him. So handsome. Lean and tall, muscular, but not overly so.

His skin was fair, and his chest had a light smattering of dark hair.

"Elena," she said, licking her suddenly dry lips. "My name is Elena Soussa."

"Well, hello Elena," he said with a sexy smile on his face despite the bruises and his obvious exhaustion from whatever foul poison those fuckers had infected him with.

"Nice to finally know your name. I'm Logan. Logan Wells."

"Nice to meet you too," she said, grinning back. The man's smile was infectious.

"Wish you wouldn't go away, but I have to," he whispered, closing his eyes, and drifting back into oblivion.

Panic gripped her for a split second. Her heart constricted. How could she feel so strongly about a man she hardly knew? But she knew how. Even if she was not quite ready to say it aloud.

Elena turned her head to find Holley waiting there with Kingston. She gestured for the woman to speak up, unable to do so as worry and unease coursed through her.

"Oh. He's fine, El. He will require lots of sleep, of course, but he will completely recover. I am almost positive."

"Oh, thank the gods. And thank you," Elena said, exhaling and nodding.

"Did he say anything?" Kingston asked.

"His name is Logan Wells," she returned.

"Okay, good," Kingston replied. "At least we have a place to start."

NINE

Logan tossed and turned. He was having the most messed up dream. Dragons and lizard men with spiked tails were fighting each other in a back alley in Newark.

Harry, the pesky bar fly, had tried to kidnap him. His beautiful bubble gum flavored stranger, the one who'd sexed him up and left his townhouse before he'd woken up after their night together, was there too.

Except instead of being the goddess of all things smexy, she was a badass superhero who'd saved his life. Fuck, she was so hot. But he knew that already. Logan's only regret was not knowing her name.

Elena. Elena Soussa.

The words suddenly appeared in his head, and he

frowned. How did he know that? Once more he heard them, whispered in his brain by her voice. More memory than made up.

Shit. When did she tell him her name? Why was he remembering it if she didn't? That's not how memories worked. His brain felt foggy, and his body burned with aches and pains never before felt. Something was wrong. Logan blinked.

The sudden influx of light hurt, and he groaned softly, aware of footsteps rushing towards him. Okay, so he was alive. And he was somewhere. What he didn't know was where. Fuck.

His head ached like mad. His body too. It was like he had the flu, but so much worse. Someone grabbed his head a little roughly, peeling his eyelids back they shined a penlight in one than the other.

"Ouch, fuck. Easy," he grumbled, but the strange man just grunted, and wrote something down.

"Are you a doctor? What hospital is this?" Logan asked, sitting up with no small amount of difficulty.

Shit.

He'd never felt so bad in all his life. The stranger didn't bother answering him, and that was when Logan began to get nervous. He looked around the room. Clean and sterile, but the mix of ancient medical technology with cutting edge was mysterious to say the least.

His clothes had been removed, and from the funk in his mouth, he guessed he'd been unconscious more than a night. As a scientist, he was not prone to hysteria, and yet, something in him was screaming that this was not right.

Logan squinted against the bright light shining over his head, and almost immediately it dimmed. Like the room was reading his thoughts.

Wow. Maybe he should think of the woman again.

"Um, excuse me," he tried to get the stranger's attention, but the man in black ignored him.

"Hello? I said excuse me," Logan managed a small smile when the uninterested stranger turned to acknowledge him.

"Thanks, uh, can you tell me the name of the hospital? Call my doctor? Or just, you know, talk to me?"

"Are you in pain?"

"What? No. Well, yes."

"I see. Is it excruciating?'

"No. Obviously," he replied dryly. "I feel like I am recovering from a bad case of the flu."

"Aches?"

"Yes."

"Mm hmm. Your name is Logan Wells? I see you are a geneticist and biochemist? But you were fired from—"

"I was not fired.! I left, but I signed an NDA, a non-disclosure agreement, so I can't give you any information without violating that."

"I see—"

"Oh, hello. You're awake!" A redheaded woman with a wide grin and dancing eyes wandered into the room. "Elena will be so happy. Hey Eg, what's up?"

She asked the angry little man who'd been pretty much an ass up till then.

"You got him?" The man called Eg asked, and the redhead nodded.

The female walked in and sat down in a lounge chair, kicking her shoes off. Well, he thought they were shoes, but to Logan, they looked like torture devices. The woman sighed loudly. She dropped a purse on the floor next to her shoes and rolled her ankles as if she'd been walking miles and miles.

Who knew? Maybe she had. Still, Logan was more interested in getting some answers. The redhead was cute, pleasant even, but she had nothing on a certain tall blonde who'd been haunting his dreams nonstop since he'd met her.

Was the woman, *Elena*, involved in some sort of fight protecting him, or had he imagined all that? He wished he had the answers. Not knowing was beginning to grate on his nerves.

Logan had never been overly emotional, but he felt panic blooming inside him as he thought of the worst possible scenarios.

Eaten by Dragon? Dragged away by Lizard men and made some kind of slave? Harry kidnapping her? Eeek! He needed answers!

Shit.

Was she okay? He needed to know, dammit. His heart raced at the thought of Elena hurt or in trouble.

And how the fuck do I know her name?

Images of her standing over him, concern in her pink gaze flashed through his mind, and he calmed a bit. Suddenly, he knew. Elena was okay. She'd been to see him, had told him her name.

Elena. Her name meant shining light. One of those useless bits of info his scientific mind stored away for whatever reason.

Logan repeated it in his mind, thinking he'd never heard anything so fitting, so perfect to describe her. From the silver platinum hair on her head to her alabaster skin and those hypnotic pink eyes. She was bright, beautiful, dynamite in bed, and from what he'd seen of her fighting skills, she was deadly as well.

He'd never met anyone like her and judging from the way she'd occupied most of his thoughts since he'd spent the night with her, he never would. The truth came blasting into his brain like it had been launched there by a rocket.

Shit.

The evidence supported his theory, and for once in his life, he could find nothing to contradict his findings. Crazy? Maybe. Odds that she reciprocated his feelings? Not good. Whatever. It wouldn't change the facts.

Logan was in love.

Somehow, some way, he'd fallen in love with a bubble gum pink eyed hottie who fought like Bruce Lee and fucked like a goddess.

Gulp.

His body reacted predictably to just the thought of her, and he adjusted his sheet and dropped a pillow on his lap, lest his visitor get the wrong idea.

There was no doubt about it. He was meant to be with Elena. But where was she now?

"Oh yeah, that's better," the redhead said, interrupting his shocking musings. She sighed contentedly now that her feet were free of her spiked heels.

"Why do you wear those things if they hurt?"

"What? Those aren't *things*, those are Louboutins!"

"What's a *Loo boo tin*?"

"OMG! Just *shhh*, okay? We're gonna take it down a notch cause getting upset is not good for the baby," she said more to herself than him.

Logan raised his eyebrows but decided to back off. He didn't grow up with his sister in the same household, but Margo was one fierce female when it came to anything she was passionate about.

Apparently, the redhead liked shoes. And Logan was smart enough to recognize something feral in the pregnant female. Especially when it came to her *Loo Boo Tins*.

Yikes.

Logan was all about self-preservation. Clearly, the woman was not to be fucked with when it came to her shoes. So, hands raised in surrender, he changed the subject.

"Uh, okay. My bad. Look, can you tell me where I am?"

"Oh, no worries. You're with us," she smiled, and he was pretty sure her incisors were a tad longer than a moment ago.

Gulp.

"Uh, so, who is us? And where is Elena?" Logan tried again with a non-threatening smile on his face.

He was getting antsier by the minute. Instant connection to his unbelievably hot, mystery woman aside, Logan had no fucking idea where he was or if he was safe. Though, he sincerely doubted she'd leave him somewhere unsafe. He wasn't sure why he doubted it, he just did.

From the looks of things, this was no regular clinic or hospital. Not even an urgent care center. The walls were made of stone, unlike anything he'd ever seen. Like something out of a medieval fairy tale, he mused before turning his attention back to the woman currently snacking on a bag of chips.

Where the hell were they, he wondered. And where could he get some of those salt and vinegar chips? Logan's stomach rumbled, and her head snapped up.

"Hungry? What do you want to eat?"

"Thanks, I am feeling a little peckish. Anything you have is fine, I don't want to put you out."

"Nonsense, the Keep loves preparing meals almost as much as Jessenia, our resident kitchen Wi-, er, chef," she said quickly, wiping her hands on a napkin that also seemed to appear out of thin air.

"Okay, how about a turkey sandwich?"

Logan was uncertain what else to say. Turkey was

like universally safe, wasn't it? He watched her scamper out and wondered how long it would be till she returned. At least the redhead spoke to him, unlike the dude who was there earlier. That fucker seemed to hate him.

"Awesome. Be right back."

As the redhead left the room, barefoot and sighing happily, Logan got out of bed. His body ached in places he didn't even know he had, places he was sure had not been hit by his assailants. Harry, that fucker.

He had no idea what that man's problem was, but it wasn't good. He'd heard of corporate espionage and was always wary of folks inquiring into his research. But Harry had seemed harmless, and Logan told him nothing.

A wave of dizziness washed over Logan, and he held on to the bed, then the chair as he made his way over to a door that opened to reveal a bathroom. Just what he needed. Why hadn't he seen it there before?

After relieving himself he opted for a shower. Unsteady as he was, the railings proved useful as he turned the water on nice and hot and stood letting the spray hit him. Dirt and blood washed away as he soaped his body and shampooed his hair. Fuck, that felt good, but it was exhausting.

He exited the shower and took a fluffy towel from

the shelf behind the toilet, wrapping it around his waist. Then he approached the mirror and found a toothbrush and paste.

As far as his life went, this was the most interesting series of days he'd had in a very long time. Let's see. First, he'd been picked up in a bar by the most beautiful and sexiest woman he had ever seen. He'd had the best sex of his life.

So great in fact was the sex, that after he'd woken up and found her gone, Logan had felt such intense heartbreak, he couldn't even begin to comprehend why. Now he knew. He'd somehow lost his heart to the beautiful Elena that very night.

Thinking of her didn't conjure the woman, but when he was in danger, she'd shown up. How and why, he had yet to answer. All he had to do was wait patiently for her to return, then he could do the first thing Logan had been dying to do since he'd seen her.

Okay. It was more like the second thing he'd been dying to do since he'd seen her. The first thing involved more of her and him naked. On the floor, against the wall, anywhere. He didn't care. He just wanted her.

Mind out of the gutter. Answers first, fucking later.

His dick softened as reason warred with primal desire. Logan shook his head. He needed to talk to Elena.

After he brushed his teeth, Logan took a good, long look at himself. He appeared no worse for wear. The one bruise visible on his temple had already taken on that yellow-gray hue that meant they were healing, and rapidly too. That was odd. He was sure he'd been hit on the head more than once, not to mention punched and kicked.

Alright. So, his ass had been handed to him. Yes, that was humiliating, but what interested him more was the fact he did not look like a guy whose ass had been handed to him.

How could he feel like he'd been hit by every car of a freight train, and not have a black eye? A fat lip? Any sort of *new* bruise or blemish?

The hair on the back of Logan's neck stood up and he reached around and touched it with his hand. Tiny electrical impulses seemed to dance up and down his spine and sweat dotted his brow. Frowning at the sudden, though not entirely unpleasant, assault on his system, he turned to see he was no longer alone.

She was there. His Elena. Though why he suddenly thought of her as his was worrisome.

Mine.

The thought invaded his brain, and he wasn't altogether sure it was his. Pulse racing, he realized he was staring at her. She was doing some looking of her own, and that alone gratified him as he turned to face her fully.

Elena stood in the doorway with a tray of food in her hands. She was so beautiful it almost hurt him to look at her.

What had he called her? A superhero? Goddess? Mystery woman? She was all those, and more. So much more.

Flesh and blood. Vivacious and striking. Tall and graceful. Her pink, bubble gum eyes flashed at him from across the room, and he felt her gaze rake over his body like hot coals. Everywhere they touched, those eyes seemed to leave trails of sizzling desire in their wake.

Especially, when they landed specifically on that part of him that had stood at attention the very moment Logan had felt her enter the room. Her eyes widened, and only then did he realize his towel had come loose.

"Shit," he muttered, reaching down for the bath sheet when a wave of dizziness washed over him.

How humiliating to wind up on the floor at her feet! Oh well, at least it was fitting. A woman like that should be worshipped. He could see her now with flowers and candles at her altar, being idolized by the mob.

No. Worshipped by me. Only me.

His thoughts turned jealous for a split second, catching him off guard. Another new for him. But he supposed that was to be expected, love being quite the emotion for a man whose last girlfriend had called him a man-sized brain wearing human skin.

It was love though. He recognized it as the truth soon as he saw her. Logan blinked rapidly, using both hands, palms flat on the tile floor, to stop his head from crashing into it.

Stupid towel. And now for the ultimate in humiliation, he thought and braced himself for impact. But before he hit ground, she was there, lifting him up with one arm around his waist, and the other gripping his right hand.

"Are you alright?" She asked, her husky voice sending shivers down his spine.

"I am now," Logan said, breathing in to inhale her subtle champagne rose scent.

It was too late to stop the lame words from passing his lips. Shit. He sounded like some lovesick asshole. But still, his body was weak from whatever had happened. So, he took her help gratefully.

Logan wasn't exactly driven by testosterone. He had no problem with strong women, and she was fierce, his Elena. He wanted to just stay there with her in comfortable silence, to bask in the warmth of her heated blush colored gaze, but he needed answers.

"Here, let's get you back in bed," she murmured, her cheeks burning pink, much like the warm glow of her stare.

Disregarding the towel, Elena helped him back to the bed, tossing the sheet over his waist, and trying to act nonchalant about it. But Logan knew better. He'd seen that telltale blush cross her perfect face, and he had to bite the inside of his mouth to stop from grinning.

At least I didn't imagine her attraction to me.

Point one for Logan.

"Uh, I brought you food," Elena said, pushing the cart holding a tray laden with more food than he could ever eat closer to him.

He took the bottle of water first and drank half of it before he spoke again. Fuck, that felt good against his dry throat. His stomach growled, and he realized he was, in fact hungry.

Elena had turned to leave, but he was so not having that. No way. He never wanted her to move out of his sight.

Baby steps, he reminded himself.

"Wait," he said, gasping for air after such a long pull from the bottle. "Please, I need answers."

"Okay," she turned, and nodded. "Ask me anything."

His head swam with things he wanted to know. Like where did she get those crazy beautiful bubble gum eyes? Why did she leave him the other night? And could he kiss her again and maybe never stop?

But Logan was a scientist. There were other things he needed to know first. He just couldn't think of them right now. And that was another first. How could one woman render his brain so utterly void of coherent thought?

"Well, I'm sure you want to know who those men were who attacked you?" Elena began.

Her eyebrows raised, and he realized they were not platinum like her hair, but black, and from what he could see, totally natural. As was the rest of her. She wore no makeup, needed no embellishments.

Her eyes were unbelievably pretty, and a color he'd never seen in nature. Not the red of albinism, or the blue violet of Liz Taylor, but pink. True, bubble gum pink.

His cock went hard again, and he was thankful for the sheet he had draped over himself once again. Logan swallowed another sip of cool water. He felt warm all over. Needy, antsy, and restless too. But he pushed back those base feelings and lasered a stare at her.

"Actually," he began, his voice deep and low. "I wanted to know why you left the other night after what was probably the best sex I'd ever had in my entire life."

TEN

Elena's face burned with embarrassment. Not only was she fighting her desire to jump him. And boy, did she really want to. Her lips tingled with the need to kiss him. Her mouth salivated as she imagined licking every beautiful, exposed inch of him. The last thing she needed to do was give every listening ear a special show.

Grrr.

When she did kiss him. If he wanted to, that was. It would not be with an audience. She stopped her growling. So, what if he'd just pretty much announced they'd fucked to a house full of supernaturals. Three of whom were just outside the door. It wasn't like they didn't already know.

Shit. Shit. SHIT.

"Uh, well, that is, uh," Elena tried, but found she couldn't really answer him.

What could she say that would even make sense to him? Let alone make up for what she'd done.

Sorry, I was embarrassed after I went into my heat, saw you, and couldn't keep my hands off you?

Wait. Did he say the *best sex* of his life? Warmth filled her and Elena could not stop the grin from spreading across her face. Even better was the return smile he gifted her with. A thousand watts of unadulterated male hotness, and it was all aimed at her. Just for her. The knowledge made her inner kitty purr.

Prrr.

Kingston walked in before she could say anything else. Good. At least the big fucker wasn't just lurking in the hallway anymore. Holley was with him, and so was Fergie, who inched her way over to where she'd dropped her shoes and bag. The she-Wolf hated going barefoot

"Excuse me, folks, gotta run," she said, then winked at Elena, who really wanted to just disappear at that moment.

"Hello. You're Logan?" Kingston addressed the normal, his voice booming with power. "Are you well enough to talk?"

"I think so yes, I was just dizzy before—"

"Dizzy? Hang on a moment," Holley said, moving towards the table where she'd left tiny bottles of potions.

"Here," she said, handing him a vial. "Drink this, it will help you fight off the poison."

"What poison? And what is this?" Logan said, eyebrows furrowed.

His handsome face paled, and Elena rushed to his side before he could tip off the bed. Something was wrong. He was not responding to the antidotes as well as they'd expected.

"You must drink that vial, Logan," Holley repeated.

He looked up, hazel eyes boring into Elena's, and she saw the question there. She nodded her head, encouragingly. Hardly expecting him to trust her, but needing him well, Elena implored him to drink it.

"We are here to help you, Logan. I swear it. And I promise, I will answer every question you have, but please, drink the vial first."

He looked at her with a serious mien, hazel eyes capturing her expression, and validating her veracity. It was like she could see the wheels in his head turning as he weighed his options and her sincerity.

"I want you to know," he said, speaking to her. "This is difficult for me. Taking a drug without knowing what it is, but if you trust her," he nodded to Elena, and a wave of humility washed over her, as she nodded.

"I do, Logan. I trust Holley."

"Then, I will drink it."

That he put his faith in her, trusted her with this decision, was momentous. He was a full human. Logan Wells knew nothing of their world, and yet, something inside told him he could rely on her.

Joy filled her. Pure happiness that made her glow with warmth as he took her hand in his, long fingers, easily capturing hers, and tossed the vial back. Elena's Panther purred, the feline proud that her mate was allowing her to take care of him.

We can't know for certain that he is our mate. Not yet, she told the beast.

Her kitty hissed at the thought, but went back to purring when she looked at Logan's handsome face. He really was good looking. Chiseled features, even a small cleft in his chin. He had plump lips that she knew to be talented. Long and lean, with just the right amount of muscle, she still remembered the feel of his strong body against hers.

"Alright?" she asked, waiting as he sat eyes closed while the potion took effect.

"Better?" Holley asked, grinning widely when his eyebrows raised, and he nodded his assent.

"Yes. I'd love to study that sometime," he said.

"Study it? Do musicians do that?" Elena asked.

"Oh, uh," he blushed and rubbed the back of his neck in that adorable manner that had her practically panting.

"I'm only a musician on Thursdays," he replied.

"Come again?" she asked.

"Actually, I'm a scientist. A geneticist and biochemist. My work is to try and uncover the origins of certain disease, birth defects and the like, and then in turn to develop ways to prevent or treat them using what I can learn from specific genes. I try to answer why certain people react specifically to certain stimuli like chemical and environmental reactions."

"I see," Elena murmured.

"Who do you work for now?" Kingston asked.

"Myself, mostly. I used to work for a pharmaceutical company but found out too late they were not as interested in helping people as they were in selling medicine to them at exorbitant prices. I left and was forced to sign an NDA."

"And you've continued this work on your own?" she asked, curiosity piqued.

Elena had no idea the man she'd been so undeniably attracted to had a big brain along with his killer bod. Maybe that had something to do with the Loyalists wanting him? She'd have to run the idea past Kingston, though one look at the Dragon told her he'd reached the same conclusion.

"Not that work, per se, but I have been trying to identify what makes some people resilient to certain diseases and injuries. For example, I recently stumbled upon a blood sample of a man who'd been in an explosion in a warehouse that should have left him dead. The man was found barely alive days later and survived his injuries far longer than any normal human being should have," Logan explained, shaking his head.

"He succumbed eventually, but not before contacts of mine got me some samples. But they must have been tainted."

"Tainted?" Kingston asked, his Dragon peeking out through his eyes.

Elena moved closer to Logan. Kingston was her Alpha, and she trusted him. But she felt an overwhelming sense of possessiveness about the human male, and her protective instincts were going berserk. Whether she was ready to admit it or not, the man obviously meant a lot to her.

"So, the men who attacked you were there because of something having to do with your work?

With this tainted sample?" Holley asked, obviously trying to lighten the tension between the Dragon and Elena.

"I don't see how, but maybe," Logan shrugged.

Elena was learning so many new things about the man she'd let fuck her stupid, she froze in place. Like she'd turned to stone as a million and one doubts came at her from all angles.

He was smart. Really smart. What would he see in her? She passed school, barely. Her dad had spent all his time training her to fight. Elena liked martial arts, and hard rock, and horror films. What did she have that could possibly interest him?

"Hey, are you okay?"

His hazel gaze found hers, and he seemed to trace every inch of her face like those strong, long fingered hands had done not too long ago. Her body came alive under that stare. Warming and swelling in places she'd never felt before.

"Do you need water or something?"

She shook her head. Elena was positively speechless. He had that effect on her. He was all beautiful male, and smart as hell, too. She didn't stand a chance.

It was part of the reason she always paired up with Byram or even Egros. They were both incredibly smart, and where she found conversations with them stimulating, she partnered with them for her superior ability to kick ass.

Storm, Furio, and Kingston, were all fairly intelligent. But Shifters tended to run on instinct and physical dominance. She did not partner with them as often for the simple reason that they stunted her in battle.

As a female Shifter, they could not help but want to protect and shelter her. But she wasn't some weak woman they needed to baby. She was fierce. A motherfucking warrior in her own right.

Elena had taken to pairing with either the Vampire or the Witch when on assignment. Neither tried to shelter her or sacrifice themselves for her. They allowed her to excel at what she did. And she was a good Guardian. She knew that without being told.

Of course, with her recent heat cycle, everything had changed. She thought sadly of Egros. She'd hurt the male Witch by turning down his offer to see her through her heat, but what could she say? She was simply not interested in him in that way. But that was a problem for another day.

Elena turned back to Logan. He was watching, waiting patiently for her attention. When she nodded, he seemed to expel the breath he was holding. Then he turned to answer Holley.

"The man who seemed to lead the attack was a guy

named Harry. He's a frequent customer at *Midnight's*, or at least from what I saw of him on Thursdays for the past five months or so since I've been playing there."

"I see," Kingston said, encouraging him to go on.

"He was insistent that I speak to him about my current research, but it makes no sense. The sample from that warehouse victim was tainted."

"Why do you think it was tainted?" Holley inquired.

"Because what I saw in that man's blood is humanly impossible," Logan replied.

"Where was the warehouse?' Elena asked, a terrible dread filling her stomach.

Kingston stared at her as Logan repeated the address, and Elena felt the walls closing in. Fuck. That warehouse was where the Guardians had battled a group of Gila Shifter Loyalists a few weeks back. There'd been no actual explosion, merely a good dousing of *Dragonfire*.

Typically, that would incinerate all evidence of supernatural battles, including corpses. Somehow, they must have missed one of the Loyalists. He probably hid somewhere in the bowels of the warehouse while Kingston unleashed his fire.

Dammit.

Elena had been there. But not alone. That was the thing about the Guardians. They worked together, and not one of them ever took the blame for a mission failed.

It was team work all around. But this was an epic fuck up. Their failure led to a human finding genetic proof of the supernatural. And that was unacceptable.

"I can tell by your faces, that I've uncovered something big, something secret," Logan began, and Kingston bared his teeth at him.

"Stop Kingston," Elena growled and moved to turn to face her Alpha, but Logan refused to release her hand.

"Before you try to threaten or lie to me, I have a question. Which one of you is the Dragon?"

At that insolent remark, Kingston roared, and Elena leaned over. Closer still to the man, who was increasingly important to her. She wasn't sure what she would do if Kingston attacked.

Well, that wasn't true. She was surprisingly very certain of what she would do in that instance. Elena was simply having difficulty accepting it.

Mine.

"What do you know of Dragons?" Kingston demanded.

"You will back away from him," Elena snarled.

After that, all hell broke loose. Before Kingston could attack, Elena leapt onto the foot of the bed, putting herself between the Dragon and the scientist.

Body trembling in rage at the threat to her mate, Elena could hardly think, let alone contain her beast. She shifted from human to Panther in the blink of an eye, stunning all there. Especially Logan.

"Holy fucking shit," he whispered, and she felt more than saw his wide eyed stare on her black furry back while she faced off her Alpha. The Diamond Dragon was not pleased. Smoke puffed from his nostrils, but Elena's Panther hissed and snarled, spitting angry at the male for baring his fangs at her mate.

Thank the gods for Holley. She was faster, and smarter than them all, she wove a spell that slammed into Logan, sending him to sleep while she pushed her mate out into the hallway.

After a furiously whispered conversation, Kingston beckoned Elena.

"Shift, dress, then my office. Now. I'll call the others," Kingston snarled angrily.

"It is okay, El. I will watch over him. He will sleep for some time now."

Holley turned spreading her arms wide and gestured for her to follow Kingston. Well, fuck. This was one shitshow she really didn't want to be a part of but what choice did she have?

"Traitor."

"I don't believe it."

"She told her lover all about us!"

"How could you think that?"

"It doesn't matter now."

On and on, the arguing went until Elena was wiped out emotionally. Byram was absent, out on assignment. Egros thought she'd betrayed them. Furio and Storm were staunchly in her corner, prepared to defend her against any and all.

While Elena appreciated the gesture, she did not need them to defend her. She'd done nothing wrong. At least, not anything that could have jeopardized them.

"I can't believe I have to say this, but I have not betrayed our secret," Elena stated to the group once the yelling stopped.

"El," Storm, her staunchest supporter so far, started, but she cut him off.

Anger and disbelief warred with the desire to simply walk out on them and go to her mate's side. But she knew she would never feel anything even close to peace if she did that now. Too many things left unsaid were bad for the soul.

"I took my vows as a Guardian of Chaos before some of you here. I have given my life to our cause, to keep magic free for all beings. You are the closest I have to family since my mother died, and my father all but disowned me—"

"And yet, you let your heat cycle control your behavior! You put us all in violation of the Assembly's strict guidelines just because you wanted to fuck a human. You put us in danger to satisfy your urges. How could you, Elena?"

Egros' growled words were like a slap to the face. She stepped back, shocked. Storm growled and yelled at the Witch, causing Furio to step between them. Then she did something she'd never thought herself capable of. She tossed her head back and roared with all the power of her beast, silencing all the voices in the room.

"You bastard," she stated quietly, more pissed off than ever before.

"How dare you be so dismissive of something you know nothing about? You are a Witch, not a Shifter. You have no idea what a heat cycle is or does to a woman."

"El, I don't think he meant—"

"I know what he meant, Storm. He's angry I turned him down when he offered to spend my heat with me. And now, he wants to try to shame me for it."

The hush that fell over them was thick and ominous. But she was done being a punching bag for the Witch. Sometimes feelings got hurt in the course of one's life. It was a bitch, but it happened, and she was finished with being blamed for not wanting him back.

"Alright, that's enough now," Kingston said.

"Is it? I am sick and tired of you males telling me what to do or weighing in on something you cannot possibly understand. Only Furio and Storm know better! Wolves and Mares in heat are nothing to joke about. Right, boys? Dragons either, I assume."

"El—"

"No, Egros is right about one thing. My heat cycle is not something I can always control, and that sucks, but who I chose to satisfy that biological urge with is no one's business but mine! I am every bit the warrior I always was, and I am loyal to the Guardians."

"Point taken. But you must admit this is more than that, Elena. You came between me and the human," Kingston asked with something close to pride on his face.

"I did that because," she said, flushing, but it was more than past time she confessed the truth. Elena turned towards her Alpha and cleared her throat.

"My Panther is pretty sure Logan is mine."

Her inner kitty purred in delight that she had voiced the words, and Elena stood tall, ignoring the hooting gasps from some in the room. Whatever happened, she needed Kingston to know where she stood. Everything inside her was pointing her firmly in the direction of the sole human inside the Keep.

Logan Wells. My fated mate.

Mine.

Prrrr.

ELEVEN

*F**uck.*

Logan blinked, head pounding as he slowly came awake. What the fuck had happened this time?

Memories flooded his somewhat addled brain, and then he knew. Perhaps he should've been a bit more tactful about the whole witnessing a Dragon thing?

"Ya think?" Someone said.

He sat up too quickly, holding his head and scanning the room until his eyes landed on two men. One had electric blue eyes, the other long hair, and a mulish expression. They were somewhat familiar, but he couldn't place either.

"Yo cump. So, you and El? Treat her right, you feel me," blue eyes said.

"Uh," eyebrows raised, Logan did not respond.

"Easy dude, we're just, you know, like her big *bruthas.*"

"I see," Logan said, clearing his throat.

"She ain't like other girls. None of us are, but you know that, right?"

"You guys turn into, uh, Panthers too?" He squeaked.

"No offense, but I ain't no pussy, bro," blue eyes snarled, and something about him screamed canine. Maybe he could turn into a German Shepherd or something?

"Okay, sorry. I, um, that is, *where* is Elena?" Logan inquired, feeling antsy under the hardened stare of both men.

There was something positively feral in their gazes, even though they were not being overly threatening. Not a pussy, huh? Logan wondered then what he could be. A Wolf or a Bear. If people could turn into Dragons and Panthers, why not other creatures as well.

The possibilities sent his mind racing. Holy shit. Questions burned his brain. About them, this place. The way the room seemed to change at whim, his or whoever entered.

Where is she?

He felt needy, restless. One night with Elena, and

he was hooked. Every time he thought of her his dick got hard, and his mouth went dry. Dammit. She showed no sign of wanting him again.

Despite his feelings, and as for those, what was he wearing a sign or something? These two fuckers could tell exactly what he'd been thinking if their smirks were anything to go by.

"Why you wanna know, cump? Miss her already?"

Yeah. He definitely had a sign on his forehead. A bright fucking pink neon one that he was pretty sure said something like *'Caution: Idiot prone to falling in love with one night stands way out of his league'* or something like it.

Either way, he had enough of these two guys. And he had no intention of divulging anything to either of them.

"Look, just tell me where she is—"

"Why should we?"

"Because I need to talk to her."

The long haired placed a big hand on blue eyes, and the latter stopped glaring. That was something at least. Logan was not intimidated, not really. And that surprised the fuck out of him.

"She'll be along soon. You know, we hear you're a scientist?"

"Yes, I am."

"You know anything about botany?"

"Um, a little, why?"

"My ma-, *er*, wife is having a hard time with her indoor herbal garden. Something is wonky with her plants. Every time she introduces anything new to the soil, fertilizer, soft water, anything really, it seems to wipe out the thyme, but not the others," the man said and pulled his long hair back from his face, arranging it in a low ponytail that the other guy pulled.

Shit. Did he just whinny? What the fuck was going on here? Logan nodded to get the man's attention.

"Thyme? Uh, sounds like she needs to introduce some diversity in the genetic makeup of the plant. Maybe by introducing different varieties in the same patch, she could crossbreed and create a sturdier plant?"

"Diversity, huh? Okay, Doc. I'll tell her."

"Doc?"

"You're a doctor, right?"

"I have doctorates," he shrugged.

"Cool. I'm Furio, this here is Storm. We'll be seeing you, Doc."

The two men nodded and walked out, and for a moment he wondered if he was going to be alone long enough to get dressed to try to find Elena. But just like that, she returned.

Logan's gaze roamed over her from head to toe. She looked different here. In worn jeans and a tank top that did nothing to hide her subtle curves and elegant physique to his hungry eyes.

Fuck, he really loved looking at her. She was like a sculpture or painting made by masters. Even better because Elena was flesh and blood. So warm and lively, beautiful in an understated way that belied her power and lethality.

"Feeling better?" She asked, and her small tongue darted out to wet her lips.

"You mean after your friend knocked me out?" He softened the remark with a smile the second he saw her face fall.

Logan was such a prick sometimes. And he really didn't want to be. Not with her. She deserved better than that and he wanted to be better to her. *For her.* She didn't need his attitude.

"I'm sorry," he began.

"Why are you sorry?"

"For being nasty. I didn't mean it."

"Are you kidding? Let's see, I basically attacked you the other night in the club. Ran out on you the next day without a word. Show up a week later without warning. Almost get you killed. Then I kidnapped you. Turned into a Panther in front of you—"

"Actually, I am pretty sure you saved my life," he interrupted.

Nerves on edge, he felt tongue tied and his stomach was in knots. Logan was breathing like a marathon runner as he watched her. He felt things he hadn't since he was a kid talking to his first hot girl.

"I'm glad you came back. To the club, I mean. I have questions of course."

"Logan, there's only so much I can tell you," she replied, biting her lip in a gesture he found both endearing and maddening.

She was so strong and fierce, but when her bubble gum eyes glanced his way, he saw untold vulnerability and that made his heart ache for her. Without thinking, he held out his hand, thrilled when she took it, allowing him to pull her close.

Elena sat on the bed, facing him, her hip brushing his. Even through the sheet, the contact sent tendrils of awareness coursing through his blood. Logan had never had such an intense physical reaction to a woman. Even if she was so more than that, so much more than what she seemed.

"Logan," she whispered his name, raising a hand to caress his cheek.

He closed his eyes, reveling at the contact, and pressed his face firmly into her palm. Fuck, that felt good. He wanted more, need more of her. Without any thought beyond that, he reached for her.

Logan pressed his mouth to hers. At first, he touched his lips to hers softly, tenderly, then with a deep, fervent desire he simply could not deny. Logan wanted her more than he wanted air to breathe.

Every inch of him was acutely attuned to Elena. To the way she moaned into his mouth, the increased frequency of her breathing, and the unsteady pounding of her heart against his. He squeezed her tightly to his chest, loving the way she molded to him.

Usually, Logan was too tall, too big for his women, but she was a perfect match. Her tall, svelte body melted into him, and he tightened his hold, dipping her head back until it rested on his arm while he plundered her mouth greedily.

She tasted like bubble gum, champagne, and roses. Like toasted marshmallows, cayenne pepper, and desire.

"Elena," he moaned her name, disbelieving she was there, real and in his arms.

Logan's cock was so damn hard he thought he was going to burst. Need and desire warred with each other as their kiss went on and on and on. And still, it wasn't enough.

He could go on kissing her forever. Despite the

growing ache in his balls and the throbbing of his dick. Just holding her and kissing her for as long as he could. That alone was the culmination of every fantasy he'd ever had.

No one ever made him feel this way. Logan had thought himself in love a time or two, but no woman had ever owned him so completely. And Elena owned him, alright. Could make him her slave if she wanted to.

The real question was, did she want too? Did she want him?

"I do want you," she whispered, slowing their kiss, and leaving them both panting and shivering with unsatisfied need.

"But we need to talk."

"I'm listening, but stay here, okay? Don't move," he begged, dropping another soft kiss to her sweet, swollen lips.

"Okay," she murmured.

And that was how she came to tell him about all the magnificent, wonderful, impossible things she and her group of Guardians were while draped across his lap in bed in a place he learned was called the Keep, a magical fortress whose only mission was to protect and serve the Guardians who dwelled within.

It was a lot for Logan to take in. Almost too much.

But then he started adding things together. What other explanation could there be?

"So, you are a Guardian of Chaos? Why chaos?"

"We protect magic in its most pure form," she explained. "From chaos comes creation, and magic is unfortunately, finite in this realm. It is needed by all supernaturals, and even normals though they don't realize it. Our biggest enemy is a group called the Loyalists. Their endgame is to control all magic, to siphon it out as they see fit. We are sworn to stop them."

"I see. I mean, I'm trying to see. It is all quite fascinating," he said, trying to wrap his mind around it.

"You think that Harry and his men are part of them, the Loyalists?"

"We know they are," she replied.

"And they wanted me because why exactly?"

"We think you learned something you weren't supposed to when you got that sample from the warehouse victim, though I would not call him that," she hedged.

"What do you mean?"

"I think you found a Loyalist, most likely a Gila Shifter, who'd been hiding from us in the warehouse. Somehow, he went undetected and when Kingston used his *Dragonfire* to cleanse the place, he survived."

"So, you guys burnt a man to death?"

"Not a man, and not on purpose," she started defensively.

"Easy, sweetheart, I didn't mean to sound judgmental. If the bastard was fighting against you, he deserved what he got," Logan stated, and unsurprisingly, he meant every word of it.

"Vicious thing," she grinned, and kissed his mouth hungrily.

Passion exploded as he wrapped her up in his arms. He had the feeling she was holding back with him, careful to not break him, but Logan somehow knew that there was nothing she would do to hurt him

And there it was again. That word whispered into his brain.

Mine.

He wanted to say it aloud. To yell it from the rooftops. Hell, Logan wanted to tell her she belonged to him and he to her. Like some barbaric caveman, for fuck's sake. And just the thought of tossing her sweet ass over his shoulder and bringing her back to his den so he could stamp himself all over her fine body sounded really fucking good.

His thoughts shocked him, but that didn't stop his dick from throbbing with need. He fought himself, hoping his rational mind would resume control of his body and brain.

Easy. She's a person not a blow up doll. Sex was great, but it needed to wait. Logan was not going to allow his base needs to disrupt or fuck with what could very well be the love of his life. For now, he would have to be content with discussion.

"So, magic is real," he said, waiting for her nod to continue.

"And you protect it."

"Yes."

"And it exists in a finite quantity, recycling itself to those who use it? Supernaturals?"

"Yes and no. The human world uses magic too, it's just not as aware of it as we are."

"I see, too many scientists among us." He grinned sheepishly.

"Oh no, there is nothing wrong with science. I find chemical reactions fascinating," she replied, and fuck him, his cock went hard again.

"You do?"

"Uh huh. Science, magic, it all blends once you know what to look for. You know, Logan, I am really interested in that mind of yours."

"You are?"

"Yes. Does that surprise you?" She whispered, and

he saw through to the vulnerability he knew she kept hidden from the rest of the world.

"That you'd be interested in science? No. That you'd be interested in me. A little, yes."

"That's the thing about Shifters," she explained. "We know when we like someone."

"And you like me?"

"I like you."

Logan's heart soared at the words. She liked him. The beautiful, magical, powerful, and sexy as hell creature liked him. Like *liked* him.

As if that wasn't thrilling enough, it was like the pieces of his life and career as a scientist were all falling into place. Every suspicion he'd ever had, as both man and back when he was a child, seemed true.

He'd always thought there was more out there than the humans controlling the world seemed ready to share with the rest of society. More to it than global warming and the effects of nuclear warfare.

"Those things are very real though," Elena pointed out, and he smiled and kissed her again.

"Yes, but so are Dragons and Witches. And, hey, what are you exactly?"

But before she could reply, Furio and Storm interrupted with a knock.

"Yo, El, we gotta run. The sensors we left at Doc's are going haywire. Someone tripped them."

"Shit," she muttered, and leapt off his lap.

"Wait. Doc is me, right?"

Her cheeks burned pink, but she nodded and slipped her shoes back on her feet. He wasn't sure when she'd kicked those off. But it occurred to him she was going to walk into danger in his house. For him.

Hell fucking no. She wasn't leaving him behind. No way, no how.

"I'm coming too."

Logan stood up, clutching the sheet.

"No," she said, shaking her pretty little head.

"Yes, I am. There are things I need from the lab in my house you won't be able to get to without me. Biometrics," he said wiggling his fingers, and wagging his eyebrows.

"Fuck. Look, it might be dangerous."

"Then I guess you'll just have to protect me, *kitten*."

The nick name just sorta came out, and Logan waited to see if she objected. She didn't say anything, so he stood and looked for clothes. Her silence disturbing, he turned and saw Elena's mouth wide open.

A wicked grin crossed his face and Logan had to admit, he was mighty pleased by her reaction to his nudity. Looked like his kitten liked what she saw if the deep purring sound she made in the back of her throat was any indication.

He took the folded pair of jeans and sweatshirt that someone had left and shrugged into them, taking his time. He liked knowing her bubble gum gaze was riveted to the lines of his body. Was proud of his thick, hard cock, liked her knowing she did that to him. Logan opted for no socks as he stepped into his worn sneakers, finally turning to face her.

"So, what are you exactly? *Panthera pardus or panthera onca?*" Logan asked as the four of them huddled into a souped up Jeep Wrangler that Storm was driving.

"Neither. I am not some cat you find in the zoo," she snorted derisively, and he laughed.

She looked exactly like his grandfather's haughty old house cat when she wore that expression. Head raised, eyes forward, so regal and confident in her beauty.

"Well?"

"*I* am a Black Panther. I have no true wild cousins. My line is strictly supernatural, but we are the inspiration for the *Panther Incensed*. You're probably familiar-"

"My tattoo," Logan grinned. "My grandfather is

descended from England. He showed me our family crest once and the *Panther Incensed* was right there in black and gold."

"Is that why?"

"Yeah, sort of. The panther is part of Wells family history. I always felt drawn to it," he murmured, eyes roaming over her fair skin and brilliant eyes.

In the din of the vehicle, Elena was all silver moonlight and pink bubble gum eyes, scenting of roses and champagne. Like a beautiful dream he could not have imagined, even if he had tried with all his might.

An ethereal vision he would never forget. Like her image was forever burned in his brain, stamped there, tattooed just like the *Panther Incensed* on his side.

"We playing twenty questions here? Pay attention, Doc. This could get dangerous," Furio warned as they pulled up to his townhouse faster than he could have imagined.

"Magic?" he asked, and Elena winked and nodded.

Damn. She was so fucking gorgeous. His cock twitched, despite it being anything but the right time for such a reaction. He couldn't help it, and even if he could, he wouldn't. Elena made him feel things he'd never felt before.

He felt virile, alive, and all fucking man. Especially when she looked at him with those crazy gorgeous eyes of hers. Right now they were glowing, and he grabbed her hand, squeezing tight before Storm parked the car, and they all jumped out.

"Stay where they can see you, I am going around back to make sure it's clear," she instructed, all business as she cased the street.

He nodded, having no intention of putting himself or her in harm's way. Logan was a scientist, that meant he was not only practical, he was also logical and methodical. He was certainly man enough to accept the fact that she was the warrior here, not him.

"No playin' hero, Doc," Furio seconded after Elena's pert ass disappeared around the corner.

Holy hell.

She was so fucking hot when she was being all superhero stealthy. Again with his dick getting hard at inappropriate times, he shrugged and pinched himself nonchalantly. Fuck, he couldn't help it though.

She was like a comic book sex kitten superhero beauty queen. His dream woman in real life with her skinny jeans outlining long, powerful legs and firm backside.

Her breasts were high and snug in the tight tank she wore, giving the most alluring hint of cleavage. A nerd's wet dream, for sure. She was Logan's every secret fantasy come to life.

"No worries," Logan replied when he caught Furio still watching him. "You three are the Guardians. I'm just a regular guy. I don't need to grab a ruler or anything."

"What?" Furio asked, cocking his head to the side.

"He means he doesn't need no dick measuring contest to see which of us is the man," Storm translated.

"Damn fucking straight, Doc," Furio nodded.

"Afraid you'd lose, horse face?" snorted Storm.

"Fuck you, Pound Puppy."

Their insults were not entirely lost on him, Logan just shook his head and jogged behind Storm as they headed for his front door. The wind whipped through the borrowed sweatshirt he wore, and he was freezing.

Logan didn't know how the three of them did it with tanks and tees, but he was grateful they'd be heading back inside. February was a cold bitch.

Storm leaned forward, sniffing the front door loudly before nodding his head and waving them forward. Logan wondered where his kitten had gone off to. Before he could worry, relief filled him as her scent reached his nostrils.

"Whoever was here, they're long gone," Elena told

the three men from her position stretched out on top of the large hutch in the dining room, reminding Logan of his grandfather's old Russian blue.

That cat was a real beauty, with tons of arrogance bred into him through his prestigious lineage. But Duke the Cat had nothing on her. His own living breathing *Panther Incensed*.

Grandfather would be so proud, he mused. He wondered briefly what Margo would say.

"Took you guys long enough." Elena winked before jumping down, landing on her feet gracefully.

Just like a kitty, he thought. Furio and Storm checked the other rooms to be sure, and Elena stalked across towards him. She leaned close as she passed, rubbing her cheek against his, and touching his chest and back.

"Where does this door go?" she asked, pointing to the entry to the basement where he'd set up his lab.

That door had obviously been busted, with what looked like claw marks and other signs of damage. Fuck. It looked like a rabid dinosaur had attacked his home. Logan followed Elena down the stairs, into the normal looking basement, to the second door.

"Shit got ugly here," Storm said, taking in the damage that had been inflicted on logan's security door.

Unlucky for whoever was trying to bust in, but good for Logan, the culprits had failed in their attempt. His biometric security system had been activated by the intruders. Judging from the angry scratches against the door and the broken mechanical arm hanging from just above the portal, the pepper spray he'd set up to keep out unlawful snoops had been deployed.

"You used mace?" Elena grinned, pointing to the empty can that was still held by the robotic arm.

"Pepper spray. It was designed to be activated in the event of a break in," he shrugged then proceeded to scan his fingerprints, type in his secret code, and lastly, the optical scan.

"Wow, this is really something," Elena looked around his laboratory, and he felt his chest swell with pride.

"Thanks," he shrugged. "Here. These are the reports I have on the sample I took."

"Okay, let's take that and anything else you think you might need to replicate whatever it was you were doing that the Loyalists might want. Do you mind doing that? I mean, we could stay here—"

"No, I think it's better we go. This place has obviously been breached."

"I am so sorry, Logan—"

"It's just stuff, sweetheart. It can be replaced. Come help me," he said, turning to gather equipment.

Elena seemed pleased he'd asked her and worked side by side with him, following his instruction to the letter. Furio and Storm kept guard, occasionally coming down to carry out a crate or two. After an hour, they'd assembled most of his files and equipment for transport to the Keep.

"I'd like to stop by *Midnight's* to get my bass," Logan said after they'd all filed back into the Jeep.

"Oh no! I meant to grab it, but I guess I got side-tracked—" Elena confessed, and her cheeks burned the same pretty color as her eyes.

"You mean with saving my life and all? No worries, sweetheart. I don't need it," Logan murmured, but it was what he'd left unsaid that really mattered.

I need you.

TWELVE

idnight's was closed to the public when they arrived, and Elena had a terrible feeling in the pit of her stomach.

"You guys keep watch, okay? I'm going to go with him."

"Sure, El," Storm said, nodding his head.

"Come on, we can go through the back," Logan said, motioning her forward.

Elena could have kicked herself for forgetting his bass the other night, but she was more worried about saving his life and all. On high alert, she followed behind her mate while he attempted to retrieve his instrument.

"That's weird," he murmured when he reached the back door.

A delivery truck blocked the far end of the alley, and Elena could not see Furio or Storm from where they were standing. The feeling of impending danger grew.

"Come on. We should go."

"What? Why? Let me just check the door," Logan said, and reached for the handle.

Then everything moved really fast. The door blew open from the inside and three half-shifted Gila monsters leapt out to grab Logan. Her mate turned around quickly, his face one of shock and horror.

"Elena, run!" He screamed at her, trying to use his own body to guard her from harm.

Sweet mate. Kill those fuckers.

Her Panther snarled, and Elena didn't hesitate to shift. She tossed her head back and roared, knowing full well Storm and Furio would hear her.

"Got you now," the man called Harry said as he cuffed Logan in shackles and started to pull him down the alley towards the van.

"Kill that bitch, then meet me at the base," he commanded his men, but something happened before he could utter another word.

Harry's hands went to his neck, and Elena saw Logan had looped the chain from his shackles around the man's throat.

"I got him," Logan yelled. "Watch out behind you!"

Realizing her mate was taking care of himself, she turned to meet the two Gila bastards who were attempting to spit at her with their venomous saliva. It was the one thing the bastards had over the Guardians. Their deadliest weapon, indeed.

But Elena was fast. Faster than ever before. She dodged a spit attack from one then two as Furio charged a third down in his fiery Pegasus skin. Storm battled another with blue rays of energy adding power to his punches. The Guardians were holding their own.

She turned when she heard Logan scream, Harry had stomped backwards on his foot and was even now trying to free himself. But her wiry mate was relentless. Even falling on the floor he pulled hard against the Shifter's shackles, choking him till he was immobilized.

Elena roared and suddenly pink flames shot from her mouth. She glanced at the door to Midnight's and caught sight of her reflection.

Holy fuck.

She had iridescent pink flames sparking at her fingertips, ears, mouth, even her hair! She felt powerful and furious. Ready to defend her mate with her newly increased magic.

Mine, her inner kitty roared, enraged at the bastards who thought it was okay to touch him.

She really was a *Panther Incensed.* The only time she'd seen a panther roaring flames out of its mouth was in heraldic images like Logan's tattoo. And what could have her more incensed than her mate in danger.

More Gila Shifters filed into the alley, but they did not stand a chance. Not against Storm, Furio, and Logan. And certainly not against her.

Roar.

———

After the battle was over, Kingston arrived with some local Enforcers. Together, they arrested and interrogated the prisoners before transporting them far away from human civilization.

"As far as people will know, there was a gas leak here and the street will be evacuated for a few hours while we clean up," Elena had explained on the way back to the Keep.

She'd been worried Logan would want to go back to his place. To be free to move on with his life and to get out of hers. The very idea filled her with dread. But he hadn't said anything of the sort, merely slid into the car, and when she sat next to him, he'd twined his long fingers with hers.

They were all safe for now. And what's more, he'd come back home with her. She would just have to be happy with that, she thought as she walked back to the car.

"You can't keep him, you know," Egros' voice had Elena spinning around to face him as she helped unload the Jeep with Logan's things.

"What?"

"He's human, El," the Witch spat. "He doesn't belong here. You shouldn't have told him about us. There are rules—"

"Egros, we both know why you are saying these things. I thought you were my friend," Elena said, her voice cracking with the thought of decades of friendship being tossed away.

"I am your friend," the male Witch yelled hoarsely, tossing a ball of energy into the far wall that left a big burnt spot in the stone.

Egros looked defeated, angry, defiant even. Not like someone she trusted or recognized. Not like the Guardian she had fought alongside of for so long. What was happening to them? She wanted to yell at him, but Elena also didn't want to explain herself to him. She shouldn't have to.

"I am your friend," he said with slightly more control. "The Assembly is convening. They will decide if he needs to be bespelled to forget-"

"What? You called the Assembly? How dare you!" Elena raged, but before she could attack him. Storm, Jessenia, and Logan arrived.

"I did it for you!" Egros yelled, but Storm was blocking the Witch.

"What's going on here? What did he do to you?" Logan asked, gaze locking with the seething male Witch in the corner being held back by Storm.

"What did *I* do? *You* are at fault here! Puny normal, you've ruined her! How can she have a future with someone so utterly beneath her on the evolutionary scale? You were supposed to be for one night! Just a nothing of a coupling to help her through her heat! Not her mate! Not her fucking fated mate! She can't even know for sure if her hormones are still whacked. How can she even think that you are hers?"

"Enough, man! What the fuck is wrong with you? He is her mate, decreed by the Fates! He is her *conpar*. You are nothing to interfere with that," Storm growled, and he shoved Egros hard into the wall, silencing the Witch who seemed stunned by his own hateful words.

"My gods, what have I done? I'm sorry, fuck.

Elena, I am sorry. So sorry," Egros groaned, pushing off of Storm and racing from the Keep.

"Oh my gods, Elena? Did Egros really call the Assembly?" Jessenia asked, crouching beside her.

Elena nodded, slumped against the wall, ass on the ground. She was unable to stem the flow of tears. A mix of rage and sorrow falling from her eyes, she glanced over at where Logan remained unmoving.

"Logan," she whispered, but his head was cocked to the side in that way he had when he was deep in thought.

"What is the Assembly?" he asked Storm.

"They're like the Council, but for Guardians. A group of elders and powerful supernaturals who oversee the various groups of Guardians situated throughout the world. They make rulings when there is discord within a group."

"I see. What did he mean her heat cycle?"

"Dude, you gotta ask El. Come on Jess, Storm said gesturing to the other woman to leave them.

Elena listened with dead ears. It was over before it had started. The Assembly was sure to rule against her and Logan. They were certain to order a spell to wipe his memory clean of everything he'd seen and heard. *Of her.*

Dammit. Just the idea of that hurt so damn bad,

she could hardly catch her breath. Elena had never been a crier. Not since she'd lost her mom. Even after she'd left her father's house and he refused to see her again. She hadn't cried then. But now? Now her heart was breaking, and the tears would not stop.

Logan remained where he'd stood when he so bravely confronted Egros. He had no idea what the Witch was capable of, but he knew he was a supernatural, and that alone spoke of his boundless bravery.

The distance felt oceans wide, and Elena cringed at the possibilities of what was going through that brilliant mind she'd only begun to skim. She'd gone through packed boxes and boxes with his tools and research. Notebooks that when she'd opened them had blown her mind with the precise details so neatly outlined.

He was indeed methodical and thorough in his work, as he'd been when he'd made love to her so expertly. Normal or supe, Elena had never had a man so attuned to her every want and need.

Her Panther yowled in despair when she thought of the Assembly and the powers they wielded. The power to take him away before she'd ever really had him.

Head hanging down, she hadn't heard his quiet approach, and she jumped a little when his hands touched her shoulders, then lifted her face to his. Curiosity and surprise shone in his hazel depths as he wiped at her tear stained cheeks.

"Sweetheart, why are you crying?"

"You heard him, Logan. You heard what he said, what he did," she explained.

"All I heard was someone blinded by jealousy rampaging over his own broken heart. He'll get over it. And, if it's important to you, I'll even forgive him for it. But why are *you* so upset?"

"Because you *heard* him," she said, confused. "He told you everything about my heat cycle, and why I was there that night, and you know."

"Elena, let me ask, do all supernaturals go through what you did?"

"No. I mean, I'm a Black Panther and we are kind of loners, but other Cats, Wolves, Mares, and more do experience a heat of some sort. Some males even go into a period of rut," she stated quietly.

She'd never been embarrassed or ashamed of her animal half. The beast was too awesome for that. But she'd always been damn angry when it came to the fact that her heat cycle could possibly dictate the terms of her life. It was grossly unfair.

"I see. So, like your wild cousins, female feline

Shifters, and I assume canine Shifters, experience this heat cycle at intense levels. Is that, right?"

She nodded. He was a scientist, surely, he knew what that meant. That for a period of her life she was completely ruled by her hormones, not her own person, at the mercy of her feline's instincts and biological drive to reproduce. Elena cringed, waiting for his judgement

"It's over," he stated.

"What?" She asked, heart stopping at the thought he was leaving forever.

"Your heat. Is it over?" He asked, and she exhaled.

"Yes. After we, um, had sex, my heat receded."

"And normally, when your cycle is present, what do you do?"

"I was taking a potion that is used frequently to stave off a female's heat cycle. But after a few years it stops being effective."

"I see, biology wins," he said, nodding.

"Logan, I wasn't using you," she tried to explain.

"You were and you weren't. I mean, you needed something, you were acting on instinct, and we clicked. That's fine. Better than," he said and smiled when she wanted to scream. "Elena, it was mind blowing. We were two consenting adults. Human or more than human, and we both wanted each other."

"Yeah," she said, hating the finality in his voice.

"And now?" His warm hazel gaze caught hers, creating fires in her soul, and Elena almost whimpered with desire.

The male was truly so pretty. All angles and hard lines. Contradictions, every last one of them. Even the angry cut of his mouth belied the softness of his lips, the tenderness of his kiss, and the heat she felt in his arms. Her panties dampened, nipples grew hard as her lust for him grew.

"Your friend said something about mates and fate?"

Logan asked, licking his lips and bringing her attention to that oh so talented muscle in his mouth.

"I used to think finding your fated mate was nothing more than a legend," she whispered in the din of the multi-car garage.

"It's not?"

"No," she replied, shaking her head. "Storm and Fergie, Kingston and Holley, and Furio and Jessenia are three pairs of fated mates who found each other. All live here, in the Keep. We are a family," she said.

"But you don't have one?"

"Well, that's the thing."

"What is?"

"I don't know, Logan. You see, I think maybe I do have a mate."

"How can you be sure it wasn't just your heat?"

His eyes seemed to burn with the question, and Elena's Panther rose within her to meet that golden edged stare of his. Strange and beautiful, never before had she seen such a thing in a human. With wonder she reached for him, kneeling in front of him now on the hard floor, she took his hand and pressed it to the center of her chest.

"Because I feel it here," she replied.

"I think we should try an experiment," he said, licking his lips. "I think we should see if we are compatible without your heat."

"Are you asking me if I'll have sex with you, Logan?" She grinned, liking his plan very, very much.

"Yeah. I guess I am," her sexy, brilliant normal replied standing before her with one hand extended.

Elena's Panther scratched at her from the inside, urging the woman to accept her mate's hand. But she needed no encouragement from the she-Cat. Elena knew what she wanted, and he was right there.

Mine.

THIRTEEN

The blood rushing in Logan's ears made him deaf, dumb, blind to everything but her. Elena pulled him along some dark, secret hallway. Thank fuck she knew where she was going, otherwise he'd never find his way through the Keep again.

"It doesn't matter where you go," Elena explained. "If you don't have a destination in mind, the Keep will take you on a ride through a labyrinth of corridors. It likes to play games."

Interesting, he thought. His scientist's brain could seriously go on overload if he started contemplating magic, and the genetics involved in the passing of magical traits down from one generation to the next.

Hell. It thrilled him to know he wasn't crazy after all, and his sample wasn't tainted.

The man from the warehouse was simply not human. And while that explained a little of what he'd found, it opened up a plethora of possibilities and theories. Decades of research, to say the least, and that was just to sate his own personal curiosity.

Still, that sort of pondering was for another time. Elena stopped in front of a door and turned around to face him, pink eyes glowing. Logan's cock went even harder, an impossibility he'd thought for sure.

Well, he'd chalk that up to one of the many things he'd recently had to cross off his *things I know for certain* list. Elena licked her lips, and his mouth watered as he followed the movement of that tiny pink muscle.

"I want you to know, Logan," she said, her naturally husky voice even deeper with need.

The rich tones stroked over him like hands, something a bassist could really appreciate. She wasn't coy or shy, didn't screech and mewl like some simpering idiot. His woman was a warrior goddess, sexy, vibrant, and powerful as fuck. All woman, and all his.

"That when I take you to bed this time, I'm gonna love you so hard, so long, and so completely, you won't know where you end, and I begin."

"You think I'm easy?" he teased.

"Easy? I don't think there's anything easy about you or this. I'm explaining things to you because I want you to understand, I want you to know, my beautiful man that once we cross this doorway, I plan to lay you bare, strip away all your defenses, and abandon mine. Then I'm gonna give you something I have never offered another living person."

"What's that?" Logan asked, hypnotized by her pale bubble gum stare.

"I'm going to show you what it means to be loved by someone who is dual natured. I'm going to show you my fangs and claws, and I am not going to hold back."

Logan paused a beat, absorbing the impact her words on not just his body, but his mind, and his heart too. He'd always thought believing was seeing, but he was wrong. It was feeling too. And he felt the magic she spoke of pulsating through the hall, flowing from Elena out into the atmosphere and back into him.

Logan was on the brink of the most important discovery of his lifetime, but it wasn't the scientist who benefit most. It was the man. And suddenly, nothing else mattered. Only Elena. Who she was. What she wanted. What she needed. Everything about her. He wanted it all. And in return, he wanted to give her his all.

"I don't want you to hold back. Never with me, sweetheart."

"Good. Because no matter what Egros said about us, I believe you are my fated mate."

"Show me," he growled.

Heart pounding, he waited while she stared, then breathed again as that slow, sexy smile spread across her beautiful face for him. *Only him.* Then it didn't matter if he was only human, and she was a Shifter because she wanted him just as much as he wanted her. And that was a motherfucking miracle.

He tried to be patient. Really, he did as Elena backed him up across the room and shoved him down on the plush comforter of her enormous bed. He had a king, this was nearly double that.

Logan swallowed, taking the shirt off his body while she went for his pants. Impatient little vixen that she was, she tore those fuckers right off, boxers and all. Claw tipped fingers danced across his skin, sending shivers down his body.

Every nerve ending was alight with sensation, and Logan could hardly react. He was drowning in it, in her. That champagne rose bubble gum scent that was all Elena teased him as she settled on her knees between his long legs.

"What are—"

"Shhh," she said, drawing circles on his thighs with her nails as she inched ever so slowly to where he wanted her most.

"Wanna taste you, love. Want you in my mouth."

Elena licked her lips, eyes watching as his cock bobbed on its own. His dick was positively begging for attention as need and desire pulsed through him, beating a tattoo across his brain like a drum. She moaned in pleasure as her lips closed over his mushroomed head, and all rational thought left his brain.

Fuck. Fuck. FUCK.

He'd already suspected he was falling for the woman big time. But if he hadn't known before, this right here was the cincher. She swirled her tongue around the tip, using the rough flat of it to lave the thick vein that ran along the shaft. With one hand around the base, she squeezed, stroked, and sucked him until he thought he was going to go mad with the need to come.

Fuck. And if that wasn't enough, the long silky strands of her silvery platinum hair stroked his thighs like silk. He watched her work him, trying to come to grips with the fact the most beautiful woman he had ever seen in his lifetime was sucking his cock.

She was gorgeous. Brave. Powerful. Sexy. Strong. And she'd picked him of everyone on the planet. He felt honored, humbled, and vowed to prove worthy of her. Fated mates? He might be new to the concept, but he believed her when she said they were meant to be. Knew in his heart she was right about that, because at that moment he also knew he loved her. Irrevocably and completely.

"Elena," he moaned her name, and she purred with her lips around his cock, deep throating him and vibrating the whole time.

He fisted her hair, holding onto the silky silver strands while her head bobbed as she swallowed his dick. The woman was gonna kill him with moves like that.

"Fuck Elena," he moaned. "Elena. Elena. *Elena...*"

Logan panted, repeating her name like a litany. The intensity of the pleasure she was gifting to him. Then the sexy siren squeezed his shaft with one hand and cupped his balls with the other, causing total sensory overload.

Logan came. Hard and fast. Again, she'd rendered him deaf, dumb, and blind to everything but her. When she lifted herself off the floor, releasing his cock with a brilliant popping sound, Logan pulled her on top of him and said the first word that came to mind before flipping their positions.

"Mine."

The singular possessive word came from his mouth, stunning him, and turning her on. They both worked to remove her constrictive clothing, he with his hands and she with her claws.

Fuck. Deadly and handy. Yowza.

Her heart pounded against his, and when he reached between them, his fingers slid easily between the wet folds of her primed sex lips.

Logan dipped his head, sealing his mouth to hers. He wanted to kiss her, needed to like he needed air. Hell, maybe more than. The scientist in him wanted to refute that, but the man shoved the geek deep inside.

He groaned as he sucked on her tongue, still tasting of him while his thumb circled her clit, flicking the tight bud to and fro. He settled his weight on her. Allowing her to feel every inch of him, as he sank into the cradle of her thighs, tasting and touching as much of her as he possibly could.

Was it love that made this sweeter than actual fucking? Maybe. He couldn't be sure. But damn it, he could kiss Elena Soussa all day and night and never ever grow tired of it. His sweet, sexy kitten growled when he turned his head, kissing her neck and chest.

"Easy kitten, wanna see you, wanna taste you," he said, rubbing circles on her sides, before lifting up to view her pretty, berry tipped breasts.

"Logan," she mewled, back arching as if trying to persuade him to move already.

But he was too busy looking. Heaven was surely missing an angel, because Elena Soussa was there in the bed with him, and she positively glowed like one.

Alabaster skin, silvery hair spread out against the bedspread in a wide circle like wings or a halo even, her pink eyes heavy lidded. She was breathtaking, and he didn't deserve her. But he was too selfish to give her up. Heat or not, he wanted her. And he was gonna work damn hard to ensure she wanted him, too.

He ran his fingers across her chest, lightly skimming her tight nipples and the undersides of each breast. He lifted one to his mouth, swallowed it down, grateful for the moan that tore from her throat.

She was a wildcat then, tugging his head closer as he ran his tongue over her sensitive buds, one then the other. She squirmed beneath him, but he was in no rush. Logan Wells was nothing if not thorough.

"Please," she begged, and he caved. She was much too pretty to beg him.

Logan dipped his hand between them, skimming over her bare mound, dipping into her honeyed heat. Fuck, her pussy was so tight, he groaned as he pressed a second finger inside. Then he was kissing her breasts and finger fucking her in long slow strokes that made his she-Cat wild. Elena panted, gasped, and even growled.

It was hard to believe that a man as alone as Logan was for most of his life could be so wrapped up in a woman he hardly knew. But he was all the same.

Fated mate.

Those words resounded in his head, and the more he thought them, the more they felt right. He never pictured himself married or tied to another human being for his whole life. Maybe this was why. Logan was not meant for another human being. He was meant for *her*.

Elena Soussa was an ass kicking Guardian of Chaos and a Panther Shifter. He was just him. A scientist and amateur musician with a mouthy twin and a pretty decent sized trust fund. But he was not a Shifter, and he had no magic.

Did he deserve her? Maybe not. But he loved her. His heart swelled with each touch and caress, and he knew he could never give her up. She was part of his soul.

Fated mate. This time when he thought it, he pictured his bubble gum eyed kitten smiling at him and he knew they belonged together down to his marrow.

"Please," she begged again, but Logan was not quitting. Not until she purred for him, coming, and saying his name at the same time.

"When I say, kitten," he replied, grinning against the delicious berry that was her nipple.

He could spend the day lavishing attention on her perfect breasts. She huffed out a snarl, but then his thumb moved to swirl around her clit, and his little kitten settled back down. She wanted him to keep going, and he would. Eventually.

Fourteen

Elena could still taste his spicy male musk on her lips when he kissed her. The fact she knew he could taste himself made her inner kitty yowl and her pussy flood with desire. She wanted him. So. Damn. Badly.

He'd flipped them over and was now working her to rid her of the bothersome clothing she still wore. Why not give him a hand or claw?

"Nice," he murmured and grinned against her lips, tugging the now torn pants off her legs and settling himself in the cradle she made there.

She felt his tight abs against her needy slit and tried pulling him up so she could feel him there, but Logan just grinned some more and shook his head. The bastard.

"Not till I know you're ready, sweetheart," he said, nipping her lip with his blunt teeth, making her nipples pebble against his chest.

"Logan," she moaned his name, feeling petulant that he was making her wait and damn near desperate for him to fill her.

"Patience is a virtue," he whispered, licking her neck and sending spikes of awareness zipping through her tight body.

Mouth wide, she watched as his tongue found her nipples licking slowly around the bud, he kissed and played until he finally sucked the whole thing into his mouth, making her cry out loud into the darkness. He paid the same attention to her other breast, kissing and licking her creamy white flesh until she almost couldn't stand it.

Then, same as before, he sucked her nipple inside the hot cavern of his mouth, pulling and tugging with his mouth, causing the most amazing sensations to spark through her flesh. The man was torturously thorough.

Going back for more, he paid close attention to every inch of her breasts. Every speck and morsel, every crevice and freckle, until he'd tasted each tiny little bit of flesh. Logan moaned and whispered sweet words to her, kissing her the whole time. Like he was stamping himself all over her ever so slowly. Maybe he was simply out to drive her crazy while he did.

Who was she kidding? Elena fucking loved it.

Sliding further down her sizzling skin, Logan slid, kissing, and licking along the way. He pressed her knees apart, opening her up nice and wide for him.

"Look at you so pretty and pink, sweetheart. Delicious," he growled much like a beast though she knew he was not.

Then he was kissing her there, and Elene was unconcerned with their differences. Her only thought was he better not stop. Not until she came, for fuck's sake. Elena leaned back, holding onto the headboard as he swirled his tongue around her clit.

So good. He was so damn good. His long body moved as he ate her, the muscles in his back rippling with each ministration. Fuck, he really was beautiful. And he was hers.

Her she-Cat roared with a possessiveness she'd never felt, and it flowed through her making everything all the more intense. She never wanted him to go, needed him in her life, couldn't wait to tell him.

Then his fingers joined his mouth, two thick ones pressing deep inside her while he doubled his efforts with his tongue lapping at her clit. Elena almost came then, but he slowed down, teasing her so good.

"Oh gods," she moaned, fisting his hair, and pushing him harder against her sex.

Elena opened her legs wider, bucking against him. She loved how he was with her, aggressive and demanding, but tender, so fucking tender even as he set the pace. She loved his reaction to her every response. When he moaned and growled against her clit, pumping his fingers harder and faster, she saw stars.

When she finally came, she screamed his name. Pulling him by his hair, he lifted his head.

"Condoms?"

"Don't need them. I don't contract STDs, and I am only fertile during my heat."

"Really?"

"Uh huh," she nodded, grabbing his cock and lining it up right where she needed him.

"Watch, sweetheart. Watch us become one," Logan commanded, lifting up so that the tip of his magnificent dick was just kissing her pussy, then, ever so slowly, he pressed inside.

Awareness, anticipation, and pure, unadulterated joy filled her as she did what he said and watched. It was the single most erotic thing that had ever happened to Elena. They groaned in unison when he filled her to the hilt. Sighing initially with relief, Elena found herself whimpering as wave after wave of desire swept through her.

"Logan," she said his name, practically begging him to move.

But her sweet, sexy normal would not be rushed. He nuzzled her neck, teeth grazing her skin, hands roaming her arms and chest, her face, her belly, breasts, and hips. On and on, his talented fingers roamed, grazing, touching, learning every inch of her. And still he did not move.

Elena growled, but he had her wrists, pinning them with one hand. Sure, she could break free, but why would she want to? She tried flexing her hips, turned her head to capture his mouth in a kiss, but he evaded her, dropping small, whisper light touches along her jaw and neck, breastbone, and nipples.

"Do you know how beautiful you are, sweetheart? I was captivated by you from the very first second in that club. Hell, I think I felt you come into the room before I ever saw you."

His words caressed her, warmed her deep inside, but it was the long, slow flex and withdraw of his enormous cock that drew a long, guttural moan from her lips.

In and out, roll, flex, withdraw. Logan fucked her ever so slowly. Talking all the while, giving her just enough to keep her from begging, and yet, he kept her wanting more. Always more. She was starving for him and drowning in him at the same time.

"So sweet, love, like bubble gum and champagne roses. Want you to purr for me," he whispered, tugging her nipple with his teeth while he increased his pace just a tad.

His big hands ran down her back, under her ass, lifting her, tilting her hips, and deeper he went. His cock felt so good, stretching her, stroking her in just that right spot. Elena's Panther pushed forward, elongating her fangs, and unleashing her claws. She growled and panted, swirling her hips every time he plunged into her wet heat. Looking for release, chasing that elusive sliver of euphoria that was just out of reach.

"Gonna get you there, baby. No rush."

"Please," she whimpered.

"When I say, kitten," he smirked, and she could've socked him, but just then he changed the angle and Elena's eyes crossed.

Fucking hell.

She'd never felt like this. Weak and at the mercy of a man's touch. She was open, vulnerable, needy for him. That alone was new. The fact she wasn't angry or frightened by the sudden shift of power told her she was correct. Her Panther knew it all along. Logan Wells was hers.

"Trust me?" Logan asked, hazel eyes blazing with passion in the dark bedroom.

"Always," she replied without hesitation.

"Hold on, baby," he growled, biting her lower lip, reaching down to lift her knees over his wrists.

Logan spread her wide, grinding into her, he pressed and pressed, swirling his hips in an erotic dance that had him hitting her spot just right. Elena's whole body vibrated then, a deep, seductive tremble that racked her from head to toe.

Starting where his cock fed her pussy, lightning bolts of pleasure began to strike out to engulf her entire body. Claws scratched at his shoulders, marking him as hers, but she couldn't stop herself, couldn't control it. Nothing like this had ever happened to her.

She'd never lost control like this, but this time, Elena let herself go. She gave the power to Logan and moaned in unrivaled pleasure as he took the reins readily. Her orgasm rolled through her, slowly and completely. So fucking hard, she almost blacked out from the strength of it.

Elena could hardly do more than ride the wave of bliss as it crashed into her. Curling her toes, arching her back, she screamed his name, then rearing up, she did the unthinkable. Elena gave him her mating bite, closed her fangs over his neck and bit down binding herself to him for life, without asking, without explaining, she'd marked Logan Wells.

"Mine!" She roared and felt him stiffen as his own orgasm exploded through him, filling her so completely.

Logan came and came, and she reveled in the explosive passion that erupted between them. After he collapsed on top of her, thoroughly spent and sated, she licked the place she bit him, closing the wound and kissing the skin there.

"That was," he panted, trying to catch his breath.

"Mmm," she whispered, kissing his shoulder and his cheek.

"I mean, I never. Even the first time, it was never like this." He grinned, kissing her hard, then slowly easing out of her.

Already she missed him there. Wanted his cock buried deep in her body. Always.

"Elena, talk to me. You look so worried. What is it?"

Shit.

She really had to explain. Needed to tell him exactly what this all meant. It had never been her life's plan to find a mate and leave the Guardians, but with the Assembly already on their way, what other choice did she have?

"I marked you," she began.

"The bite?" His eyes narrowed as he listened.

"Shifters, other supes, sometimes bite during sex. But the bite I just gave you was a mating bite. Shifters give that bite only to their mates."

"So, I'm your mate. You know now it wasn't your heat," he grinned, and her heart pounded in response.

Dammit. He was so beautiful. And he didn't seem angry in the least.

"I should have asked you first. I am so sorry. I just got, well, carried away." Elena winced at how idiotic she seemed.

"Hey, look at me," Logan traced her cheek, then with a firm forefinger on her chin tilted her face toward his.

"I love you, Elena. I want to be yours, so if that means you biting me and giving me the most intense orgasm I have ever known, I am so down, baby."

"Yeah?"

"Oh, yeah. In fact," he cupped her face in his hands and kissed her again, his renewed passion jutting against her hip, and Elena moaned in pleasure.

Her future might not be in stone, but this was.

Logan belonged to her now, and she to him. Whatever else happened, that was a truth no one could deny.

Many hours later, wrapped around each other, someone knocked on her bedroom door.

"El?" Fergie's voice called to them, and Logan sat up, but Elena stilled him with a hand on his arm.

"El? The Assembly representative is here. Kingston said you should come to the conference room."

Her heart pounded in her chest as she thought of the implications. There was no way she was going to let them take Logan and bespell him. Panic filled her, making her tremble, then he was there, in front of her.

"Hey, look at me. Whatever happens, I am with you, Elena. Me and you, together. Got it?"

"Okay."

Fifteen

"Elena, Logan," Kingston opened the door to the conference room and stepped back to allow them both to enter.

The Dragon's face was a mask, and she felt her nerves tense. Storm, Furio, Byram, and Egros were there as well. Each male looked at her and nodded, except the male Witch. His shamed eyes did not meet hers.

Traitor, she thought angrily, but Logan's fingers gripped hers and she knew forgiveness was not far away. Egros was misguided, but he was not evil. Still, she was not quite ready to make that leap. Not when her whole life was about to change forever.

Sitting at the long conference table was a stranger. The Assembly representative, she concluded. The man was dressed in a long robe with a mask over his face, hiding his identity. She looked at Kingston curiously, but he was impassive.

"You are Elena Soussa?"

"Yes," she answered the stranger.

"This is your *human*," the Assembly rep spat the word as if it were dirty, angering Elena.

"My name is Logan Wells. You are?"

"You dare address me? Silence. This does not concern you," snarled the man.

"Sir, I think if you take a moment to listen you might be pleasantly surprised. You see, I'm a scientist, a geneticist and biochemist to be precise. I believe I can help the Guardians in this fight to keep magic free."

"How could you possibly hope to help?"

"For one thing, I spent a few minutes analyzing the Gila Shifter saliva, and after talking with Holley, I believe I can help make a preventive elixir to ward off the paralytic effects of their venom."

"That is insane. No Witch has ever been able—"

"That's because each potion will need to be created for each individual. Time consuming, but worth it, sir."

"Don't interrupt again, normal. My concern is for the Guardians as a whole, and you are not even supposed to know about us, *normal*,—"

"That's it. You will stop calling him that, right now. His name is Logan."

Elena's pink eyes flashed angrily and before everyone gathered pink flames began to lick her skin coming out of nowhere at all. Her eyes blazed, the reflection in the glass hutch behind the representative, and she watched in awe as pink flames billowed from her ears and from between her parted lips.

"You! You are fate marked!" yelled the shocked Representative.

"I am," she replied. "He is my fated mate, and I am a Guardian of Chaos, sir. The Keep is our home, and I shall do my duty with my *conpar* by my side."

"And you, Kingston Baldric? You are the leader of this group. What say you?"

Elena blinked as her flames receded, noting Logan had held firm to her hand the entire time. The flames had not hurt him. Joy pulsed through her as she realized that, if anything, he seemed to think she was really cool.

"Love you," he murmured, and she felt herself blush all the way down to her panties.

Storm cleared his throat, and Elena's eyes flashed to their Alpha, who waited for her attention before turning to the Assembly representative. This was going to be tricky, and she tensed waiting for her leader's response.

"Our group is more than just the average Guardians, sir. My team is a Pack, a family. So before I answer, I will ask their answers," then Kingston turned to the other Guardians, some of whom had suddenly been joined by their mates. "What say you of Elena's mate?"

The hush in the room grew exponentially as each Guardian eyed one another. Elena held in her next breath. Her entire future was now in the hands of those she'd called family for so long.

As with all families, they'd had their difficulties over the years and decades they'd lived and worked together. But this was the first time she was unsure of the outcome. She supposed it was because nothing had ever mattered so much to her.

Logan squeezed her hand, and she silently thanked the gods for him. He was the only man who had ever been there solely for her support and comfort. It meant so much to her. She hoped to pay him back in kind, or to at least be afforded the opportunity.

One thing became quite apparent to her in that long stretch of silence. If the strange Assembly Representative ruled against her, against Logan, she would walk away from her vow and from the Guardians forever.

And the second she owned that, peace settled over her. Logan stood, brows furrowed, but she caught his gaze. He watched her silently, then a small smile teased the corner of his mouth, and somehow, through their *matebond* perhaps, Elena knew he understood her. Even better, she knew in her very bones that he felt the same. No matter what, they would be together, and that was enough for both of them.

"Doc's cool," Storm replied, blue eyes flashing at Fergie. He was the first to break the silence, and Elena's pulse raced with joy.

"I agree. He's awesome. Even likes my shoes," Fergie answered with a playful wink at Logan, earning her a stern growl from her mate.

"Oh hush," she told her besotted Wolf. "You know you're the only one for me."

"I better be."

"We think Doc is the man, too," Furio stepped forward, rolling his eyes at the Wolf pair. He had his hand on the small of Jessenia's back, and the kitchen Witch nodded in agreement.

"He's already helped me with his knowledge of genetics to improve my herb garden. I expect our elixirs and potions to be exponentially stronger this coming year," she added helpfully.

"Apologies, I have not yet made Logan's acquaintance," Byram, the only Vampire among them spoke up. "However, if Elena vouches for him, then I see no problem. She has proved herself a hardworking and dedicated Guardian time and again. I trust her implicitly," Byram bowed slightly, and Elena nodded.

The Vampire was perhaps the most secretive of them all, but that was simply his nature. He was powerful, strong, and he'd never treated her as anything other than equal. She respected him. The fact he trusted her and said so aloud made her very happy to call him friend.

"I think Dr. Wells is just brilliant," Holley offered. "And if our Elena says he is her mate, then that is what he is, and I see no issues for their future. Neither do the *manetuwak* who've already acclimated to Logan's preferences." The Witch spoke with a twinkle in her eye.

The moment Holley mentioned the spirits of the Keep, the lights fluttered, changing from a gold color to the soft white glow that Elena knew Logan liked better. The Representative gasped, head turning to Kingston, but the Dragon smiled lovingly at his mate.

Elena felt Logan's hands tense around hers as Egros stepped forward.

"Sir, I am the one who called you here," the male Witch. "My name is Egros Pyke. I who called the Assembly to investigate the normal Logan Wells and his relationship with Elena Soussa, my fellow Guardian. I want to offer my sincere apologies to them both. You see," Egros said, clearing his throat and glancing at Elena and Logan before quickly turning his remorseful eyes to the Representative. "I was overcome with jealousy. She'd refused my offer to help see her through her heat cycle, and I was wounded. I see now that my affection was misplaced and ill advised. Elena Soussa was never anything but loyal and professional. A true Guardian that I would do well to model myself after."

"I see Mr. Pyke," the Representative replied. "And what say you, now of Logan Wells?"

"I say Dr. Wells is the true fated mate, the *conpar* of Elena Soussa, Guardian of Chaos, Panther Shifter, and my friend, if she will forgive me. I am hoping they both will, actually." He grimaced then reached behind him and held out his offering.

"Uh, I know it's not much, but I retrieved this for you," he said, holding Logan's bass out to her mate.

"Thank you," Logan said, and he moved forward

to retrieve his *Rickenbacker Fireglo*, highly polished and looking good as new, from the Witch.

Stepping back, Logan's arm came around Elena's waist and he nodded encouragingly. She inhaled his spicy scent, calming her Panther, and relieving some of her anger. She was still upset, but she knew she could not stay angry with Egros and remain there. And she very much wanted to do just that, with Logan by her side.

"I see. So that leaves me then," the masked Representative faced Elena and Logan. Tension had her straightening her back, she felt her newly mate given powers circling them both and looked down to see pink flames dancing at her fingertips.

"I have one question for the couple," he said in a voice that suddenly seemed quite familiar to Elena.

Like something lost from a memory she had pushed to the foremost corner of her mind. Elena stepped closer to the tall stranger. Tears unexpectedly pricked her eyes, as he reached behind him and removed his mask.

"And that is, can you forgive an old fool?"

"Papa?" Elena cried out, throwing herself at the man who'd forced her to choose a life without him when she took her vows.

"Elena, mija, can you ever forgive me? I was so lost

in my fears and my grief, I forgot what was important, my daughter. I've spent years trying to gather the courage to approach you."

"But the Assembly? How?"

"I have contacts," her father shrugged, and wiped his face unashamedly.

"Hello, sir. I'm Logan," her mate stepped forward offering his hand, but Anthony Soussa grabbed him in a hug and kissed both his cheeks.

"Thank you, son. You be good to my Elena, now."

"Of course," he replied, smiling as she tucked herself into his side, sighing happily while the rest of their group erupted in conversation and laughter.

Champagne was opened, and glasses shared as they toasted the end of the inquiry and a new chapter for one of their own. After a few hours of catching up, Elena's father left with a promise to visit for Easter.

That night as she lay wrapped around her mate, Elena sighed and snuggled into his warm skin. Logan grunted and opened his sleepy eyes to gaze at her with such love and emotion, she could hardly dare to believe it was real.

"It's real, kitten. I love you so much. More than my life," he whispered, kissing her temple.

"I love you too. I'm so happy, I feel like I could

burst. Are you going to be happy here though? I mean, I am asking you to give up your life—"

"What life? Elena, I work for myself and the lab the Keep has already started putting together for me is better than anything I ever had at home or in any office. I am going to be working with Byram, Holley, and Egros on new potions that will help all of you, protect you, my love, and I couldn't be happier. As a matter of fact, look," he leaned over and picked up a vial, handing it to her.

"What is it?"

"It's a new potion to stop a female Shifter's heat. I ran an analysis of the one you used to take that stopped working and discovered why the potion was losing its effectiveness. We just needed to apply the principals of precision medicine, personalizing each dose to the different Shifter species," Logan said, sitting up as his excitement grew.

He was so brilliant and gifted. Elena sat up with him, lost in his energetic speech. To say she was surprised was a gross understatement. This meant so much to her and would mean as much to so many other females. Having to go through a heat cycle robbed many of their choices, but this would offer to put the control back in their hands.

"The one size fits all method was not working efficiently because you are all so genetically diverse. We had your sample on file, so I was able to tailor this to you."

"What about when I want to," she said, blushing furiously.

"Have children?" He asked with a wide, warm grin.

"You simply stop taking the potion. From what I can see, your Shifter genes are hardwired to heal and protect you. The second you decide you want to have kids, sweetheart, all you do is let your heat cycle start and let nature take its course."

"And you're okay, waiting?"

"To start a family? Yes, I am more than okay doing whatever you want, my love. I want children with you, but there is no rush. Being with you has made me the happiest man in the world. I would do anything for you," he said, cupping her cheek and kissing her softly.

"Do you mean that?"

"Of course."

"Then make love to me, Logan. Show me how you feel about me."

And he did. Again and again, until she came purring his name.

Prrr. Logan. Mine. Mate.

EPILOGUE

Holley grimaced and rubbed her belly as she, Jessenia, and Fergie waited for Elena to step out of the cubby where she was trying on her wedding gown. The *Ladies' Room* had the *Rat Pack* softly playing in the background and snow was falling outside the large windows that faced the woods.

It was a chilly March morning, but the friends were more than happy to gather around the cozy fireplace to plan Logan and Elena's upcoming nuptials. He'd proposed almost immediately after moving into the Keep, and she'd said yes.

"Come on, El. I'm starving," Fergie bellowed despite the bowl of buttery popcorn on her lap.

"You're always hungry," Jessenia teased.

"*Shyaddap*," Fergie snorted, throwing a kernel at her bestie.

"Will you two, quit it," Holley grumbled, hand on her back.

"Are you, okay?" Jessenia asked.

"Yeah, yeah. I'm fine. My little one is just messing my back up," Holley tried to laugh as she grasped her back with one hand and clutched her enormous belly with the other.

"El? You might want to speed this up," Jessenia called out, her eyes still riveted to the heavily pregnant Witch.

"She's nervous, isn't that cute? Hey, El, can I ask you something?"

"What is it, Ferg?"

"Well, since you're now a one man gal, does that make you *pussy whipped*?"

"*What?*"

"*What?*"

"*What?!*"

All three women replied but Fergie was on a roll, munching popcorn and talking to no one in particular, she continued.

"Yeah, I totally think *pussy whipped* applies to you. I mean A) you have a pussy, and B) you turn into a pussy, and C) the aforementioned pussy is being fucked by one guy which essentially makes you—"

"Uh, Fergie, no," Jessenia said. "That is so not how you use that phrase!"

"What? I think I'm totally right," the redhead said but before she could really get into it, Elena roared, grabbing everyone's attention.

"Thank you! Alright, I am coming out now. No one laugh," Elena called, and stepped out onto the runway.

All three women stopped and stared. There was no laughter at all, not even a smile. Elena bit her lip and tried not to fidget.

"Well?" she asked, nervously looking down at the vintage, off the shoulder, mermaid gown.

It was made entirely of Leavers lace and silk, the color a blush tinted ivory that made her eyes glow. Of the five gowns the Keep had offered, one look, and she'd fallen in love with it.

"Oh El!" Jessenia sighed, clutching her hands to her chest.

"You are so beautiful!" Fergie said.

"Holley?" Elena's eyes went to Holley, who was tearing up as she gazed at her friend.

"It's perfect, El. Take it off."

"What?"

"Take it off, now," Holley growled.

"Why?" Elena asked.

"Holley!" Fergie barked.

"Because I'm in labor! Ooooh!" The Witch bellowed.

Everyone moved like lightning. Jessenia called Furio who went to get Kingston from the greenhouse. Fergie put her arm around Holley to help her stand, while Elena stepped out of the wedding dress, shrugging into her tank top and jeans before going to pick Holley up and off the ground.

She'd barely stepped into the hallway with her when Kingston came flying down the hallway. He took his mate and headed to the infirmary.

"Byram is waiting in the medical wing, love. Just hold on. Elena, call Logan and Egros!"

"On it," she yelled back.

Logan and Egros had developed a tentative friend-ship that had allowed both males to work together to create potions, elixirs, and medicines that would help supernaturals the world over. One of them was designed to lessen the risk of complications during labor since birthrates were dangerously low for some supes.

We're on our way.

She reread Logan's text and immediately calmed.

Her mate was coming, and he would do all he could to help her friend. Apparently, when he'd told them about his doctorates, Logan had failed to mention graduating from med school.

"I never got my license to practice."

He'd said and shrugged it off. This was after she'd confronted him when her mate had helped set a bone in Furio's leg when he'd unexpectedly broke it after engaging with some Loyalists during a mission. Logan was full of surprises, and so far, she loved every one of them.

Hours later...

The sounds of a baby's cries echoed through the halls as Storm, Furio, Elena, and their mates gathered in the kitchen for some snacks. Soon, Egros and Byram shuffled in after them.

It had been an exhausting process for everyone, but none more than Holley and her dragonling. The baby, named Greyson Mount Baldric, was resting now with his doting parents.

"How are they?" Elena asked Egros, and he smiled and nodded.

"Mother and babe are very well. Kingston looks like he needs a stiff drink though," he said with a snort of laughter echoed by the others.

Happiness seemed to overflow the Keep as Jessenia

prepared some grilled cheese sandwiches and home-made tomato soup. Furio helped his mate by dishing up the food and serving everyone. It was delicious, and they ate and joked around as a feeling of complete serenity washed over them.

Snow continued to fall, and Elena sat on Logan's lap, feeding him bites of grilled cheese and kissing him every chance she got. She looked at the pink sapphire on her finger and smiled.

He'd worked with Egros to bespell the band to stretch when she shifted to her Panther, and to shrink again when she switched back. So thoughtful, she sighed kissing his soft lips once more.

"Are you sure you want to wear it all the time?"

"I'm sure. It's a sign of our commitment to each other. I'll never take it off," she murmured, pleased when she saw his happiness in the radiance of his smile.

So lost in their glow of love, neither Logan nor Elena noticed the woman drop from the sky right outside the window. That was not until she busted right through it pointing two military grade weapons, one at Elena's face and the other at Egros' balls. The male Witch snarled angrily, having jumped up to defend the couple as soon as he realized what was happening.

"Get the fuck off my brother!" snarled the female.

"Margo! Margo, what the hell are you doing?"

Why did Elena recognize that name? Shit. His sister. That was his sister, Elena thought curiously. The short woman had gold brown skin and a head full of glossy black curls. The only similarity between them was her large hazel eyes.

"Rescuing you from these people. You don't know what they are, Logan—"

Elena jumped off him and stood in a defensive position. No way in hell was anyone taking her mate. She felt her Panther's anger, looked down to see pink flames swirling around her fingers.

"Oh shit. I've never seen a Shifter do that!"

"How the hell do you know about Shifters?" Logan asked her.

"How do *you* know about them?" She asked back.

Brother and sister bickered while the rest of the Guardians and their mates shrugged and went back to their food. The window repaired itself, and only Egros and Elena remained with Margo and Logan.

The male Witch seemed paralyzed, maybe because of the gun still pointed at him, or maybe because the violent little woman was truly something to behold. Elena grinned, then stepped beside her mate.

"My name is Elena, and Logan and I are mated."

"Mated? OMG! She brainwashed you," Margo said through gritted teeth.

"What? No, I did not!"

"We're engaged, Margo," he said proudly.

"Engaged?"

"Yes, and I think you better sit down and tell us what the hell is going on," Logan said eyes narrowed at his now squirming sister.

"How did you find us?" Egros asked, reminding everyone of his presence.

"Okay, fine. I will tell you everything, but do you have anymore of that soup? It was cold as hell out there."

Elena laughed and took her new sister-in-law by the hand. She and Logan led her to the dining room table, Elena fully aware of Egros' eyes on the small human. Once she had her settled with a bowl, deep in discussion with Fergie about the latest Ferragamo boots, she called Logan over.

"Well? How do you think she knew about us?"

"Margo has been involved with secret government ops for years. Your guess is as good as mine," he shrugged.

"I have another question," Elena said, loving how he took her waist and pulled her flush against him.

"What's that, kitten?"

"Will she be okay on her own for a few while you and I sneak back to our room?"

Logan glanced at his sister, then back at his mate. His grin wicked as he took her hand and headed down the hall, calling out to Fergie to find Margo a room for the night and telling his sis that he'd see her in the morning.

"But Logan—" Margo yelled after him.

"Tomorrow," he called back.

Lifting Elena in his arms, he took off at a run to their room. She giggled and held on, not used to that sort of thing. But her human mate was full of surprises, and she looked forward to more with each passing day.

"Now, what did you have in mind, kitten?"

"Let me show you," she said, mashing her mouth to his.

Her inner kitty purred deeply as their matebond pulsed and swirled around them. Logan and Elena's love, so precious and new, was strong and pure, and full of loyalty and integrity. She kissed him with every one of those things in her heart, pouring all her love and desire into it. Making sure he knew just what he meant to her with every slide and swipe of her tongue against his.

"I love you, Elena."

"I love you too, Logan. I would die for you."

"Don't do that, mate. Live for me instead. My own *Panther Incensed*. And I promise to live for you, every single day."

The end.

Did you like the story? Read the rest of the Guardians of Chaos today!

READING ON A BUDGET?

Hello Readers!

I am so excited to be able to offer you exclusive bundles available only on CDGORRI.COM for readers using my BUY DIRECT option.

Right now, I have several bundles available at a whopping 30% off the listed prices and there are several series bundles to choose from.

Orders will be delivered via BookFunnel email. Just download to your favorite app and READ!

Thank you for buying direct. Have an awesome day!

xoxo,

C.D. Gorri

Join the Pack!

Looking for a Paranormal Romance series that is loads of growly fun?

Welcome to the Macconwood Pack!

These stories are split into two series, the Macconwood Pack Novels Series, and the Macconwood Pack Tales. Each story features one or more Pack members their journey to their one true and fated mate. They can be read alone, though they are better read in order, as characters may show up in each other's stories.

Pack is family for the Macconwood wolves, and when you read their tales, you become family too. What are you waiting for?

Join the Pack today!

https://www.cdgorri.com/series/the-macconwood-
pack-novel-series/

No cliffhangers. Steamy PNR fun.
Go and read your next happily ever after today!

Beware... Here Be Dragons!

The Falk Clan Tales began as my stories surrounding four dragon Brothers and how they find their one true mates, but when a long lost brother arrives on the scene, followed by a few more Shifters...what can I say? The more the merrier!

Each Dragon's chest is marked with his rose, the magical link to his heart and his magic. They each have a matching gemstone to go with it.

She's given up on love. But he's just begun.

In The Dragon's Valentine we meet the eldest Falk brother, Callius. He is on a mission to find a Castle and his one true mate, one he can trust with his diamond rose....

His heart is frozen. Can she change his mind about love?

In The Dragon's Christmas Gift our attention shifts to Alexsander, the youngest brother of the four. He has resigned himself to a life alone, until he meets *her*.

Some wounds run deep. Can a Dragon's heart be unbroken?

The Dragon's Heart is the story of Edric Falk who has vowed never to love again, but that changes when he meets his feisty mate, Joselyn Curacao.

She just wants a little fun. He's looking for a lifetime.

We finally meet Nikolai Falk and his sexy Shifter mate in The Dragon's Secret.

She doesn't believe in fairytales, until a Dragon comes knocking on her door.

Meet Castor Falk, the long lost brother of our original four Dragons, and his sassy mate Josette. The Dragon's Treasure is full of adventure and laughs.

Nothing can surprise this six hundred-year-old Dragon, except maybe her.

Devine Graystone meets his match in Sunny Daye, an irrepressible Wolf Shifter with a heart of gold. Read their story in The Dragon's Surprise.

He's a hardcore realist until she dares him to dream.

Nicholas Gravestone doesn't know what to think when he spies Minerva Lykos on the property his Dragon covets. Can this unlikely pair come to a truce? Find out in The Dragon's Dream.

Thanks for reading.

xoxo,

C.D. Gorri

*Dragon Mates & Dragon Mates 2 boxed sets are now available in hardcover, paperback, and ebook.

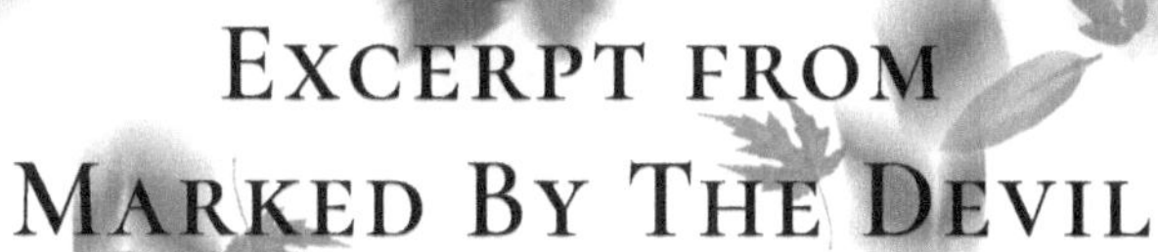

EXCERPT FROM MARKED BY THE DEVIL

*S*nap! *Flash! Snap! Bang!*

"*Over here! The Dark Prince is by the window!*"

Click! Bang! Snap!

"Oh, for fuck's sake," Avail growled. He could feel that secret part of him pushing to be released. Power pulsed through his veins, his beast demanding to be set free, but he fought the temptation.

Snap! Flash! The horde of paparazzi swarmed outside the entrance to the Leeds Foundation, snapping pictures and banging on the polished reinforced glass doors in hopes of catching a glimpse of him—*like he was their prey.*

If they only knew.

He growled aloud, eyes flashing at the throng below. The man they hunted was not the useless, spoiled playboy they took him for.

Avail Leeds was something more. A predator. Not like those uncouth vultures circling with their cameras and cheap shots.

He was the real thing. A creature humankind built into legend with stories of midnight encounters. He snorted a harsh laugh.

If only I could show them. Grrrr.

They'd been there since daybreak hoping to get a statement or a picture of him, but Avail had managed to dodge them. He was no stranger to this kind of game.

Unfortunately for me. Sigh.

They'd dubbed him the "Naughty Dark Prince" years ago, recording his exploits and reporting them with more than a touch of exaggeration, as a constant source of entertainment for *normals* the world over.

As heir to the Leeds fortune, Avail had been in the spotlight since birth. Especially after his parent's tragic death when he was an infant.

His grandparents had brought him up with the finest education and surroundings a boy could have.

So, yes, he was known to indulge in a bit of luxury

and sport in between his family's foundation and other philanthropic works.

The Leeds family was enormously wealthy. The money had come to the family at first from the land itself. Natural resources like coal and oil had started the family's legacy.

Later on, they'd dabbled in manufacturing, then real estate and development. Now the family was known for their charity.

Avail himself had increased their holdings by playing the stock market and investing in several internet start-ups. He certainly had a marvelous head for figures. The mathematical and the female kind.

He gritted his teeth at the reminder. The latter had, once again, caused him this current headache. Women would surely be the death of him, or so his grandmother promised. Often.

Oh dear. Grandmother is certain to be angry this time.

"Denise!" Avail groaned his secretary's name as he looked out his office window.

So many of them are here this time. Ugh. He slumped back in his Perigold executive chair. The exotic French walnut was highly polished and smelled of lemons. The seat was made from the leather of a sixteen-point stag that his great-grandfather had taken down himself. He remembered that day.

Hunting with Grandfather was often the best time of his life. After all, he'd taught Avail everything he knew about controlling his inner demons, so to speak. He sure missed the old man.

His darling grandmother ordered the leather made from the buck's skin to be turned into this bit of posh office furniture for Avail when he took over as president of the Leeds Foundation. Conditioned with only the best mixtures of Mink and Neatsfoot oils, the chair was fucking amazing, if he did say so himself. Soft and strong, perfect for his six-foot four-inch, two-hundred and forty-pound frame.

He was certainly grateful for it as he slunk down into the buttery depths and cradled his head in his hands. It was only seven o'clock in the morning. How did those vultures find him so quickly?

"What have you done now?" *Why does her voice have to reach that pitch?* He cringed.

"Just the usual, Denise," he answered with a grin.

His silk shirt of the night before hung open revealing a large expanse of his muscled chest, evenly covered in a dusting of black hair.

It matched the midnight dark strands atop his

head that earned him the hated moniker *"Naughty Dark Prince"*.

Of course, if he'd bothered to stay out of the public eye the name would probably be forgotten. *Fat chance.* Avail couldn't help himself. He simply loved life, women, and parties. Usually, in that order.

He didn't bother to button his shirt or his pants as Denise stomped across the floor in those ridiculous heels she wore.

The older woman had seen him in far worse shape. He could use a shower and shave, ooh, and some breakfast.

A bloody steak and half a dozen eggs should do it, but even as he thought it his stomach revolted. *Ugh. See what happens when we mix whiskey and magic!* His Devil growled inside of him and Avail groaned aloud. The magic had been a bit much, but the little Witch deserved it. Taunting him for not being interested in her obvious wiles.

The glare coming from Denise had him refocusing his attention on the motherly woman. *Ouch.* She could singe toast with that look! *So loving*, he thought. His secretary of seven years cared about him. That was nice.

"Well, Denise, I suppose you want to know what happened."

"Oh, a night of wining and dining the little trust fund baby? What's to know? Did *little pookie* not like getting kicked out of bed at 3AM?"

Denise Reynolds stood over Avail with a large, steaming mug of his favorite French roast, served black, in one hand. In the other was a large cup of tomato juice and six aspirin. Otherwise, he might have growled at her insolence. *As if.* He loved the crotchety older woman.

Her white hair was sprayed straight up like spindles guarding a castle. The sight was a bit harsh on his poor bloodshot eyes.

Yes, he'd had far too good a time last night, but it wasn't with *little pookie* as much as it was with the whiskey he'd imbibed.

And the magic he'd wielded.

It was nearing the last quarter moon and Avail's beastie had been up for some good old-fashioned debauchery. As was the little Witch he'd brought along for the ride.

Bambi was a trust fund baby and a Witch. He'd met her at *The Thirsty Dog* where he'd gone to partake in some booze and dancing, perhaps a little nookie with a stranger.

He thought he'd found the perfect partner for the evening in the wicked Bambi. The woman had been down for just about anything. Including skinny dipping in the frigid Blue Hole which was just a few miles from his home.

He'd used a few tricks with some ancient runes and conjured a little light show while they swam. He'd even allowed his Devil to play a little bit as well. Hoping for a little suck and blow afterwards.

Not the card game.

And then it had all gone wrong. Bambi had wanted promises with her sex. That was a serious no in his book. Then the taunting came and out she went.

Like a light.

"Well?"

"Oh Denise, what can I say? She wanted more than an evening's entertainment. I simply didn't see us headed that way."

"Well, normally I'd say the girl had standards, but uh, I don't think so."

He stretched as he swallowed his aspirin and downed the tomato juice. Avail held his hot coffee carefully. Denise had a sadistic side and he'd caught her trying to burn his Devil once or twice over the years.

"Humph. How is *that* too hot for you?" She rolled her eyes and gathered the empty glass as he continued to wait for his coffee to cool down.

"I told you before, I'm not that kind of Devil,

Denise," he murmured and sipped the brew as it reached the perfect temperature.

Heaven.

He continued to sip with his eyes closed ignoring everything but the smooth warm liquid as it slid down his throat.

"Really, Avail? You took *that* silicone doll to the Blue Hole! Your grandmother is going to be furious with you."

"Yes, yes, I know. Wait, how did you know?" He frowned.

The swimming spot had been shunned by locals for decades, but the Leeds family still enjoyed the crystal-clear waters.

They were fed by an underground glacier though some still claim to be baffled by its existence. *Whatever.*

Still, he knew better than to take a normal to one of his family's private haunts. He also knew better than to use magic in front of anyone. But he'd figured it was alright since Bambi was in fact a Witch.

Even better, she had her own money. So, he didn't need to worry about her motives. Ideally, she'd been looking for a little light fun on a Friday night. That was all!

How wrong he'd been.

"Avail, you need to see this."

"Hmm? What?" He turned and looked at the older woman who was staring at the television with her mouth hanging open.

"Pookie took pictures! *Ha!* Looks like you've finally did it this time. And look, an interview too!"

"Oh fuck! Turn it up!"

"Leedsy is a very naughty boy! Mmm hmm. He fed me whiskey and oysters on a silk sheet by the pool...

I tell you the truth I didn't mind spanking him, but the ball and gag was where I drew the line. I like it when my men talk dirty, you know?...

Of course, that's true!...

Well, he insisted on wearing my thong as a choker...

Yes, I'd be willing to go out with him again. He is a big boy after all, and his endurance is divine...

I found his size to be more than adequate though his oral skills were slightly exaggerated...

but that is nothing compared to what happened afterwards...

yeah we both saw him...

the actual Jersey Devil..."

For fucks sake...

Continue to read here https://www.cdgorri.com/series/purely-paranormal-romance-books

The Maverick Pride Tales:

Dire Wolf Mates:

Wyvern Protection Unit:

Jersey Sure Shifters/EveL Worlds:

The Guardians of Chaos:

Twice Mated Tales

Hearts of Stone Series

Moongate Island Tales

Mated in Hope Falls

Speed Dating with the Denizens of the Underworld

Hungry Fur Love

Island Stripe Pride

NYC Shifter Tales

A Howlin' Good Fairytale Retelling

Standalones:

Witch Shifter Clan

Young Adult/Urban Fantasy Books

The Grazi Kelly Novel Series

The Angela Tanner Files

G'Witches Magical Mysteries Series

Co-written with P. Mattern

Witches of Westwood Academy

with Gina Kincade

<u>Blackthorn Academy For Supernaturals</u>

<u>*Be sure to check out my BUY DIRECT BUNDLES*</u> *and get 30% off when you buy available only my website.*

ABOUT THE AUTHOR

USA Today Bestselling author C.D. Gorri writes paranormal and contemporary romance and urban fantasy books with plenty of steam and humor.

Join her mailing list here: https://www.cdgorri.com/newsletter

An avid reader with a profound love for books and literature, she is usually found with a book in hand. C.D. lives in her home state, New Jersey, where many of her characters and stories are based. Her tales are fast-paced yet detailed with satisfying conclusions. If you enjoy powerful heroines and loyal heroes who face relatable problems in supernatural settings, journey into the Grazi Kelly Universe today.

You will find sassy, curvy heroines and sexy, love-driven heroes who find their HEAs between the pages.

Wolves, Bears, Dragons, Tigers, Witches, Vampires, and tons more Shifters and supernatural creatures dwell within her paranormal works. The most important thing is every mate in this universe is fated, loyal, and true lovers always get their happily-ever-afters.

In her contemporary works, you will find fiercely possessive men and the smart, confident, curvy women they are crazy about. As always, the HEA is between the pages.

Thank you and happy reading!
del mare alla stella,
C.D. Gorri

http://www.cdgorri.com
https://www.facebook.com/Cdgorribooks
https://www.bookbub.com/authors/c-d-gorri
https://twitter.com/cgor22
https://instagram.com/cdgorri/
https://www.goodreads.com/cdgorri
https://www.tiktok.com/@cdgorriauthor